Oberheide

OPENING HER EYES

Rodric took her chin in his thumb and forefinger. "You have beautiful eyes, Ainsley, eyes that beguile and transfix."

"Do they beguile you, my lord?" she asked, knowing even as she did that she should not be teasing him so.

His answer was swift in coming, and her heart raced as one strong, sun-browned finger trailed down her cheek, then under the fragile line of her jaw and forced her chin back. She sighed when his mouth found the vulnerable cord of her throat and barely knew it when his hand slipped into the front of her low bodice, but she tensed to rigidity as his fingertip touched the soft mound of her naked breast. She felt her nipple spring to life, and she began to tremble.

"Please, please . . ." she managed somehow, without knowing for sure what she begged.

"Yield to me, Ainsley," he said. "Let me love you."

Still Ainsley shook her head, even as her body cried *yes . . .*!

Lilacs on Lace

Linda Ladd

A TOPAZ BOOK

TOPAZ
Published by the Penguin Group
Penguin Books USA Inc., 375 Hudson Street,
New York, New York 10014, U.S.A.
Penguin Books Ltd, 27 Wrights Lane,
London W8 5TZ, England
Penguin Books Australia Ltd, Ringwood,
Victoria, Australia
Penguin Books Canada Ltd, 10 Alcorn Avenue,
Toronto, Ontario, Canada M4V 3B2
Penguin Books (N.Z.) Ltd, 182–190 Wairau Road,
Auckland 10, New Zealand

Penguin Books Ltd, Registered Offices:
Harmondsworth, Middlesex, England

First published by Topaz, an imprint of Dutton Signet,
a division of Penguin Books USA Inc.

First Printing, June, 1996
10 9 8 7 6 5 4 3 2 1

 REGISTERED TRADEMARK—MARCA REGISTRADA

Printed in the United States of America

For my husband, Bill, with love—for his help, support, and encouragement, for always being there when I need him, for two beautiful children, and for twenty-five wonderful years of marriage.

Chapter One

⸙

Argyll Peninsula,
Scotland
May, 1691

As dark blue and brilliant as an intricate mosaic of
polished turquoise and sapphire stones, the deep
waters of Loch Awe wore ruffled whitecaps
formed by warm spring gusts whipping down the
high, barren crags mirrored in doubled splendor
upon the surface. Boulders strewn along the rocky
shore embraced the gentle lap of waves. The
beach spread into a carpet of spongy emerald
grasses that inched toward a thick forest tract edg-
ing a portion of the long valley. Fields of broom
waved with peaceful contentment in the late afternoon as the sun dropped low to be swallowed
by the jagged mountain peaks. A herd of small
red deer grazed leisurely among the wispy-
stalked foliage.

When the first muffled thuds rumbled with
faint echo through the quiet hush of early twilight, a majestic stag lifted his impressive rack of
forked antlers, alerted by the impending danger.

Flared nostrils sniffed at the wind, his uneasy stamping of hoof transforming his followers into a still-life portrait of poised sentinels. As an immense white stallion exploded from tree cover to thunder like an avenging, bolt-wielding Norse god into their midst, they disappeared with silent leaps and bounds into a thicket of brambles.

Ainsley Campbell barely noticed the exodus of the roebuck, nor did she glance twice at the covey of ring-tailed pheasants fluttering to wing from a patch of whin alongside her path. Her sole concern was returning to the nunnery before her absence was discovered. Hugging leather-trouser-clad knees tightly around her mount, she leaned low across the horse's neck until her cheek was slapped by the streaming white mane.

Although she well knew the severity of her punishment would go unchecked if the abbess caught her outside the convent again, she tried not to dwell on that eventuality but exhilarated in the rushing cold air. With pale cheeks flushed pink and eyes bright with pleasure, she laughed aloud with the sheer joy of such freedom. Months of prayers and nursing the sick had passed since she had escaped her stifling world in the nunnery, and she meant to relish and savor each moment spent in the real world where the heavenly smell of cedar boughs spiced the breeze and great eagles winged and soared in glorious plunges above the lovely blue lake.

"Go, Saracen!"

At the sound of her cry and the kick of her heels the powerful stallion lunged forward with great strides. His sleek muscles worked between her thighs, and his hoofbeat drummed a hypnotizing cadence as they seemed to take off into the sky and fly into the heavens. Her heart leapt with wild excitement as the death-defying gallop kicked up sand alongside the curling waves, pure joy filling her from head to toe.

Inside her heart she gave thanks to her friend and beloved mentor, Brother Alfonse, for leaving her this magnificent Arabian. He had succumbed to fever three years come Hogmanay Eve, but she missed the dear old man still, and so intensely that she would gladly give up the prized animal to have him back again with his age-dimmed eyes and shuffling step.

With his gift he had given her the only moments where she was able to do exactly as she wished, and the longing to stay outside the abbey was so intense that it bit into her heart with the sharpness of Toledo steel. This was the only pleasure in her life, the reason why she risked the nuns' wrath so many times since her guardian, Lord Hugh Campbell, the great Earl of Strathmorton, had placed her under the care of the abbess.

On her twenty-first birthday she would wed the Englishman, Randolph of Varney, but that would only be a different kind of cloister where her husband would become her master. The blood pumping so violently through her veins brought yet another rush of recklessness, and she had to fight off her desire to turn the regal horse south again to the hills and glens of Strathmortonshire, where her patron earl lived in his ancient stone castle.

She had sneaked out today to collect herbs and flowers needed for the medicinal concoctions Brother Alfonse had taught her would help ease the pain of the unfortunate souls brought to the abbey's hospice to die. In the deep-pocketed short apron tied at her waist were many roots and leaves needed to refill Brother Alfonse's earthen apothecary jars. She had promised him she would continue his work with the sick until she left the abbey for England, and had tried her best to do so. But without the kind friar there to protect her from the superstitious nuns, she had constantly suffered accusations of witchcraft when she healed the diseased and fever-ridden with the medicines.

The unusual appearance of her eyes frightened them, and well she knew it. Even the crofters of the surrounding farms and hamlets had heard of her appearance, and ignorantly designated her as the witch of Kilchurn, despite the fact that she had successfully treated many of their neighbors with the monk's potions. And they continued to blame her for every plague and pox that ravaged the peninsula.

Of late she had learned through Jeremy that she was being cursed and vilified for the latest outbreak of fever running rampant from Dalmally to Ingott since winter's end. The primary reason she had ventured out to gather fresh medicines was to cure the fever. She was used to the foolish peasants and their ridiculous beliefs. In truth, she had been accused of having the evil eye ever since she came to Kilchurn Abbey as a tiny bairn. Only her stalwart ally, Brother Alfonse, knew the truth, and now her new friend, Myrna Campbell, whom the earl had sent the year before on her twentieth birthday to become her companion and then lady-in-waiting on the day of her wedding.

Though on every occasion she sneaked from the abbey she rode along the shore facing Strathmorton Castle, she was yet to see or meet the man who had provided for her education and arranged a most suitable marriage for her with a wealthy Englishman of high rank. The abbess had explained that he had taken her well-being to hand because her own parents had been murdered in a bloody massacre perpetrated by the worst of their enemies, the heathen devils of Clan MacDonald. As a man of wealth he pledged his aid to the young girl

Ainsley drew up on the reins and slowed her gallop when off to her right she caught a glimpse of a crofter driving a one-wheeled cart down the rutted track toward Ingott town. When the crofter noticed her so near, he hastily crossed himself, then hastened to veer away from her path. As if she were as unlucky a symbol as a cat of black, she thought with a shake of her head. How ironic that she was feared so universally when she was the very one who had healed so many villagers under the apprenticeship of dear Brother Alfonse.

Even now she hazarded their wrath and persecution by venturing unescorted outside the protective walls of the abbey, not to mention a beating by the abbess herself for disobedience. Even Brother Alfonse had not allowed her to leave the haven of the abbey after the peasants became aware of her eyes, for fear she would be attacked with stones or captured by the English witch-hunters, who used—in the not-so-distant past—to travel the Highlands in search of witches and warlocks.

Ainsley shivered at the thought, disliking the hatred and fear, but she felt a certain safety atop her fierce Saracen. She forced from her mind the horrible stories Brother Alfonse had recounted of his youth in England when mass burnings of witches and heretics oftentimes sent a pall of black smoke over the land.

Now her primary concern was returning to the abbey in time for vespers. If she was discovered outside the walls, she would surely pay the price, for the exalted abbess of Kilchurn, Mother Mary Catherine, considered Ainsley her personal responsibility since she was put under her care by Lord Hugh Campbell. A delicate shudder shook through Ainsley at memories of the last time she had been caught out collecting her herbal remedies.

Of all her restrictions, leaving the nunnery was the one most emphatically demanded by the earl himself, and in punishment for such a weighty infraction, the abbess had caned her most mercilessly and sentenced her to a month of fasting but for a wooden bowl of unpalatable gray gruel at eveningtide.

Ainsley's stomach tightened at the thought of

the thin, tasteless broth and the lonely days spent suffering in a prayer cubicle. She had been truly repentant when the abbess had finally relented and allowed her to resume her work in the hospice. She had also been given permission to rejoin the other girls in their tower dormitory, although sleeping there was not much better. Nearly all the haughty heiresses in residence were afraid to look her in the eyes, for fear that she would stop them from conceiving after the saying of their vows. Only Myrna stood by her side as friend and confidante, and never believed the whispers about Ainsley's bedevilment and evildoings.

Kicking her mount to a faster gait, Ainsley muttered a silent entreaty that she had not been missed. She was supposed to be in her chamber, praying upon her knees, these last two hours. With Myrna guarding her portal there, she would not be missed until the girls lined up for chapel.

Ainsley's heart warmed at the thought of her one loyal friend. Myrna was a Campbell born, the daughter of a soldier of Strathmorton. He had died defending Campbell lands from the MacDonalds, the very demons who had murdered her parents when they had raided and pillaged her home village of Carinth when she was still in the cradle. All her family and kin had been murdered in cold blood, and only she had been lucky to survive their villainous swords.

Within the year, however, her life would change drastically when she became the bride and moved to faraway England. Often she wondered if her betrothed had heard the tales of the witch of

Kilchurn and if he might renege on the marriage contract.

A tingle of alarm crept down Ainsley's spine at the thought of spending all the rest of her days among the nuns, and she quickly thrust such ideas away and turned her horse straight toward the tall hedgerow that impeded her path. She had no time to ride the length of the bushy barrier to open the gate.

With a daredevil thrill coursing through the pit of her stomach, Ainsley took the gallant stallion flying over the hedge. When his front hooves landed safely on the other side, her heart overflowed with the elation. If only she could ride forever and ever, away from the boring convent school, away from the village of Dalmally, down the whole length of Scotland to the farthermost tip of England, where her unknown husband awaited her. Perhaps he would be young and handsome and kind; perhaps he wouldn't be afraid of her eyes like everyone else.

Her honey-colored hair flew from its staid anchor of pins and whipped free down her back, the sun illuminating its natural streaks of gold while the dampness of the wind riotously wove the long tresses into ringleted tangles that would take hours to comb out. Ainsley cared little about her dishabille. She was tired of the tight coils of braids deemed pious enough by the abbess to please God instead of lustful men who sought to vent unmentionable carnal desires upon innocent young girls. She didn't know much about unmentionable carnal desires, but she had a feeling she might prefer them to lying on her stomach on the cold floor while the abbess prayed endless hours to exorcise her of the devil inhabiting her eyes.

Within minutes the towering walls of the church tower loomed high and rectangular in the distance, the tiled rooftops of Dalmally just visible on the hill beyond. Many a day would pass before she would get another chance to bribe Jeremy into sneaking Saracen out of the stables. Though the horse belonged to her, the abbess refused to let her ride him. This time the young stable boy had not demanded his usual bribe of a fat haggis stolen from the refectory, but had merely demanded a kiss from her—a request she found most peculiar.

Despite the abbess's constant threats of hellfire for those allowing men to take such liberties, the slight brushing of Jeremy's adolescent lips against her own had seemed neither pleasant nor offensive. Actually she thought the sensation more like setting a moist clam atop one's mouth, and considered it at best a rather unhealthy habit to be pursuing. On the other hand, the quick kiss was a good bit easier and less complicated than filching the haggis or his favorite crispy-crusted blueberry tarts from underneath portly Sister Colleen's nose.

When she neared the field where the abbess's skinny cattle were grazing, she slowed and guided Saracen toward the back of the abbey, where thick blackberry bushes and sturdy ivy vines obliterated the ancient stones. Years ago when she was little more than a child, she had sought out the easiest place to scale the enclosing wall. Still agile and fleet of foot, she made her way through the bushes, where she could unbridle Saracen and let him find his way back to the stable.

"I'll come for you again soon, my beautiful friend," she whispered, pressing her cheek against the great white's velvety muzzle. Carefully she removed the leather strap, then retrieved from her pocket the apple she had purloined from barrels in the dark, aromatic depths of the convent's root cellar.

"Ainsley, be quick with you! The abbess has already rung the bell!"

At the low-pitched directive, Ainsley found her friend atop the age-pocked wall. Myrna gestured frantically for her to hurry, and Ainsley hastened to oblige, alarmed that the girls had already been summoned for prayers. With years of practice, she found the familiar cracks and footholds between the old paving blocks and ascended with practiced expertise. Within seconds she was over the top and crouching beside Myrna.

"Why have they rung the bell so early?" Ainsley peered anxiously toward the church. "They've never chimed before sunset."

"Maudie MacArthur said that important visitors have come, so we'll be in dreadful trouble if we show up late and embarrass the abbess! Please, you must hurry, Ainsley, everyone was already donning their cloaks when I sneaked away to find you!"

"But I can't go dressed like this," Ainsley objected, pushing tangles of windblown hair off her forehead.

As if noticing her attire for the first time, Myrna stared down at the old shirt and tight leather breeches Ainsley had bribed out of Jeremy last winter with a filched pan of shortbread and a jar of gooseberry jam. The look on her face was so horrified that Ainsley would have smiled if she were not in such dire straits.

"Oh, Sweet Mary, Mother of God, where did you get such disgraceful garb? The abbess will surely cut your back to ribbons if she catches you dressed up like a stable boy! And where is your eye patch? Oh, Ainsley, what are you thinking? Quick, you know how hysterical the other girls become when you leave your eye uncovered!"

Ainsley grimaced but reluctantly pulled the black patch out of her pocket. She slipped the scrap of leather over her left eye. Though she was rather embarrassed by her unusual eye color, she loathed wearing the ridiculous patch. Their fear of demon possession was absurd. She was not a witch, and certainly possessed no magical powers. Sometimes she wished she did. It would have been enjoyable indeed to turn some of the more vengeful of her tormentors into toads or spiders or equally loathesome creatures. Surely that would serve the more vicious nuns right for wielding the cane upon her backside with so heavy a hand.

Now that she was inside the convent school and facing the abbess's punishments, Myrna's trembling trepidation abruptly shocked Ainsley back to reality. Not only would she be punished when she was found outside the walls, but poor Myrna would receive a few whacks as well for reneging on her sacred duty as lady-in-waiting. And the nuns felt free to strike Myrna with more force, for she was not the ward of such an important personage as the Earl of Strathmorton.

"Do not worry, Myrna, they will not find out where I've been this day. Soon we will be out of this place forever, as soon as my English betrothed takes me to wife."

"I hope you are right," Myrna murmured as she wound Ainsley's thick honey tresses into a knot and tried to secure it with a few pins left intact after her harrowing ride. "If they see such scandalous clothes upon you, we will wear bruises on our back for days to come. I thank Holy Jesus that I thought to bring your cape with me. Oh, Ainsley, how can you be so wicked as to wear a man's trews instead of a skirt?"

Throwing the cowl over her tangled hair, Ainsley did not answer but wrapped herself in the long charcoal dark folds that hung to her ankles. She had meant to return in plenty of time to don her drab gray gown for chapel, and if the bell had not rung so early, none of this would be happening.

As they hurried across the courtyard that led to the prayer chapel off the side of the nave, the final chime died melodically on a wind current. The last girl was entering the door, and though they scurried to catch up to her, the easily provoked Sister Gertrude scolded them in harsh, nasal tones, then rapped Myrna's head with the knotted end of her walking cane.

At Myrna's cry of pain, Ainsley furiously jerked off her eye patch and sent a narrow-eyed, threatening glare at the mean old woman. Sister Gertrude gasped and averted her own gaze, making a quick sign of the cross as she backed away. Ainsley relished the nun's look of fear. She deserved to be frightened. She was the most vindictive, hateful of all the sisters, and she took special delight in punishing poor Myrna.

"Go on with you, you wicked girl," Sister Gertrude rattled out sharply, but it was Myrna she pushed forward hard enough to make the girl stumble. She kept a goodly distance from Ainsley, and Ainsley smiled to herself, thinking that sometimes her perceived kinship with Satan was gratifying in its own way.

Assuming a prayerful mien that she rarely felt after an altercation with the less than beneficent Sister Gertrude, Ainsley followed the other girls down the side aisle of the small chapel. *Forgive my sins, Mary, Mother of God,* she added quickly to herself as she anointed herself with holy water, genuflected, and crossed herself before kneeling obediently beside Myrna. She would have to admit her transgressions as soon as the priest came to hear confession, and in her case that would take a good deal of time.

The nuns were already seated in straight-back benches facing the girls, looking like a flock of hungry vultures in their stark black robes and white wimples, Ainsley decided irreverently. She already dreaded the long droning prayers, knowing full well how badly her knees would ache after hunching so long atop the hard stone floor. The abbess stood at her customary place at the raised pulpit, but Ainsley's attention was captured by the two strangers sitting in the chairs carved of mahogany and cushioned in royal blue velvet trimmed with rich gold braid.

The haughty bearing of both visitors indicated they were of aristocratic lineage. She could see better the one who sat closest to her, and from beneath her long lashes observed his neatly trimmed wheat-colored hair, which he combed straight back from his forehead. He was rather young with cheeks clean-shaven but for a narrow downward-pointed mustache of a darker shade of blond. His scarlet uniform identified him as a soldier—one of the English dragoons who fought as allies with her own Campbell clansmen. The fancy braid upon his shoulder epaulets designated him an officer, and her curiosity was piqued by the peculiarity of seeing a fierce Dragoon sitting so casually in a chapel among pious nuns.

When she leaned forward enough to examine his companion, she found the second man was half hidden by his blond-haired friend, but he was dressed in fine civilian clothing tailored in what must be the very height of Edinburgh fashion. His black wool riding coat was of the finest cut and fabric, and she could see the tight-fitting gray breeches were immaculate atop tall Hessian boots that were polished to so high a gloss that the black leather actually reflected the flames of the votive candles burning in the prayer niches. She wondered what it would be like to be rich and noble enough to wear such garb.

While she had observed him, he had been scanning the row of girls in front of her. When his gaze suddenly found her place, she was riveted beneath the intense glow of his silver-gray eyes. He did not look away, nor did she, and she saw something in his expression that could have been recognition had she not known that she would definitely remember meeting a man who looked so magnificently attractive. He did not break their gaze but watched her with such a narrow-eyed scrutiny that Ainsley was forced to lower her own contemplation. A hot, embarrassed flush rose to burn her cheeks. Who was this man who could make her heart pound so erratically?

Chapter Two

❦

" 'Tis my privilege to announce the arrival of two most distinguished guests at our humble abbey. I beg all present will strive to represent the courtesy and deference for which our order is so well respected."

After her brief, smilingly applied introductory remarks, the abbess presented to her young charges a visage so sternly appointed that no human mortal would dare do otherwise. Ainsley could not stop the bubble of mischief oozing up from deep inside her, an overpowering inclination to lurch to her feet and shout some wonderfully awful gibe that would echo in an endless, sacrilegious litany around the vaulted rafters. Even the mere thought of how the hefty abbess's ruddy face would darken to hot bloodred crimson brought an inordinate wave of satisfaction. Indeed that sight would be suitable recompense for the hours spent on her knees in endless exorcisms meant to send the demon screaming out of Ainsley's dreaded ocular orb.

When the abbess's eyes, as jet-black and forbidding as the oily surface of a peat bog, found Ainsley's face, however, Ainsley made sure her expression revealed nothing but pure reverence and piety. Such scandalous behavior would earn her a painful trip to the iron whipping bench, and an equal punishment for poor Myrna as well. Her throat tightening convulsively, she folded her hands at her waist with newfound humility.

"My Lords." When Mother Mary Catherine inclined her veiled head respectfully to the noble visitors, Ainsley marveled at the abbess's obsequious behavior—displayed even more noticeably now than when she groveled before the wealthy Campbell benefactors and important lairds who secretly still supported Catholic monasteries.

Since the Reformation when Scotland joined England as a Protestant country such support was rare indeed and dangerous to those with lingering loyalty to the Roman church. Pushing those thoughts aside, Ainsley revived her interest as the abbess continued her recitation.

"We are most fortunate to have among us one of the most notable of our English neighbors and esteemed colonel of the Forty-second Regiment of Royal Dragoons, the Earl of Shreveshire, Lord Richard Lancaster."

The man wearing the crisp scarlet uniform stood and bowed formally from the waist, and Ainsley peered curiously at him from beneath her hood as he reseated himself in the throne-like ornamental chair.

"I am particularly honored to present our second guest, a man of great nobility and highest character, and envoy of our most honored and celebrated countrymen, the Earl of Strathmorton. We welcome you, Lord Rodric Campbell."

A representative of Ainsley's guardian? Here at the abbey? Ainsley smiled with not a little pleasure as Myrna leaned close, and whispered, "Lord Rodric is a most handsome man, do you not think so?"

Ainsley had no time to answer for Sister Gertrude was quick to apply her knobbed cane in a jab at the small of Myrna's back. The nun's action brought a dark frown to Rodric Campbell's noble features; enough displeasure, in fact, that the abbess was forced to tender explanation.

"Your pardon, my lord, but often times we must remind our charges of the blessings of piety. 'Tis our duty to school them in Godly behavior."

In any case his obvious annoyance saved Myrna further abuse from said walking stick, but Ainsley knew full well that both she and her friend would receive the brunt of Sister Gertrude's ire once the important personages departed sight of the abbey gate. She returned her attention to Lord Campbell as he rose to his feet and stood a true giant of a man, a startling three or four inches over six feet. She could never remember seeing a man so tall, nor so broad of shoulder. Now thoroughly intrigued by the man with such vivid pewter eyes and close kinship to her patron earl, she was intensely curious as to the reason for his visit.

Though he did not glance in her direction again—almost as if he had not noted her so fully only minutes earlier—she could not seem to ignore his person. He was obviously a refined and genteel man, but seemed to her more a personification of some great warrior-king, such as Alexander the Greek, who ruled in the ancient land of Macedonia.

She took a moment to enjoy a mental vision of him—standing feet braced apart in short leather tunic and silver breast armor upon a battlefield, his finely sculpted features relaxed and confident as he surveyed the enemy, with no fear whatsoever in his extraordinary eyes. When she looked back at him, however, she only sensed a growing impatience in his manner, as if he longed to finish his business in a hurry and be gone from the abbey.

Ainsley forced her regard toward the floor and studied her fingers folded demurely in her lap, but was chagrined at herself when moments later she sought to steal a furtive peek at the gentleman who so fascinated her. His hair was as black as Mother Mary Catherine's robe, and rather long, though he wore it tied neatly at his nape with a leather thong.

The symmetry of his facial structure, lean of contour and tanned by the sun, seemed nearly perfect—at least in her opinion—but his eyes were what arrested her overly much, the shiny silvery color of mountain lochs brightened by wintry moonbeams. His nose was strong, well-formed, and slightly aquiline, his lips firm and chiseled—she felt sure they would not feel like wet clams atop her mouth—and a strong jaw that bespoke a tendency toward stubbornness.

Aye, he was handsome, 'twas true, as much as any man she had ever seen. Which were few indeed during her years cloistered in the abbey, she reminded herself. The sisters spoke often about how physical attractiveness could not be trusted, that Satan enjoyed assuming beauteous forms to entice his victims. Though she had always sneered at such tales, now she wondered if they did not bear some truth, for her gaze seemed unable to focus on anything but Lord Campbell, especially now as he began to speak.

"You flatter us, my dear abbess."

He politely inclined his head in the abbess's direction, one corner of his mouth tipped up in a faintly mocking smile that etched a deep indentation on the left side of his mouth. Inexplicably Ainsley's flesh ran rampant with a rash of prickly goose bumps. To her surprise, Mother Mary Catherine also preened with pleasure and returned a most cloying smile, all the more shocking because Ainsley had never seen the stern woman adopt a pleasant look. Never, not once in all the years since she had been in the convent school.

"Our time here at Kilchurn is limited," Lord Rodric continued in the deepest and most mellifluous of baritones, "and I am quite certain that you will wish your vespers to begin at the appointed time."

"Please, my lord, consider all of us here at the abbey at your service." Incredibly, the abbess was beaming again.

"As I made mention of when first we spoke," Lord Campbell went on, "my cousin and I have traveled here at the request of the Earl of Strathmorton as escort to Lady Ainsley Campbell, a duty we both consider an honor."

Ainsley's jaw dropped, and she gaped open-mouthed at him until Myrna's elbow landed sharply against her rib cage. A surprised titter was born among her fellow students, several of whom turned to stare curiously at her. All the girls quickly resumed bowed heads when the abbess leveled a lethal gaze upon their ranks, one that surely could have stopped a horse at full gallop.

"Escort Lady Ainsley? But to where? I received no word that she was to leave us so soon . . ."

"His lordship wishes her taken to London, where she is to meet her betrothed," Lord Rodric interrupted carelessly, cutting off the abbess's objections, "and with all due haste, I might add."

Both Ainsley and the abbess stared at him in stupefaction. "But, my lord, 'tis not until the end of this year when she is to wed. His lordship was most clear in his last missive to me."

Please, dear Lord, do not let this be a misunderstanding. Please let the handsome man take me out of this awful place. To London, the great city that Alfonse had described with hundreds of church bells and great ships afloat in the river channels. She would like to see the legendary land. Her prayers continued with more devout vehemence than she had ever demonstrated before, and the handsome noble's words showed that her exhortations had borne grace from above.

"Aye, Reverend Mother, his lordship has decided it is necessary that she should join her betrothed at this time. He did not share with me his reason nor did I demand he do so."

Ainsley nearly held her breath as she watched the abbess shake her head, apparently caught in a quandary of consternation. What if she refused to let her go? The idea was most horrible and brought Ainsley's heart up to block the base of her throat.

"Surely you cannot expect me to release an innocent young girl such as Lady Ainsley into the care of two gentlemen . . ."

"That's exactly what I intend, abbess," his words held a sharpness in them now, the tone of a man who was not used to being denied his requests. "The earl has inked his wishes upon paper and sets forth the same with his own seal. I would not think it wise for you to question his decree and hardly think it necessary to remind you that Lord Campbell of Strathmorton is your primary benefactor at the abbey."

Ainsley watched Lord Rodric unfurl a piece of parchment and verify the signature and seal. The thread of impatience woven into the nobleman's imperious words was readily detectable, and the startled expression on the abbess's face gave Ainsley secret pleasure. She realized that this man, this Lord Rodric Campbell, was indeed a powerful personage if he felt so secure in speaking with so unveiled a threat to a churchwoman of the abbess's stature. The abbess apparently knew his authority well-founded, for after glancing over the formal document, she relinquished her objections with a respectful bow.

"Of course, my Lord Campbell, as you wish." She turned and looked straight at Ainsley. "Come forward, child, and do not dawdle. The gentlemen have indicated they have little time to linger with us here at the abbey."

Terrified to approach yet overjoyed to be escaping the nunnery at last, Ainsley rose and walked quickly toward the nobleman. Excitement possessed her, but once she stood alone at the forefront of the assemblage, she remembered the eye patch and was acutely humiliated to have the two men see it upon her.

A myriad questions ran through her head as she fixed her attention on the gold trim decorating the front of Rodric Campbell's white silk shirt. Starched lace spilled from the sleeves of his fine jacket, and she stared at two huge emeralds gleaming from the signet ring he wore upon the forefinger of his right hand. A beautiful Celtic cross had been engraved between the two precious jewels.

"Are you Lady Ainsley Campbell, ward of Hugh Campbell, the Earl of Strathmorton?"

"Aye, milord." Ainsley curtsied, nervous in a way she rarely had been before, and in truth, wondering if the two gentlemen could hear the excited thuds inside her chest. As hard as her heart was beating, she was surprised they couldn't see it moving her chest up and down. Her pulse lurched to a standstill when Rodric Campbell caught her chin with his forefinger and thumb, and raised her face so that he could study her features.

"I have heard that you possess unusual eye color. Remove the patch so that I will know you are truly the one I seek."

Ainsley tensed all over as he bracketed her chin inside his strong fingers, then she forced herself to raise her gaze. She stared into pale silver pools and felt her heart hammer even faster. His steady gaze seemed to immobilize her, and she could not make her lips move enough to reply to his question. She was glad when the abbess intervened in her behalf.

"Surely you know the girl is marked by Satan, my lords. 'Tis a fact known widely through the whole of the Highlands."

Lord Rodric looked visibly startled by her explanation. "I have heard of the witch of Kilchurn, of course, but I must say such notions are antiquated by men of reason, Reverend Mother."

For the first time the abbess appeared affronted by the young nobleman. "The girl possesses the evil eye and has displayed healing powers throughout her years in residence here that have no other possible explanation. I have seen such magic potions as she uses with my own eyes, and believe me when I say, sire, that we have tried our best to eradicate her affliction since she was brought to us as an infant."

Rodric Campbell's eyes narrowed slightly as he returned a speculative gaze upon Ainsley. "Remove the patch, my lady, and let me judge for myself this mark that so frightens the devout abbess."

Ainsley was loath to let the handsome man see the peculiarity of her left eye. " 'Tis said that those looking upon my eye will suffer ill fortune," she felt obligated to warn him.

"Don't be absurd. Take the thing off, I say."

Ainsley wondered if he would back away in dread as so many others had done upon first sight of her eyes, or cross himself and intone a hasty prayer of deliverance, or even run wildly in the opposite direction as the superstitious villagers usually did if they were unfortunate enough to encounter her unmasked. Somehow she could not picture the big man doing such as that.

"Obey Lord Campbell at once."

At the sharpness of the abbess's command, Ainsley slowly lifted the black patch, now perversely curious as to what his reaction would be. Very few people had demanded to look upon her eyes once they had heard the stories of how it harbored a demon. He was brave indeed to face her without fear.

"Look at me, lass." Again Lord Rodric showed impatience.

Slowly, with her eyes opened wide to heighten the effect, Ainsley raised her regard and awaited his look of abject terror. She saw it, too, or was it something else? Whatever the emotion it was quickly hid from her as he turned to the abbess as if he had seen nothing untoward at all.

"We should leave now since time is of the essence," he ordered, quite calm and unaffected, yet the import of his words would change the course of her life. "Have someone pack Lady Ainsley's belongings and load them onto the carriage."

Now even Ainsley was surprised at his great haste to whisk her away. Did he mean to say they were to leave now, that very moment, without even time to ready herself for the journey?

The abbess was quick to voice Ainsley's inner doubts. "What mean you, sire? That you would take her this very evening, as dusk is beginning to fall?" Mother Mary Catherine actually gave a small chuckle. Ainsley contemplated how strange her mirth sounded. " 'Tis true that Ainsley is under his lordship's protection, but it is hardly acceptable that she leave here alone with two gentlemen and no chaperon to protect her virtue . . ."

Ainsley's initial reluctance turned to joy when she remembered that she had every right to include her friend in this rescue mission. "Mistress Myrna Campbell has been my designated lady-in-waiting this year past, my lord. I would be grateful if she could accompany me on the journey and act as chaperon."

To her pleasure, and surprise, too, Lord Rodric was readily agreeable. "So be it. Have both lasses ready, Reverend Mother, for I am hard-pressed to make good time south into the Cheviot hills."

Ainsley turned and found Myrna beaming at her. She thanked Lord Rodric from the bottom of her heart. "I am truly grateful, my lord."

Rodric Campbell's eyes raked over her face, but she tensed when his gaze dropped to her cape-swaddled figure. When she followed his regard, she found with some chagrin that the front of her cape had parted to reveal her attire. Before she could draw it together, he had tugged away the cloak, causing her long hair to spill down around her shoulders. She could only stand frozen in humiliation as Lord Rodric stared speechlessly at the dirty leather trews she wore upon her legs.

The girls and nuns were not so circumspect nor so closemouthed, and a scandalized, collective gasp was heard. In addition, the easily provoked wrath of Sister Gertrude was swift in coming.

"You wicked, evil girl," the angry nun cried furiously, bringing her cane down across Ainsley's back. Ainsley cried out but before the second blow could land against her shoulders, Rodric had the nun's wrist captured tightly in his fingers.

"Enough, Sister. The lady is no longer in your charge. She answers to his lordship now."

Grateful for the man's intervention, she was pleased when Myrna ran forward and clung loyally to her arm. When Rodric again looked down on her, she saw different emotions lurking deep in the silver-gray eyes. Again she found him difficult to read. Was it kindness, or pity, or triumph, perhaps? Somehow she thought it the last, and something about that realization seemed unsettling and sinister.

Lord Rodric obviously sensed her foreboding, because he bent close and mouthed a reassurance so softly that even Myrna could not hear him. "I have no intention of harming you or your friend. Come along willingly because being difficult will only complicate matters. You have no choice but to obey the earl's command. He is your legal guardian."

"But why has the earl changed his mind at this late date?" she dared to ask. "I do not understand."

"You can trust me, my lady. I have no cause to harm you, only to take you to your new home."

Still uneasy, Ainsley glanced at the abbess then at Sister Gertrude's pinched, vindictive frown as the other girls continued to whisper excitedly among themselves. Whatever she thought, she had little choice but to follow the directives of her patron lord.

When Lord Campbell took her elbow and led her down the aisle, she walked docilely at his side. Myrna clung to her arm, and the scarlet-coated dragoon followed in their wake. The most overwhelming sense of unreality flooded through her as they neared the huge stone archway that led outside the nunnery and into the real world. This cannot be happening, she kept thinking over and over again. It has to be some wondrous dream. I will awaken on the cot in my cell, disappointment will flood over me, and I will want to cry.

Then they stood outside on the worn cobblestones, where a shiny black coach awaited them. She had not trod these stones since she was a small child and the gate had closed behind her. Just down the path she could see the village of Dalmally with its thatched rooftops and stone chimneys streaming the black smoke from supper fires. She was free, she thought with a joy that brought her face alive with happiness. She could walk along the streets like any other maid of the Highlands, she could mingle with real people and ride horses if her husband approved. She was free at last!

Chapter Three

A good bit more relaxed now that they had the girl safely inside the hired traveling coach, Rodric MacDonald leaned back against the black leather squabs and stared across the cramped interior at Ainsley Campbell. The abduction had gone according to plans and easily enough thus far. Bloody well better than he had ever expected.

No one had detected the Strathmorton seal as the fine-honed reproduction it was, thanks be it to the saints for the expertise of Rodric's clansmen at Balluchulish. The discovery of the forgery would have ended the hoax before Rodric had even gotten himself and the two girls out the convent's barricaded gate.

At one point he had feared the girl herself would become the major obstacle in their plot, but apparently she did not particularly savor the cloistered life. The fact that she wore such scandalous garb told him more than a thousand words about her willful disregard for the abbess's authority, knowledge he had better keep foremost in his mind if he meant to keep her captive. Though she had seemed most eager to see the last of the nuns and their sticks, now that they rolled and jounced over ruts in the road, she surveyed him warily, her eyes openly reassessing him. Was she questioning his motives?

From where she sat huddled in the opposite corner with her red-haired, freckled friend, Ainsley Campbell watched him with the same amount of curiosity that he had scrutinized her earlier while in the chapel. The expression she now wore was openly distrustful, as if he was some dragon ready to fry her crispy with one fiery blast of his breath. Could she truly have no idea what family name she truly bore? Or of the magnitude of her importance to the clans of Skye? For truth, to the whole of Scotland?

Young Lady Ainsley had received the startling word of the escalation of her impending marriage with admirable aplomb, that was true, but would she accept so readily once she realized he was not transporting her to the Englishman to whom she had been betrothed for the last decade? In his mind he acknowledged the fact that he was damnable fortunate that she was so bonny a lass, for by law she was already his own bride, if not yet announced by the banns of the church. How would she receive that crucial little tidbit of news? Not well, he feared.

Her unusual left eye had startled him at first but certainly not because of its unique coloring. In truth, he found it more beautiful than peculiar. What shocked him more was its parallel to the ancient legends told for generations before the hearth fires of his mother's clan. A tale he had heard the MacLeods quote first when he was but a tiny lad clinging to his mother's skirts.

Without warning he suffered the most overwhelming need to gaze into those prophesied eyes once more, to verify what he thought he had seen. Even stronger was his desire to rid the lass of the ugly black eye patch, for it gave her more the look of a swashbuckling, rum-swilling buccaneer on the Spanish Main than the lovely young woman she was.

"You no longer have need to hide your eyes under this scrap of leather," he told her, leaning forward and looping the strap off her head before she could prevent it. The other lass, Myrna, gasped at his bold act, obviously horrified, widening her eyes and covering her mouth with both palms. Lady Ainsley seemed startled indeed by his unexpected action, her soft lips parting in silent shock as he wadded the leather inside his fist, then carelessly tossed it through the opened window.

The surprise on her face ran slowly into pleasure, or perhaps it was merely relief to be rid of the thing, and Rodric found himself again caught up in those eyes of hers, absolutely entranced by her large azure eyes fringed with long golden lashes. This time he barely noticed the spot of copper-brown that marred the bottom half of her left iris. Evil eye, indeed, he thought, contemptuous of the ignorant people surrounding her. The MacLeod Lady of the Legend sat before him in the flesh, he knew that now by the mark inside her eyes. Moreover she was his wife. Triumph overwhelmed him as he realized he now had the final proof that they were destined to wed.

He wondered if some of the stories bandied about concerning her were true, for the tenets of the legend bore out the whispers spoken in many a crofter's wattle-and-daub hut throughout the glens and mountains of the Highlands. He could not seem to take his gaze from her face and began to wonder if that was part of her power, to beguile, or was it simply that he had rarely seen a woman so beautiful?

God preserve him, had she already bewitched his mind? Lady Ainsley was called the witch of Kilchurn by many Scots, well he knew that without the verification of the abbess. Her fame had spread all the way to his own Isle of Skye, but little had he known then that she would become his wedded wife. Was she adept at the other feats prescribed by the MacLeod legend of the fairies?

" 'Tis said by many that the witch of Kilchurn can heal the sick by merely touching their flesh. Is that true?" Personally he had never believed the stories of magic spells bestowed upon the witch of Kilchurn, but this tale was different because the Lady of the Legend was purported to have such a gift.

In the wake of his question, Lady Ainsley's soft mouth tipped at the corners—a smile designed to enchant—but that also bestowed not a little mockery. "Do you harbor fear of me now, my lord, since you have cast off the protective patch over my demon's eye? Do you fear from this day I will haunt you as you lie abed in the dark night?"

Rodric felt a twitch of inner amusement at the audaciousness of the girl's taunt. Haunted by her he would be, but not for the reasons she cited. She was a comely lass, and he felt sure, a virginal maid after so long cooped inside a convent. Though few of that sort would make allusions to a gentleman's couch.

To her surprise she would soon be sharing the very bed of which she spoke, for the ink upon their marriage contract was long dry. Not a fortnight had passed since the legal wedding document had been set with her true father's signature and sealed in wax with his own signet ring. Lady Ainsley had been told many lies by the Campbells, even the name she had grown up with was of false origin. She would soon enough know the truth from his own lips. The truth and the husbandly kisses that he was already beginning to crave. Now, however, was not the time to think of the pleasures they would one day share.

"I believe in neither demons nor witch's spells, though every other soul hereabouts seems to fear you. There was well nigh talk of you in every village we passed through, and blame heaped upon your head for the pestilence presently ravaging the countryside. I do not believe such things of you, but I am most curious to know if you are the healer others have sworn you to be."

"Nay, I cannot heal by touching flesh. 'Tis a silly tale, as you say." Ainsley's denial seemed a bit too quick and too vehement. Why? The answer

to his question was forthcoming, he found, not
from Ainsley's own lips but from the mouth of her
friend, Myrna.

"The abbess rarely lets Ainsley touch the sick
brought to our hospice, for fear she got her powers from the devil; but 'tisn't true, my lord. She
is learned in herbs and remedies by the old Knight
Hospitaller, Brother Alfonse." Myrna glanced protectively at Ainsley, but Ainsley was watching
Rodric so closely that he began to feel vulnerable
beneath her intelligent, unblinking stare.

"Am I really known throughout the realm?" was
her query, one that surprised him, though it
seemed uttered with little motive other than
curiosity.

"Aye, that you are. Tales of the witch of Kilchurn are told from the lairds of Fife to the mer-
chants of Edinburgh, and probably as far south
as those inhabiting the English capital," Richard
interjected into the conversation with an affable
grin, blithely unaware that his innocent remark
could very well have given away his ruse.

Rodric hoped the girls did not notice his cousin's slip of tongue, but he knew Ainsley had as
she immediately transferred her keen gaze to
Richard, her delicately arched blond brows knit-
ting with a perplexed frown. "You speak of the
English as foreigners when you wear the scarlet
of the Royal Dragoon? Why is that, my lord
Lancaster?"

"I suspect that Richard has ridden alongside us
Scots for so long that he feels a Highlander at
heart, my lady." Rodric glanced at his cousin with

a nonverbal warning for him to consider his comments before speaking again. They could not let down on their charade, not yet. They had the girl in their hands, but they would not be safely away until they left Campbell territory, and that meant the whole of the Argyll peninsula.

Richard's startling transformation into a member of the dragoons would need continue until they were aboard the boat and out to sea. Even on such short acquaintance Rodric knew the girl to be bright and lively of intellect. Another slip of tongue would alert the fair Ainsley of their trickery, and they were much too deep in Hugh Campbell's domain to allow that to happen.

"But 'tis no secret that the peasants hereabouts say your eye is the blame for the pestilence ravaging the shores of Loch Awe this past winter."

He fully expected her to laugh at the absurd story, or at least deny any involvement, but something in the way she looked at him sent a cold chill undulating down the length of his spine.

"Is that the reason the Earl of Strathmorton has sent for me? To gaze into my evil eye and watch me perform my witchcraft?"

His gut told him that she was trying to intimidate him. "I am looking into your eyes as we speak. Perhaps you should demonstrate to us now what awful deeds are prompted by your kinship with the devil."

Instantly Ainsley lowered her gaze. He watched her draw her lower lip between her teeth. His own eyes latched hungrily on those softly moist lips and mentally traced them with his own tongue.

As she answered his challenge, he wondered if her lips would tremble the first time he kissed her. Someday he would taste her sweet mouth at will, and every other part of her, and the power of that mental image sent his blood surging warmly with erotic anticipation.

"I am not a witch, but I have always feared that the earl would come to believe such tales. Is that the reason he has never come to visit me, though he has been most generous with his patronage?"

Strathmorton had lied to her, had tricked her, had locked her inside a nunnery so that she would never get the opportunity to learn about her true destiny. Rodric could not tell her that now; 'twas much too early. So instead he asked her another question he had pondered since he had learned of her existence.

"How came you to live at the abbey? You must have been quite young, for stories of the witch of Kilchurn have circulated for years."

"I was orphaned as a newborn babe after Mac-Donald savages spilled the blood of my parents. They are heathen murderers, not worthy to walk the same earth as other Highlanders. I curse them to the last man who draws breath, and place a pox upon their sons, and the sons of their sons, and any who suffer them to live."

Rodric made a valiant attempt not to wince under the viciousness of her curses. His muscles tensed considerably, and he exchanged a furtive glance with Richard. Though he took great pains to keep his expression inscrutable, he swore inside. Hugh Campbell had trained her well to hate

Clan MacDonald—no doubt to keep her loyalty if ever the truth were revealed to her—and in doing so had soured any notion Rodric might have had about easily winning the affection of the beautiful young woman across from him.

His hopes withering rapidly, he already began to dread the long, difficult task now facing him. He would have to convince her of the truth with very little time allotted to do so while he fought hatred instilled in her by the Campbells for an entire lifetime. How long would it take him to transcend the lies she now believed so vehemently?

Their marriage had been accomplished with ease, her abduction almost as effortlessly, but the consummation would not be so forthcoming, not with anger distorting her mind and heart. Unfortunately his ultimate success involved the physical union and getting her with child, a feat, he mused gloomily, that would be doomed from the beginning once she knew his real name.

On the other hand he had always been persuasive, especially where women were concerned. There was much she did not understand about her life and parentage but would find out soon enough. She had been lied to at will, about everything of importance in her life. Yet she was quick of wit as well as pleasing to look upon. Given time he might be able to convince her that MacDonalds did not sprout forked horns and cleaved hooves and certainly were not as despicable as the English-loving Campbells who had raised her as their own.

"I am sorry that you lost those beloved of you."

He watched her face intently, wondering just how much of the truth she did know.

"I do not remember my family at all, except recollections of the nursemaid who raised me until I was eight years old."

She spoke now of Ellie MacLeod, he realized with an overwhelming tide of relief. Initially he had not been wont to believe the wrinkled old woman who had come to his kin at Skye and related the sordid tale of treachery and betrayal. It was a tale that had embroiled both him and Ian MacDonald full force into a mission of intrigue as well as his own hasty marriage to the girl with the haunting, different colored eyes sitting across from him.

When he became aware of the way Richard was shifting uncomfortably under the course of the conversation, Rodric strove to change the subject away from Ellie MacLeod.

"You have suffered much in your young life, but we will take good care of you from this day forward. I can promise you that you will not be the object of fear or ridicule when we reach our destination. I give you my solemn word upon that, my lady."

She seemed discomfited by his courtesy, her face troubled. "Even at Strathmorton, which lies so near the abbey? Surely many inhabitants of the castle have heard rumors of my witchcraft?"

Rodric could not tell her the truth, not until they reached the hamlet of Taynuitt, where the boat lay moored. She had already vilified the Mac-Donalds like a vindictive zealot, and after only a very short time in his presence. Escape would be her goal at the mere inkling of who he really was, and he wasn't in the mood to chase her down.

"You mean you cannot divine such answers with your famous evil eye?" he challenged in lieu of veracity.

Richard's chuckle sounded more nervous than amused. "You best watch your boldness, Rodric," said he, "for if she is truly the witch of Kilchurn, she might lay bare all of our secrets."

"Taunt my powers and perhaps you alone will taste my magic."

Ainsley Campbell's threat had been quite calm, but Rodric could tell that she was angry by the way she tossed her head and sent riotously tangled sun-streaked tresses swirling back over one shoulder. She looked directly at him, almost daring him to respond as she sat before him, legs clad in a man's trews, one foot propped on her opposite knee as any soldier might do. Something about her pose and the way her slender thighs looked in the tight leather sent a stinging brand of desire into Rodric's body, and acted more to strengthen his resolve to have her as a willing partner in wedlock.

Despite her unusual eyes, Ainsley Campbell was a woman who tantalized men by her mere essence. He allowed himself a long moment to admire her delicate bone structure and fine white skin, fair and creamy and so dewy soft that he had to stop himself from stroking his fingertips along her high, elegantly formed cheekbone.

The fragility of her brow and classical lines inherent in her profile were not indicative of peasant stock, which only bolstered old Ellie's farfetched tale that had lured him so far into the provinces of his worst enemy. Once the cheeky lass was adorned in a shimmering hooped gown sewn with pearls and lace and sat in her place as mistress of Arrandane Castle, she would shine as brilliantly as a winter constellation.

Undeniably she possessed the mark of nobility, and she was now his, forming an alliance that would not only cement his place as heir to the MacDonalds as lord of the isle but also strengthen ties between the MacLeods and the MacDonalds, so long torn by strife and war. Now that he had seen her in person, Rodric had no doubt that Ian MacDonald would claim her as daughter. All he had to do was look upon her face.

"When will I meet the Earl of Strathmorton? I have always dreamed of such an honor. I would thank him for his generosity." The object of his rather heated perusal had asked the question of him, and he garnered his thoughts back to the problems at hand.

"My lord is more than anxious to see you." True, Ian no doubt paced the floor in eagerness for her arrival at Arrandane. Someday Rodric would remind Ainsley that he did not lie at this moment but merely circumvented her questions.

He could tell she was pleased by his answer. Could she really have no idea of her real identity? Though that seemed implausible, Ellie's story was an ugly one even from a villain of Hugh Campbell's caliber.

"I am surprised you have not visited at Castle Strathmorton since the island lies so near Kilchurn?" He hoped to find out as much as he could about her past before the truth prevailed, and she raised her guard against his interest.

"I was not allowed to leave the nunnery for fear the peasants would attack me as a witch," she admitted with a sidelong glance at Myrna, "but I did sneak out on occasion. In truth, on this very day I rode beside the loch and gazed at the walls of Strathmorton. That's why I am dressed so peculiarly, but I beg permission to change attire before I am presented to his lordship. I do not wish to disappoint him after the kindnesses he has shown to me."

"You had access to a mount?" Rodric asked, more than surprised.

Ainsley smiled broadly. "The abbess forbade me to ride, of course, but Jeremy helped me sneak away with Saracen, my great white Arabian. He is my one possession, for he was left to me by Brother Alfonse."

"Pray tell who is Jeremy?"

"He is the boy who cares for the stables, and it is from him that I got the trews and shirt in which to ride."

His bride continued to shock Rodric, on purpose he feared, but he turned the subject again to elicit more about her life. "And you have no other living kin? What about the nursemaid you mentioned?"

"I never saw her again after I was brought to

Kilchurn. The earl sent word of her death through the abbess not long after I arrived."

More deceit, Rodric realized. The poor lass had been fed nothing but Hugh's self-serving fabrications. Now he, too, was embroiling her in deception, but would she believe the incredible story once he revealed the truth? Would she be grateful to Rodric for rescuing her and giving her a rightful place with her true clan? He had a feeling she would not.

"Rest now, my lady. 'Twill not be long before we reach the crossroads, where you can step down and refresh yourself at the travelers' well."

As he abruptly ended their discourse, the two young ladies leaned their heads together for a session of hushed whispering, too low for the men to overhear. Richard crossed a booted foot atop his knee, much the way Ainsley had, and leaned his head back against the cushion. Rodric eyed his beautiful bride, certainly finding a great deal about her that gave pleasure to the senses.

Now that he had heard her mind about his kith and kin, he knew their marriage promised to be little other than an intimate battleground. But he had expected that from the onset, and happy or naught, their union was set and sealed and would put him and his sons in line to rule as the lord of Arrandane and leader of MacLeod and Mac-Donald alike. Any marriage would be worth such a prize.

He shifted his gaze to contemplate the passing scenery as they rode for a time in silence, but he was glad when the carriage rolled to a stop near the traveler's well of St. Barnabas, where they were to meet an armed company of his own men. Once astride, they could make excellent time back to Taynuitt. As the soldier acting as footman jumped down and opened the door, Rodric gestured for Ainsley to precede him. Rodric watched her jump down with lithe grace, more than appreciative of the way the worn deerskin breeches fit snugly over her slender hips. The thin wool shirt did little to conceal the fact she wore none of the proper feminine undergarments that genteel ladies donned for the sake of modesty. It did reveal, however, that her body was as well formed as her face, and the sudden aching sensation plaguing his body bore witness to his approval. The ridiculous quickening of desire did not fade quickly, even after he was on the ground with Richard watching the two women walk together toward the covered well.

"Do you think she suspects our ploy?" Richard queried softly, unfastening the top button of the English uniform. "By God, I shall be glad to cast off this bloody uniform, even the scarlet color sickens me."

Rodric glanced up at the sky. Dark clouds hastened the falling dusk, and he could detect the damp scent of a storm coming on the rising wind. Down the road in the direction from which they had come, he knew that a small contingent of soldiers, volunteers from the MacDonalds of Glen Coe, were following them at a distance. He had ordered them to keep out of sight but close enough to assist if they skirmished with Campbell forces.

After a moment, he decided to dip a cup of cold water from the well, but the clipped cadence of galloping hooves brought him up to a standstill. He muttered a low oath when he saw his lieutenant, Robert MacDonald, break from the trees on horseback and bear down on them.

"I told him to stay out of sight," he ground out between set teeth to Richard, spinning to see if Ainsley had recognized the red plaid of MacDonald tartan Robert used as a saddle blanket.

Neither Ainsley nor Myrna seemed to make the connection, but only watched curiously as Rodric's lieutenant thundered to stop and leapt from the back of his prancing mount.

"A company flying the pennons of Hugh of Strathmorton are headed this way! They're armed to the teeth and mounted to the man," he cried breathlessly. "We aren't enough to win against them if a fight is challenged!"

"Damnation," Rodric growled, well aware they were in for serious trouble if they encountered the enemy, a fight he would relish if he was not so anxious to get Ainsley locked safely inside a MacDonald stronghold. He strode rapidly toward the women, then paused in his intent when he found Ainsley staring hard at Robert's accoutrements. She swung back to face him. Her countenance drained of color as realization hit her, and she cried out in warning to Myrna. Before Rodric could react, both women turned and fled into the darkening forest.

Cursing, he grabbed Robert's reins and swung onto the saddle, holding the skitterish horse in check with one hand as it sidestepped in alarm. His command came low, terse. "Robert, get the men back to the ship. I'll catch Ainsley and meet you there. Richard, try to find the other girl but don't waste time on her if she evades you. Be quick, damn it! We cannot risk a fight this close to Strathmorton!"

Wheeling his horse toward the trees, he spurred it in pursuit of his fleeing bride, cursing his own bad luck. Twilight was nearly gone now, the sky darkening quickly to cloak the landscape. The woods were thick and uncharted, a black, impenetrable undergrowth with a million places for a slender girl to hide. A miracle from heaven would be required for him to catch her before she found an armed Campbell to rescue her.

Chapter Four

Her blood was surging so violently through her veins that Ainsley could actually feel the thunder of her pulse. Still she ran hard, propelled by fear, like a fox fleeing hounds through the thorny tangles and dense undergrowth. The growing darkness helped conceal her desperate escape as she angled through tree trunks and scrambled over fallen logs.

Thankful now for the trews and shirt protecting her skin from sharp brambles, she bent low and endeavored unsuccessfully for stealth. But her thrashing course was not to be silenced as she jumped through piles of dead leaves and fallen branches while she rushed onward. Constantly glancing behind her, she kept up the pace until her throat burned with such raw pain that she could barely suck in her breath.

When a huge oak tree loomed as shelter not far ahead, she rounded the trunk and pressed her back against the gnarled bark. Impending nightfall was the only thing that could save her, and the thunderstorm brewing to the south would darken the day prematurely. Already the winds tossed the thick boughs high above her head in a wild, rustling dance.

Panting like a wolf on the run, she knelt and sucked in deep breaths to calm the riot of her heart. The hamlet of Ingott was nearby; they had passed through it not long before they stopped at the well, but could she risk going there for help? The crofters of Ingott hated her, blamed her for the pestilence that was decimating their villagers.

Cowering at the base of the tree, shivering uncontrollably, both with fear and exertion, she hugged her shoulders and continued to gulp great lungfuls of air. She had to think, to calm her fright. Where was Myrna? Had they taken her already? The men were MacDonalds, she had seen the red tartan of the arriving horseman very clearly, a design she had recognized as evil since she was very young. But why were they so deep inside Argyll, where the Clan Campbell reigned supreme?

Had the MacDonalds come to kidnap her? she wondered with rising horror. They had demanded her by name! Why would they want her? She was no heiress of great wealth, many of the other girls at the abbey had far more. Why would the man Rodric take such risks in order to abduct her? She had no relative with gold coin enough to garner a ransom.

Or was it merely an act of vengeance for which the MacDonald devils were so well-known? A life for a life, perhaps, as had been their motive when

they massacred her parents? Who among the
MacDonalds would even know of her existence,
locked away in the abbey since early childhood as
she had been?

Ainsley found no credible answers to her questions. Panic, simmering thus far, rose inside her
like the contents of a fiery cauldron, rising in bub-
bles of raw terror that immobilized her. She shut
her eyes and huddled among the rootwad of the
tree, trying to get hold of herself as the storm
bore down upon her. Cold drops pelted the
ground around her, gaining force as she raised her
hot face to the cooling rain.

She peered through the forest, worried for Myrna's safety. Would the other girl perish somewhere
in these dark trees, a MacDonald broadsword
thrust through her breast? If not for Ainsley,
Myrna would be safe in the convent instead of
fighting for her life. Was that the intent of their
mortal enemies? To murder helpless, unarmed
maids? But would they dare face the wrath of a
man as powerful as Strathmorton after perpetrat-
ing such cowardly acts?

Distant lightning illuminated the deepening
dusk, and Ainsley peered through the falling rain
at the ghostly gray woods with its mist-shrouded
trees. Echoing thunder rumbled and rolled like
avenging angels across the heavens. Another flash
of white filled up the encroaching darkness, and
Ainsley came to her knees when she caught sight
of the man Rodric heading toward her. He rode
a horse now, and as the flash of lightning died

away, he saw her and spurred his mount in her direction.

Ainsley scrambled to her feet and took flight, oblivious to the thickets where stickers slashed her face and arms. Her only thought was escaping the MacDonald. She could hear thrashing as his horse trod through the thickets, and she twisted her path again when she saw a clearing in the distance. Though twilight had nearly faded into night, she could make out a group of riders moving slowly away through the trees. The pennon flew high and proudly, and she nearly collapsed with relief when she saw the tusked boar of Clan Campbell emblazoned on the flag.

"Help, help," she cried, but the wind took her screams and hurled them to the treetops. The riders continued upon their trek away from her. She had to get close enough for them to hear her! She took off toward them, yelling desperately and waving her arms, but she had not made it ten yards when she heard her pursuer just behind her. Fingers closed in the loose fabric at the back of her shirt, and she was jerked off her feet.

A moment later he was on the ground with her, his left arm jerking her back against his chest as his horse reared and crashed sideways into the bushes. He held her tightly, one hand clamped over her mouth as he took her with him to the ground. She grunted as her breath was knocked out of her, then he was atop of her, his weight pinning her facedown in wet leaves. Sobbing, and twisting hysterically, she struggled, but his grip was too strong.

"Hold still, damn it, or you're going to get hurt!" They were hoarse, breathless words muttered viciously through clenched teeth.

When she refused to yield to his strength, he flipped her onto her back and held her there with his torso. Trying to bite his hand covering her mouth, she flailed at him, hitting him in the face with her fist then drawing blood with her nails before he managed to pinion her wrists together above her head. He held her mouth with his left hand and peered at the Campbell soldiers, who were nearly out of sight as they rode through the downpour thirty yards away.

Though she continued to try to free herself, he was far too strong. Finally she lay still, heaving ragged breaths and staring wide-eyed into his face. No longer did he seem the handsome gentleman whose face she admired. Blood trickled from a long scratch on his left cheek, and he was angry now, his expression so rigid with rage that she felt sure he was moments from strangling her with his bare hands as she lay helplessly at his mercy.

His head bent closer to her face; she could feel his labored breaths against her cheek even as his eyes remained fixed on the retreating riders. He lay against her, his powerful muscles leashed in check but ready to fight in the space of a heartbeat. Squeezing her eyes shut against the driving rain striking her face, she knew despair inside her heart. Her clansmen had not seen her. She was in the hands of the MacDonalds with no one to help her.

For what seemed an eternity they lay thus,

pelted by the storm, the heaviness of his limbs
holding her unmoving on the muddy ground. By
the time he dragged her to her feet, their clothes
were soaked and she was shivering uncontrollably.
Though saturated to the bone and stiff with cold,
she managed a weak attempt to tear her arm loose
from his grip, but his fingers tightened brutally
around her elbow.

"Listen to me, lass, I do not want to harm you.
I know you're afraid and for good reason, but if
you come along without a fight, I swear I won't
hurt you."

"Think you that I would give credence to the
word of a MacDonald devil! I would rather perish
here than go willingly with you!"

Rodric frowned and glanced back at the de-
parting company now swallowed up into the dark
fog. He loosened his white neck cloth, now blackened with mire, and jerked it off. "Then I have
little choice but to keep you quiet the only way
I can."

Ainsley fought the gag as he settled it over her
mouth and knotted it tightly behind her head. She
stared at him defiantly as he pulled the leather
thong out of his hair and bound her hands in
front of her. His hair hung long, dampened by the
rain until it straggled loosely around his shoulders, making him appear the barbarian he was. To
her surprise, he did not grip her arm so harshly
now that she was subdued but merely led her to
where his horse stood with hanging bridle nearby.

Boosting her up over the leather saddle, she lay
there upon her stomach until he mounted behind

her and settled her in front of him like a deer carcass. She hung there, pummeled by the rain, blond hair struggling over her eyes until she could not see. She was exhausted from her dash through the woods, but fearful, for all her life she had heard tales of the MacDonalds' cruel treatment of their enemies, horrible massacres where women and children alike were murdered with knives and swords. Now she would die the same way.

The storm worsened as they plodded onward through the wind and rain. Her body gradually turned to ice under the deluge, and she could no longer feel her muscles beneath her wet, clinging garments. Despite the fact that he was inside enemy territory, Rodric MacDonald seemed to know exactly where he was going. After what seemed an eternity, he brought the horse out of the woods and into a muck-clogged road. Through the drizzle she thought she recognized the outskirts of Ingott.

Surely he would not be so bold, or so stupid, she thought, to bring her into a Campbell village, where most lived under the liege and protection of the Earl of Strathmorton. He would be seized at once, and though she was feared by many there as a witch, perhaps they would not harm her once they learned she was the ward of the earl. Questions revolved through her mind like a wind spiral as he guided the horse around the perimeter of the village. No one was about, but still he circumvented the single thoroughfare that meandered through the midst of the stone and thatch buildings.

Not long after, she realized exactly where he was taking her and was appalled at his destination. The Black Boar Inn lay at the crossroads between Dalmally and Oban, which lay to the west. Even she, raised innocently in the cloisters, knew it to be a place where men took care of their baser needs with women of ill repute. What had he in mind to do with her there? The obvious answer sent her cold with disbelief, and she looked around, frantic for help, but no one was venturing from their warm beds on such a cold, inhospitable night. What could she do if she saw someone anyway, gagged and trussed as she was?

With necessary stealth he pursued his intention, with so much care in fact, that she knew he was wary of discovery. If that were so, why come there at all? He said not a word to her as he wended his way through dripping, swaying trees to the back entrance of the inn. A thatched-roof shed gave them respite from the storm, and he dismounted and pulled her down beside him, as if she was a wisp of eiderdown. Though she stood still and docile as he secured his reins to a stall, Ainsley's eyes darted around anxiously for any avenue of escape. She would run the moment he gave her opportunity. Unfortunately he was not so careless to do so, but bent and hoisted her like a sack of barley across the broad plane of his shoulder.

Grunting under the gag as her cheek hit against his back, he settled her where he wanted her with his forearm across the backs of her thighs then strode casually out into the rain again as if he was taking her strolling on a sunny afternoon. When they reached the inn proper, seemingly deserted for an abode so infamous, he entered a small, enclosed stairwell half hidden by shrubbery, as if he knew the place well. He toted her to a door at the top of the steps where he knocked softly. She squirmed until his arm tightened around her legs.

Barely a moment passed before the door swung open to admit them. She was carried into warmth and bright light, and blinked against the glare after so long staring into darkness. When her eyes adjusted, she realized she was inside a chamber filled with a bed and other furniture. She lay still when she heard a woman's voice speaking to Ainsley's abductor.

"By the saints, Rodric, have you lost your senses? Bringing the girl here is dangerous!"

"Our plans went amiss, Bess. And I know the area not well enough to find my way to the boat in this bloody downpour."

"You are a lucky man that the storm has kept Campbell soldiers out of the taproom this night, when usually they are leaning against the bar by the cartload." She sounded angry, and a bit frightened, too, Ainsley realized as Rodric unceremoniously dumped her on the bed. She twisted at once and rose to her knees.

"God's teeth, Rodric, did you have to truss her up like some felon? Poor little lassie."

The woman was older than Ainsley, but not by much, probably nearing her thirtieth year or somewhere thereabouts, and pretty of face with curly blond hair caught in a topknot and fine violet-blue eyes that peered curiously at her. Her expression changed as Ainsley gave her a hostile glare.

"She does have the mismatched eye as purported," Bessie noted to Rodric. "No one must see her here, for the witch of Kilchurn is despised in Ingott."

"She's no witch but a willful girl who's already given me a black eye."

Bess looked quickly at him, then touched the bruise forming at the corner of his eye. Her touch was tender. "You cannot blame her for that, my lord. You did abduct her with trickery and malice."

Ainsley sat back on her heels, distressed to know how far-reaching the plot was against her. Why, why, why? Again the same questions with no answers to end the litany.

"Easy there, lassie," Rodric said, as if he sensed her sudden despair. "No one here will hurt you, and we'll be off again as soon as the rain yields."

"By Saint Columba, what did you do to the lass, Rodric? She is covered with mud and wearing leather trews!"

"I didn't choose her garb for her nor tell her to take flight in a rainstorm."

"Martina just filled the washtub for my bath. The water's hot and plentiful in the kettle there on the fire, and I've plenty of warm clothes that'll fit you." Bess leaned closer to Ainsley, then frowned at Rodric. "The poor lass looks the worse for your company. Her face bleeds from scratches."

Rodric lifted Ainsley's face, and though she glared at him with every ounce of hatred she felt and tried to wrest away from his fingers, he held her chin tight as he searched her for injury. "She fled through thickets of thorns to escape me." He let go and turned away, drawing the pistol in his belt as a knock sounded on the door.

Bess held a finger to her lips, then moved to the portal. "Aye? Who is there?"

"Martina, it is. Glennie be wantin' ye company and asks if ye finished with ye bath, is all."

"Tell him I will come shortly," Bess answered, then turned back to Rodric.

"You'll find clothes in the chiffarobe there for the both of you, and you'll be wise to keep the door bolted till I return. There's bread and cheese left on my supper tray and a pint of ale to wash it down with. I will make sure no one disturbs you here with the tale that you are a gentleman in secret tryst with a married lady."

Those words brought color up underneath Ainsley's muddy cheeks and a new fear at being left alone with the big MacDonald.

"You'll be paid handsomely for this night, Bess, my love" was her enemy's parting remark to the woman Ainsley's eyes widened as he smacked the woman's backside as she turned toward the door, but Bess only giggled as she let herself out the door.

Rodric turned to Ainsley, and her breath caught at the way he stared at her. She shivered, not from cold, though she felt half frozen, but because she realized she was now completely under his control.

Chapter Five

When her MacDonald captor moved slowly toward the bed, Ainsley inched back away from him until the wooden headboard stopped her cautious retreat. Her eyes never left his face as he stopped and stood towering over her. Defiantly she tried to dispel her rising trepidation but could not prevent a long, drawn-out shudder that crept like a writhing snake up her spine to the base of her neck. What did he intend to do now?

"You're cold."

His remark was not the one she expected, but she stayed still and continued to watch him, her eyes full of distrust. The corners of her mouth ached from the mud-stained neck cloth stretched tightly through her teeth, not sure how she could counter any advance he might make. She went rigid when he sat down on the edge of the bed and stared at her for a few tense moments.

"As I told you before I don't want to hurt you, but for our safety and for Bess's, I cannot let you reveal our presence here. If I take off the gag, will you give me your solemn vow not to cry out for help?"

All very reasonable and civilized after his dastardly deeds against her, she mocked him inwardly yet could not help but feel astonishment that he would trust her so on the basis of her word. Giving one stiff nodding motion with her head, she adopted a look of earnestness when she felt no compunction at all about fleeing him the first moment she got a chance.

And she would scream her head off as well, and in a thrice, except for the fact that her infamy among the inhabitants of Ingott made it dangerous to do so. After Bess's words, she feared she would be treated more harshly as the notorious witch of Kilchurn than he would be, a MacDonald discovered in their midst, and he no doubt knew that well. Still, she could never escape his clutches while bound and gagged. She would bide her time. He would eventually let down his guard.

For the space of a trembling heartbeat he appeared to mentally weigh her trustworthiness, and Ainsley tried not to squirm beneath his measuring silver regard. No longer did he awe her senses with his fine look of nobility, but seemed nothing more than a dangerous outlaw spattered with mud and lethally armed with sword and brace of pistols.

Her body tensed, her muscles ready to do battle, as he pushed her head to one side and carefully untied the knotted gag. As it dropped away from her face, she moistened her lips and stroked the tip of her tongue against the ache at the sides of her mouth. When she realized he was watching her do so, standing very still, she stopped it at once, and again their eyes met. Neither spoke, though the tension was as thick as batter.

"Why are you doing this to me? What is it you want?" Her whisper was low, but she had to know his answer. She swallowed hard, convulsively, in fear of what he might say.

When he moved suddenly, bringing up his arm toward her head, Ainsley cowered slightly, instinctively expecting a blow. His hand stilled in midair, his expression startled by her defensive reaction, and it was at that point that she realized he had merely meant to push away the wet tangles hanging in front of her face. Again he stared deeply, unafraid, into her eyes, and she realized very few others in her life ever dared to do so.

His voice came softly, his eyes fixed on her left cheek. "The thorns cut deep." A pause followed, then he gave a deep, heaving sigh. "It was not supposed to happen this way. I never intended you to get hurt. If you hadn't fled me, you would not have suffered injury. 'Twas a foolish thing to do."

Foolish?, she thought with a scathing kind of anger that she dared not reveal. He no doubt thought her docile indeed to go easily with a murderous abductor. But she would be wise to show fear if she wished him to lower his guard. "I was frightened. I knew not whether you sought to murder me, or ravish me, or hold me for ransom. I still do not know what you intend."

His strong white teeth flashed briefly, and the

wretch had the gall to laugh at her very legitimate fears. "You have naught to concern from me. You have been ill taught in your low regard for us of Clan MacDonald, a sorrowful consequence of birth that I intend to remedy."

If he had tried for a millennium to astonish her, he would have had no better luck. "You overestimate your powers of persuasion, my lord, if you think you can make me forget the blackhearts who murdered my parents and now have taken me prisoner against my will."

"We will see if you hold to such unfortunate conclusions once you learn the truth."

"Truth? Pray tell it to me now, if you please."

Suddenly the moment for discourse passed, and his face returned into an inscrutable mask impossible to decipher. He stood up, fists braced on his hips, looking at the flames darting and dancing in the hearth. "We have time to bathe and don dry garb, perhaps even rest for a time if the storm plays out. We have a long journey ahead of us this night."

"Journey to where?"

Rodric simply ignored her question.

"I have a right to know my fate," she insisted forcefully.

"You can use the wash barrel first if you please, but heed well my warning, my lady. Do not try to escape me again."

His words were spoken calmly, uttered innocuously, but with a subtle thread of iron-hard threat. His gaze surveyed her steadily, as if he attempted to deduce her intentions.

Unwilling to give away herself, Ainsley frowned and glanced around the room, noticing for the first time, and with a great deal of interest, the draped casement window.

"Unless you covet a coffin to lie inside, 'tis not worth the trouble to contemplate fleeing through yonder window. 'Tis a long drop to your death upon the paving stones below." When she said nothing, he added impatiently. "Be about it. The water's growing cold."

"Am I to bathe like this?" She held up her bound wrists and sent him a glare.

Without comment he proceeded to unfetter her hands, and Ainsley gloated with inward triumph, for each of his concessions put forth better conditions for her eventual escape. A slatted dressing screen stood at one side of the fire, and Ainsley positioned it around the washtub to block his view. She warmed her numb hands close to the fire, glancing longingly at the waiting bathwater, but was mightily afraid to ungarb herself with him so close by.

"You need not worry, for I have no intention of molesting you."

Refusing to give an answer, she peeked through the screen and found him removing his filthy black surcoat and stained white shirt. She averted her eyes, then looked back again as his bare back appeared. She had never seen a man naked, nor did she want to, but she did not think he meant to ravish her or he would have done so already.

Ainsley looked down at herself and grimaced at the mud that covered her from head to toe. Even her hair was caked in strands heavy with black mire, and she looked longingly at the warm water. Never had she, nor any of the other girls at the abbey, been allowed to submerge themselves in such a way. The abbess thought the idea of nudity, even in the bath, much too sinful to consider, so instead they had made do with cold basin water, even upon the most frigid January days. Still, how could she possibly trust the man? When she peered at him again, he sat on the edge of the bed in his breeches and boots, cleaning dried mud off the barrel of one of his pistols.

Quickly, before she could change her mind, she unbuttoned the trews at the waist and stepped out of them, then hastily pulled the filthy shirt off over her head. She stepped into the tub, careful not to make a splash to alert him that she did so, and nearly swooned with pleasure as the warm water enveloped her cold, clammy skin.

Bess had set pitchers of water beside the tub, for purposes of washing her hair, Ainsley realized, and near the cauldron of water warming on the tripod lay a round bar of soap. When she put it to her nose, she found it scented of lilies. Wishing she could luxuriate forever in the hot bath, she knew she did not dare, so she quickly lathered her skin even as every nerve remained poised and on edge for any hint of Rodric MacDonald's approach.

To her relief she heard no sound from the other side of the barrier, and she took a few moments to soap her hair, then used a pitcher to sluice out the lather. She groaned in pain when the soap stung into the open facial cuts.

"What is it?"

The man now stood close, but still on the other side of the screen. Ainsley grabbed the white linen towel warming by the fire, sloshing water as she clutched the thin cloth desperately against her breasts. Fortunately his footfalls took him away again, but no longer did she linger in the warm water. She was quickly drying herself when a blue gown landed atop the screen, followed by a white petticoat.

"These are probably too big for you, but better than those damned deerskin trews."

Ainsley was tempted to retort, but thought better of it as she drew the soft undershift over her head and hurriedly stepped into the dress. Royal blue with ruched white lace around the low neckline, she fumbled with the laces on the front of the bodice, binding it as tightly as possible, but still deeming it immodest compared to the gray serge habits of the abbey. As she tied her rather dirty apron with its pockets of collected herbs at her waist, she admitted that he had been true to his word. And now that she was clean and clothed, she was much better prepared to escape.

Hesitant to face him again, she reluctantly stepped around the edge of the screen. He turned quickly from his place at the window and stared at her, his eyes dropping almost at once to where her breasts mounded provocatively above the loose neckline. More than aware that he was half-naked himself, she turned away and moved across the room in the opposite direction. She paused near the gate-leg table set against the wall.

"Partake of some cheese and ale while I tend to myself, but I warn you again, I will be watching your every move and I hold not to the maidenly modesty that you display so charmingly."

In other words he would come after her completely naked, if need be, she thought with a blush as he folded back the screen and began to wash his torso in the tub in full view of her. Averting her eyes, she wondered if she could get away while he was so engaged. She thought it wiser to bide her time, however, and her stomach rumbled as she caught the scent of the fresh baked scones hidden in a napkin-covered basket. She fetched one and tore off a piece, tasted it, and found it palatable, though not as light and tasty as Sister Colleen's oatmeal scones. A pot of honey stood open beside it, and she dipped a portion in it, realizing how famished she was. She needed her strength for when she decided to run, she decided. When her eyes found the earthen jug of ale, she wondered if plying him with drink might help her cause.

"Well, now, I'm pleased to see that this terrible ordeal I have put you through has not robbed you of appetite."

Ainsley heard the amusement underlying his assessment. She shrugged defensively. "I have not eaten a bite since I broke fast early this day."

As he moved around the table and sat down across from her, she saw that he had donned a clean brown shirt and dark brown riding trews.

"Your clothes seem to fit you better than this gown," she commended dryly, wondering if he left a change of garb with his lover for nights such as this.

"I find the way yours fit rather appealing."

Self-consciously Ainsley tugged at the front of her dress, pulling it up, embarrassed and humiliated. When she stole a look at him, however, he was rubbing the bridge of his nose with his thumb and forefinger, as if very tired. Outside the inn, the storm was gaining in fury, rain beating wrathfully against the windowpanes in great sluicing currents. Inside she watched him slosh a good libation of ale into a pewter tankard, then drain it with a couple of deep drafts. Perhaps he would make it easy for her if he was of a mind to imbibe. Yet somehow she knew he would not be so careless. He was not a stupid man. She watched him sit down in the chair across from her and bite into a scone. The irony of the situation was not lost upon Ainsley. They sat together like old friends enjoying a visit.

"I would know why you have gone to such trouble to abduct me."

He stopped chewing and replaced his empty flagon upon the table. He poured more ale into it. "And I will tell you again that you will know in time. We mean you no harm, so you have no reason to fear us."

For some reason she believed him, but that did not make her wish to stay with him long enough to find out the purpose behind his actions. At his next pronouncement, however, she froze, her greatest fears realized.

"Lie down on the bed."

Ainsley shook her head. "Nay, I will not."

"Aye, you will." Uncompromising.

"What do you have a mind to do there, sir?"

"I have in mind getting some rest, because I have slept little for two days past."

"Stealing innocent maidens breaks into your slumber, my lord?"

A faint glimmer of mirth shadowed his eyes. " 'Tis trying work, I must agree."

"Do you intend to lie upon the bed with me?"

"Aye, with your hands tied to my own. I can think of no other way to keep you with me once my eyes are shut."

They observed each other in silence, gauging the intent of the other, and Ainsley decided then that she would have to make her move before he bound her again. When he turned to reach for a sash draped around the bedpost, she lunged for the bottle, grabbed it, and swung it at him with all her strength.

The bottle smashed against his temple and sent him sprawling sideways onto his hands and knees on the floor. He stayed down, and Ainsley did not pause to see if she had rendered him unconscious. She fled for the outside hallway, scratched desperately to throw the bolt, then flung the door open. Voices and guffaws of laughter filtered up from the ground-floor level, and she avoided the crowded taproom, dashing instead for the steps leading down to the back entrance. By the time she burst out into the backyard, the rain had faltered to a light sprinkle. No one was about, and she avoided the stable and ran instead down the muddy road toward the village.

It was late, and she doubted that she would encounter any villagers, but if she could find a horse, she could make her way back to the abbey on her own. The earl had to be alerted to the trespass of his dominion. Bunching her skirts in her hands, she ran as hard as she could, and when she caught sight of a light moving to her left, she changed her direction toward it, hoping it might be the Campbell soldiers she had seen earlier.

Once she came close enough to realize the lights were from swinging lanterns, she pulled up for fear of being recognized by the peasants. She had always avoided villages when outside the abbey, indeed had avoided any contact with anyone. What if they knew her as the witch of Kilchurn?

"Who goes that way?"

The voice came unexpected from behind her, and much too close for comfort. Frightened, Ainsley whirled at once and found herself facing three men. Their presence had been hidden behind a tall wall of stones, and as one man thrust a lantern toward her face to illuminate her, she realized they had come out of a graveyard. Her courage faltered, and she stumbled backward as the smallest of the men walked straight to her.

"What be yer business out so late at night, lassie?"

Ainsley did not speak as her gaze found the

shovel in his hand then shifted behind him where a coffin sat near an opened grave. Another lantern sat on top of the casket. *Grave diggers,* she realized, sick in the pit of her stomach. *She had stumbled upon the interment of a fever victim.*

Fingers suddenly closed hard upon her shoulder, and she slowly turned her face toward him. He was short, strong, as solidly built as a bull, and he dragged her with him toward his companions.

"Please help me," she begged, glancing behind her. "I've just escaped from MacDonald soldiers. They're here in Ingott, armed, and they tried to kidnap me. I escaped him, but we must warn Strathmorton! Please, you must believe me!"

"MacDonalds? In Ingott? They'd have to be daft to come here." The second man stepped closer to her. He bent and peered into her face. His features and expression were nearly indistinguishable because of his bushy black beard that straggled halfway to his waist. His coarse hair was oily and smelled rank with grease, and when his breath fanned her face, it was vile with grog and garlic.

"Sweet Jesus protect us, she looks just like the witch of Kilchurn! Look at 'er eyes, Jemmer, she's got it, she's got the evil eye! I seen her once before, I did, when I was totin' grain to the abbey's stores. She had herself a black patch o'it that day, she did, but I'd know her anywheres. I would."

A third man—leaner, and wiry of build, more obviously drunken than the others—grabbed her arm. "She be the witch of the abbey? The one who caused the pox that put near our whole village into the ground?"

Two of the men immediately backed away, as if afraid of her, and when the third let go of her arm and made the sign of the cross, Ainsley backed slowly away from them, fear closing tightly around her heart. They blamed her for their pox and pestilences. They believed all their curses and misfortunes were caused by the demon in her eye.

"She kilt my poor sister's wee Will, with 'er magic and hexes," the big bearded one cried furiously, forgetting his initial timidity as his voice rose shrill in the quiet night. "And he were just a bairn in arms, hardly old enough to hold his own spoon."

"Nay, sirs, you are wrong about me. I am no witch." Her voice quavered perilously as she realized her own danger at the hands of drunken men. "I am not, I swear it upon the Virgin. 'Tis only ugly rumors that are said about me . . ." She got no further because the big one grabbed her by the throat.

" 'Tis her evil eye that done us the harm. It be spoken of and feared far as Galloway. We must pluck the devil out of her afore she puts Satan's hex upon us, everyone!"

Sheer panic made Ainsley able to tear her arm loose from his grasp, and she struck off blindly for the trees. Her entire body shook, and she looked back as the sky brightened with a flare of distant lightning. The three grave diggers were running down the road after her.

Chapter Six

🎵

Fleetness of foot got Ainsley to the edge of the trees ahead of her pursuers, but before she could disappear in the darkness of the woods, she ran headlong into a downed log, sprawled over it, skinning hands and knees and cracking her forehead on a rock. Momentarily stunned, she lay still until a shout told her how close the men were. Frantically she wriggled bodily into the leaves against the trunk.

She held her breath. The running footsteps were closer now, and she could see their lanterns swinging and throwing light all around her in erratic, shadowy patterns against the tree trunks. She did not move, could not, as the bearded man stopped his search just on the other side of the log. She could see his legs, only inches from her head.

Screwing her eyes shut, she prayed as she had never done before, a silent litany to the Virgin Mary, to Saint Columba and all the saints she had ever known. Heavy boots shuffled through wet leaves, near enough to smell the wood smoke on the man's clothes. She lay, as rigid and cold as the stone effigies on the sarcophagus in the abbey, her breath suspended in her lungs as he braced a foot on the log.

Rotten wood cracked under his weight and sent a shower of soft splinters onto Ainsley's hair. Not courage, but utter terror, kept her scream of horror frozen, unuttered in her gullet, as he crossed the log and stepped down inches from her head. He turned away from her when another grave digger approached him in a thrashing run, flaming torch in hand.

Ainsley's body ached with the awful tension of lying completely still, her teeth cutting into her bottom lip until she tasted the coppery tang of her own blood. Her limbs lost all rigidity and began to tremble of their own accord as Brother Alfonse's vivid descriptions of the tortures perpetrated on innocent women by witch-hunters flooded her mind. Awful things—red-hot irons against bare flesh, dunking stools where women were strapped and lowered into the water until they drowned . . . oh, please God, save me and I will never commit another sin . . .

Her prayers ended abruptly when she felt a hand grab her hair. She screamed with utter, unbridled horror as the big man jerked her to her feet. He whispered in her ear, the softness of his words making them all the more frightening.

"Ye canna hide under the eyes of the Almighty, daughter of Satan."

Ainsley knew then she was about to die, and

she fought for her life as she had never done before. The man was much too big, his hands huge and brutal upon her arms. He held her immobile, as if she was not struggling with every ounce of her remaining strength, his muscular forearm tightening around her throat.

"Hold yourself still, wicked witch of Kilchurn," he intoned harshly.

Ainsley panted and gasped for breath as his grimy fingers bracketed her face and forced her into the lantern light. She renewed her fight, and he muttered a filthy curse and backhanded her with enough force to send her flying to the ground. Swirling stars sparkled and spun through her vision, disrupting her ability to think as they dragged her upright again.

Thunder growled as it angrily retreated with rain and bolts of lightning to strike fear into the denizens of the next valley, but the damp wind still whipped through the branches and played havoc with the candle flames in the tin lanterns.

"Open yer evil eye, girl!"

The bullish man made the demand, his ragged Campbell plaid of dark blue and green fluttering over his shoulder. He had the torch, and the fire at the end blew backward in a billow of black smoke.

"Please release me! I've done nothing!"

Ainsley's hoarse words went unheeded as she was jerked backward and pinned across the log. She groaned as they held her down, then struggled again as one thrust the torch close into her

face. She turned her head and moaned as the
acrid odor of singeing hair filled her nostrils.

"Open yer bloody eyes, witch, and show us the
mark of Satan! Or feel God's fire burn your flesh."

Ainsley shook her head from side to side, but
one of her tormentors pried open her left eye and
leaned down to peer into her face.

"God have mercy, it is as told in the stories of
her evildoings."

The actual sight of her demon eye seemed to
derail their dire objective, and Ainsley sought her
voice in the dregs of her terror.

"I am no witch but only a lass from the abbey!
I swear upon the Bible most holy that I am not
akin with Satan! 'Tis only a mark of birth you see
in my eyes, a spot of brown upon blue, 'tis all, I
swear! Mercy, I beg you. I've done naught to you,
naught to anyone. I am a Campbell born, the
ward of the Earl of Strath—"

"Silence yer lying tongue or have it cut from
yer throat." The bearded man's voice had become
more gruff, cruel, and deliberate. "Tales of your
perfidy have come to us since the day you were
brought into the abbey as a newborn bairn, and
Ingott's suffered naught but fever and plagues of
boils and pox since that evil day. 'Tis your witchcraft that brings the pestilences to us, but God
Almighty has given us remedy of it on this night.
We will cast the demon from you forever."

Ainsley's heart vibrated in her ears as her eyes
held fixed on the short dagger he now held above
her face. He had heated it in the torch until the
blade glowed red against the dark sky.

"I am innocent." She could only whisper her last denial as he lowered the dirk toward her eye.

"In the name of God and all his avenging angels, we close this open portal to hell. We banish Satan back to his fiery depths and forever free this poor lass from his evil bidding . . ."

Somewhere from deep inside her throat, Ainsley heard a most terrible shriek rip free from the fabric of her despair. She tried to close her eyes but her eyelid was pried apart, forcing her to watch the glowing tip come closer and closer.

She sobbed with hopeless, helpless horror, then cut off her own cry as a different sound exploded nearby; a gunshot, its report echoing over the wind. The knife paused above her, and she stared into the face of the bearded man and watched his evil expression fade into shock. A slowly widening crimson circle bloodied the front of his dirty hide tunic, and he staggered back a step then crumpled to his knees, felled by a pistol ball through his heart.

Then she was free and sobbing with relief. She fell to the ground on hands and knees as her other tormentors yelled before the slashing steel of Rodric MacDonald's broadsword. Stunned, she saw him wield the heavy weapon, swinging it in great forceful arcs, his long black hair blowing in the wind, his features so twisted with rage that she hardly recognized him.

A massive swipe of the sword sent one man to the ground unconscious, and Rodric turned to dispatch the other, but not before the man in tattered tartan snatched up the hot dagger. He flung

the knife, and Rodric groaned as hot metal
plunged deep into the muscles of his side. Despite
his injury he assumed a defensive stance, but the
attacker took flight, leaving the others sprawled
lifelessly upon the ground.

Ainsley remained cowering beside the log, her
limbs trembling as the MacDonald took a step
toward her. She watched him grunt as he jerked
out the small dirk, then slung it away. Without a
word, he pulled her up and to where his horse
now sidestepped with flared nostrils at the scent
of fresh-spilled blood. He steadied the mount with
a hand on the bridle, stepped into the stirrup,
and swung himself into the saddle. Bending, he
grabbed Ainsley's arm and lifted her up behind
him. She barely had time to grab the back of his
shirt before he kicked the stallion to full gallop
and headed out of Ingott.

Still shaken from the ordeal, Ainsley clung
tightly to his waist, horribly aware that the sticki-
ness soaking her arm was blood oozing from his
fresh knife wound, but still she pressed herself as
close against his back as she could. He was her
enemy, a MacDonald, and she did not want to
think about where he was taking her and for what
purpose. Whatever was her fate to be, surely it
could not be as terrible as the one from which he
had risked his life to save her.

The village of Taynuitt lay within a mile of the
salt waters of Loch Etive with ready access to the
Firth of Lorn. Grinding his teeth together against
the burning agony just above his waistband, Rod-

ric pressed on relentlessly for the boat landing. He had to avoid the main road, but he traveled parallel to its course, using the direction as a compass. Fortunately the inclement weather had acted his friend and encouraged Campbell soldiers to remain inside, warm and dry, and unaware of his presence.

Ainsley gave him no more trouble and said nothing as she clung to him as if she were strapped to his back. When the storm intensified again, he drew up long enough to unroll his plaid and throw it over both their backs to protect them from the cold downpour.

The driving rain caused him to miss the turn that led down to the loch, and he was forced to backtrack several miles. With a long litany of curses raging through his mind, he rode on and on, growing light-headed from loss of blood as the hours lengthened. His body felt numb except for the hole of fire where the blade had sliced through his flesh, and he appreciated it when the girl used her wet hem to help staunch the blood flow. Thank God the man had held the blade in the fire, or the bleeding would have been severe. A small blessing, 'twas true, but everything else had surely gone amiss that night.

Relief flooded through him when he finally caught sight of the old mill house on the point. The grueling ride was near an end, and he walked his exhausted mount down the steep incline to where a long wooden dock stretched outward into the deep waters of the loch. He did not dismount but guided the horse onto the wide wood planks, not sure he could sustain himself on foot all the way to shipside, especially if the girl decided to run again.

Halfway to the boat, a sentry called alarm and a handful of armed men came running. Richard reached him first, and took hold of the bridle as Rodric swung a leg over the horse's neck and slid off. He pulled Ainsley down beside him.

"I see you had better luck than I." His cousin peered down at the wet, bedraggled girl standing between them. "The rain helped the one named Myrna evade me."

"Aye, I got the lass all right, but not without a dagger in my side to show for the trouble."

"She stabbed you!" Richard exclaimed, taking a firm grip on Ainsley's arm.

"Nay, not her. A couple of ignorant Campbell louts decided to put an end to the witch of Kilchurn, and 'twas up to me to save her skin."

"Did they harm her?"

"The fools were set to plunge a dagger into her eye when I tracked them down. If I had tarried a moment longer, she would have perished at their hands." He explored his wound, then pressed his fingers against the jagged hole as he took Ainsley's elbow with his other hand.

"Are we set and ready to sail?" he asked as he led her up onto the gangplank.

"Aye, the rain's played out enough for a safe sail to the firth. Are you all right, cousin?"

Rodric nodded without comment. All he wanted was to get belowdecks where it was dry and warm, bind his wounded side, and get some rest. Yet he wasn't about to let Ainsley out of his sight after all he had gone through to get her there. She was quiet now, so subdued by her near demise that he doubted she would risk another flight. However, he bloody well wouldn't take any more chances with her until they landed safely on the Isle of Skye.

As the captain shouted orders and the crew rushed to ready the small fishing boat for disembarkation, Rodric held her tightly by the wrist as he negotiated the companionway leading down to his cramped quarters. He pushed her inside the cabin ahead of him, then followed her, turning the key and pocketing it in his breeches. She showed no reaction, but stood silently near the door while he crossed the cabin and poured himself enough whiskey to make a good start in deadening the pain. The brew was mellow and true, and went down warm inside his gullet, helping to warm him, inside and out.

He drank another glassful, then poured a third before he turned and faced the girl. She looked like a filthy little street urchin. Her dress was drenched in his own blood, and her face was scratched and streaked with mud. It looked like she had sustained an abrasion on her brow as well, and despite his anger at her, his compassion was stirred. She had been through a great deal, faced her own death, yet still stood upon her own two feet. One of his flannel shirts lay discarded over the back of a chair, and he picked it up and took it to her. Up close he could see the lump

on her forehead encased a superficial cut already
purpling into an ugly bruise.

"Are you all right? Did you strike your head?"

She nodded but still did not weep. She wouldn't
meet his gaze.

"There's a bowl and pitcher there on the stand
built into the wall. Towels are just beneath. You
best dry your hair and don something warm if
you're to get any rest."

Ainsley finally looked up at him, but did not
reach for the proffered shirt.

"Please yourself then," he muttered, not in the
mood to coddle her. He dropped the dry garment
on the bunk, turned, and grimaced as he pulled
up the tail of his shirt and found his side a bloody
mess. He picked up the bottle as the ship lurched
with wind-filled sails, then braced an arm on the
bulwark as he tipped the whiskey to his mouth.
He drank several deep drafts. While gritting his
teeth, he tilted the bottle and sloshed a goodly
portion of it into the open wound.

Pain jolted in a direct current to his heart, and
it felt for an instant as if he again had the burning
dagger lodged in his muscle. He clamped his jaw
tight and doused the bloody wound again. Exhal-
ing hard to keep from groaning, he took the towel
and pressed it hard against the wound. He sucked
in a few more deep breaths before he drank again
and finally looked at Ainsley.

She had donned the flannel shirt while his back
was turned and was in the bunk covered to her
chin with a navy woolen blanket. Bess's wet gown
lay in a muddy, bloody heap on the floor. He sat

down on the bunk and stared across at her. She was leery and cautious, her strange-colored eyes wide and wary as a doe cornered by a dog pack. He leaned his head against the wall, sighed deeply, and closed his eyes. Silence reigned until she surprised him by speaking.

"I wish to thank you for saving my life. I am sorry that you were hurt."

Her words of gratitude surprised him. "They were ignorant, superstitious fools."

"For thinking me a witch?"

He gave a curt nod and lifted the bottle again.

"I do possess a gift for healing. I can help your side mend if you'll allow me to tend to it."

Rodric wasn't sure he trusted her sudden show of kindness. "I don't need any magic potions. I'll heal on my own."

"I can relieve the pain far better than will the emptying of a whiskey bottle." Despite her helpful offer, she appeared very nervous now. Her fingers fiddled self-consciously with the edge of the blanket. That made him nervous.

"You seek to minister to a MacDonald. A murdering devil is what you called us, was it not?"

"You saved me from a most wretched fate. I will not forget that you took the knife meant for me." She paused for a short time, then said, "I do not think you mean to harm me or you would have let them blind me, leaving me to die."

When he stared suspiciously at her, she averted her gaze, providing him with an opportunity to study her delicate profile. She had another small bruise on her cheek.

"Please let me help you."

Her plea was very low, and Rodric watched her push a wet strand of hair behind her ear. He was startled when she suddenly met his regard, her eyes intense upon his face.

"You need not be afraid. I am not evil. I only want to ease the pain in your side."

"Just how do you intend to do that?"

She stood and wrapped the blanket around her body, which only emphasized the slender curves hidden beneath the soft wool. Then she walked to him and went down on her knees in front of his bunk.

"Will you lie back so that I can examine the wound?"

The boat was already at sea, and she had no weapon with which to finish him off, so he relaxed back against the wall in a half recline. He remained alert and wary, just in case she suddenly remembered who he was and how much she hated him.

Ainsley raised herself slightly and brought her hands toward him. Palms downward, she didn't touch him at first but slowly examined the torn flesh. After a moment she pressed the heel of her hand against the hard ridge of his lower chest. Immediately he felt a gradual warmth spread over his skin, and his pain lessened noticeably. Slightly unnerved, Rodric grabbed her wrist. She jerked her eyes upward.

"What are you doing?"

She shocked him again with an answering

smile. "I am not possessed by the devil, but was simply taught ways to help the sick and injured."

Eyes locked on hers, Rodric continued to hold her wrist.

"I will not harm you, I vow that before God."

He let her go, and she shut her eyes and continued her strange pressures against his chest, then more upon the inside of his left arm. As she retrieved her pocketed apron from the floor, he remembered her having it on at the abbey. She took a pinch of dried brown powder and shirred it in her palm with a small amount of water from a decanter on the table. Mixing it thoroughly, she took some on her fingertips and reached for his punctured flesh. He was quick to stay her hand.

" 'Tis naught but a salve made from roots and bark. It will help close the flesh, though the heat of the metal helped to do that as well."

Rodric hesitated an instant longer, then hoping she did not apply a substance designed to rot his flesh away, he released his grip. Very gently she applied the thick paste to his side and folded a clean towel to place against his wound. "Sleep now and you will feel better in the morning. I mean you no harm. You will see."

"And give you opportunity to escape while my eyes are closed?"

"Escape? Where, pray tell? I am not so foolish as to jump into a storm-tossed sea. I cannot swim, and even if I could do so, I am much too exhausted this night to strike out for an unknown shore."

With that she recrossed the cabin and climbed

into bed. She turned to face the wall and lay still. Rodric stared at her back with lingering consternation, then lifted the towel and examined his side. The throbbing ache had lessened somewhat, and he replaced the bandage. Was she indeed the witch of Kilchurn as purported? Had she worked some poison into the wound that would send him to his death before the night was done? Knowing that she very well could have done just that, he relaxed back onto the bunk, fairly certain he would enjoy little sleep that night.

Chapter Seven

Despite the deep rocking motion of the ship plunging through storm-wrenched seas, Ainsley finally fell asleep from sheer emotional devastation. Sometime later when a sudden dip to starboard took her rolling hard against the wall, she came awake and hastily struggled to sit up. She stared groggily at Rodric MacDonald, whom she found now occupied a chair drawn close to her bunk. He still wore no shirt but had bound the towel over his wound in a makeshift bandage. Red stains darkened the linen strips and the waistband of his breeches.

Her abductor looked more exhausted than she felt, with black beard stubble darkening the lean contours of his jaw and neck. He simply stared at her with his tired, bloodshot, weary eyes, but said nothing as she pushed straggles of hair off her forehead and drew the blanket closer around her shoulders. Muffled shouts from top decks indicated they were soon to seek landfall.

"How does your wound fare?" Her query was

tentative, for his unblinking stare left her un-settled.

"I do well enough since you placed your healing hands upon me."

Then there was more silence, with only the splashing sounds of seawater deluging the hull and intermittent shouts of busy crewmen. His gaze remained riveted on her face. "Every four-score a lady of Skye will be born, her eyes mismatched in hue, sent by the angels to heal the sick and forlorn."

Agape, Ainsley stared at him, for she had never heard such a rhyme before, but she had no need to speak as he went on with an explanation.

"You are the MacLeod Lady of the Legend. Every man, woman, and child on Skye knows your story. The last healer of the legend lived in the very castle to which I take you."

"I don't believe you."

"Then tell me you do not have the gift of healing. My wound is better already because of your ministering."

"Not by my touch but by the knowledge taught to me by a Knight Hospitaler at the abbey. He is dead now, but he shared the secrets he learned from the Arabs when traveling in the Holy Land. 'Tis not magic or witchcraft, though most think it is the powers in my eyes."

"I care not from where the gift comes. I know only that you seem to possess all the features attributed to the Lady of the Legend."

"I am a Campbell, not a MacLeod."

He gazed steadily at her. "To Clan Campbell

you are possessed by the devil and were nearly blinded by their ignorant fears. Upon Skye you will be considered an angel touched by God's grace. I think the latter belief much more healthful for your future, considering what happened to you only hours ago."

"I am a Campbell born and pledge my loyalty to my lord, the Earl of Strathmorton," Ainsley insisted stubbornly, even as a shiver flit wildly up and down her spine as she remembered the terrible moment when the bearded one held the knife above her eye.

"You defend louts who persecute you as the witch of Kilchurn? I do not think that a great show of your wisdom."

Ainsley was tired of his querulous questions and veiled accusations. "You are not a MacLeod but a MacDonald. Why have you abducted me? What do you want?"

"My mother was of the Clan MacLeod, and the healer is never born on Skye but brought there from afar. You are not a true Campbell. If nothing else, the strangeness of your eyes proves such. You will accept the truth in time and realize you are our Lady of the Legend."

Though she considered his words absurd, Ainsley could not contain her curiosity. "Have there really been others like me? With different colored eyes? Those who heal the sick?"

"Aye. Your great-grandmother was such a person until she was murdered by superstitious fools."

Shocked, Ainsley stared at him. "I know nothing of my forebears. Who murdered her?"

"She was burned by English witch-hunters sent to Skye to work their evil against innocent Scots."

Tiny hairs stood on edge at the back of Ainsley's neck as his revelations chilled her heart. Brother Alfonse had told her of the cruelty of the English constables who had ridden through Scotland in olden days accusing women of witchcraft. But that had been long ago. Did it still happen in the wild reaches of the Hebrides?

"She was revered on Skye and healed both with herbs and remedies and by laying on her hands. Legend says the first healer was a maiden from the Dark World. A fairy princess who fell in love with the mortal who saved her from death."

Ainsley had heard tales that the enchanted Isle of Skye harbored the Dark Land of the Fairy Kingdom. "Do fairies really roam the hills and lochs of Skye as 'tis said?"

Her remark earned a small grin from Rodric. "So now 'tis you who fear superstitious nonsense, Campbell witch that you are."

The sound of knuckles rapping the door brought Rodric to his feet, but after he had donned a red flannel shirt and unlocked the door only Richard moved into the cabin. Ainsley huddled deeper into the bunk.

"We've come to berth safely near Maycairn." Richard kept glancing over at her. "The rain has fallen to a wet mist. Do you intend to take the lady to Arrandane this night?"

"Aye, though she is fearful of being set upon by the fairies on the way."

"You will be treated far better by us than you were in Kilchurn and Ingott, my lady," Richard promised, his reassurance followed by a respectful bow. "Now that our deed has been accomplished and we are safe at home, I will leave you and allow Rodric to present you to Lord Ian."

"Garb yourself and join me on the deck," Rodric ordered without looking at Ainsley, then departed the cabin with his friend, leaving Ainsley to ponder the mysterious events that had transpired during the last hours. She stood and picked up Bess's blue dress, then quickly shivered as she drew the damp garment over her warm flesh.

After she finished lacing the bodice, she slipped Rodric's huge flannel shirt over her shoulders, though the immense proportions nearly swallowed her petite figure. She rolled up the sleeves and tried to rectify her wild tresses by combing her fingers through the tangles, with little success.

Ready to depart, she paused with her hand on the doorknob and contemplated what faced her now. Though she had heard many stories about the Enchanted Isle and the Dark Land of the Fairy Kingdom, she was not afraid. At least not while Rodric MacDonald stood by as her protector. He had saved her once from a most awful death. Surely he had no desire to harm her. She opened the door and found her way up to the hatch and into fresh air cleansed by the smell of spray and salt. Rodric stood nearby with several crew members, but he left them at once and strode toward her.

"Arrandane is but a short ride from the quay. You'll soon find yourself snuggled in a nice warm feather bed." As he spoke he swung a heavy cloak of black wool around her shoulders, one lined with the MacDonald red plaid, a garment so long that it swept the ground around her ankles.

"Who is the man called Ian? What does he want with me?" she asked of Rodric as he took hold of her arm and led her down the gangplank.

"Ian MacDonald is the present lord and chieftain of the MacDonalds of Arrandane."

"Is he the one who bid you abduct me from the abbey?"

"Aye."

His answer was abrupt and uttered in a manner that discouraged further inquiry, as did the firm grip his fingers pressed upon her upper arm. He led her past several men working to secure the ship at anchorage. No one else joined them, but a small pony cart stood at the bottom of the ramp. Rodric lifted her to the seat with no concern for his wounded side, then turned and lifted an arm in farewell to his companions aboard the ship. When he took his place beside her, the small cart dipped precariously under his weight. He was so big, his shoulders so wide, that he dwarfed the slight conveyance.

"Please tell me why I have been brought here? Is it because of the strange legend of the fairies?"

"You will know everything soon enough. 'Tis not my place to reveal the answers you seek."

Rodric slapped the reins on the horse's back, and they were propelled at a trot up the steep and winding dirt track. Ainsley lapsed into silence and tried to make out the surrounding terrain. It was too dark to see much and rolling clouds of eerie gray mists hugged the ground all around them, as if the cumulus had drifted to earth to hang in wispy ornamentation among the tree boughs. All the spooky tales of the Fairy Kingdom came back to haunt her, and she shivered and peered through the shadowy fog for glimpses of wee creatures afoot from their lairs in the Dark Land.

As they drove along, ascending slowly from sea level, Ainsley marveled at the strange course her life had taken so abruptly. Without warning, without understanding quite why or how, she had been swept into this frightening abduction. What would happen to her? Rodric had been a protector thus far, but he was an avowed enemy of her clan. He would no doubt kill her if the unknown man named Ian decreed she should die. The MacDonalds had murdered every single person in her parents' village, only she had somehow survived. She could not let herself forget their ruthlessness, not ever. She had only Rodric MacDonald's word that nothing dire would befall her among them. What if he lied to keep her docile?

"Are you going to stay here with me?" she asked, sounding terribly breathless and afraid but unable to hide the sudden alarm at the thought of being left alone in such a ghostly place.

Rodric glanced in her direction. "Aye. This is my home and will be yours, too, soon enough.

And a much better lot you face here than you suffered in the abbey."

"But I don't belong here! His lordship will be furious that I have been taken by force and trickery against my will. He will surely declare clan war upon you for this affront."

"When he knows not who we are or why we have you in our keep?"

His quiet remark gave her pause. She asked no more questions but watched him furtively, wondering who he really was and what sort of man he was. He had handled both pistol and sword well, had displayed the courage of a warrior, and had exhibited expertise in battle skills, yet earlier that evening he had borne the manner of a cultured gentleman of manor born.

While he handled the reins, she studied his profile from the light of the tiny lantern swinging behind them, and found it aristocratic and pure of line. He looked a nobleman even now in his plain red shirt and stained breeches. A sudden thought occurred to her. Was there a woman waiting here for him? A wife, perhaps? With sons and daughters who had inherited his dark good looks? Who was he really? Why had he been the one chosen to come after her?

Perhaps a quarter of an hour passed before he slowed the cart. The fog was so heavy that she could see little of the structure to which he had brought her. Only a tall wall of gray stones set with steps that disappeared upward into the swirls of mists.

Rodric climbed slowly from the seat, leaving the

conveyance trembling, but this time he held his injury protectively with his palm as he assisted her to the ground, as if it pained him. The knife wound would heal quickly now, especially if doctored regularly with her remedy. Although, even under the best circumstances, the sliced flesh would take many days to knit before it no longer gave him trouble.

As they climbed curving steps winding alongside the steep wall, she felt as if she were entering a fortress and hesitated in her step until Rodric's hand touched her back and gently nudged her upward.

At the top of the stairs a plain planked door set with great hinges of black iron remained closed until Rodric pulled a bell cord above the portal. Within minutes a face appeared in the small grilled window. The door opened at once to reveal a sleepy-eyed servant on the threshold. The small man was dressed in a rumpled white nightshirt that hung to his bony knees, and his white hair stuck out in every direction imaginable, as if he had just risen from his bed. He held out his candlestick to light their way.

"Lord Rodric, thanks be to God that you have returned safely! We have all been anxious. Did trouble find you?"

"Aye, Arnolt, but I've brought back the lady I sought."

"I see that, milord. Welcome, milady."

The manservant, already bent with age, acknowledged her with a deep waist bend more suitable for royalty. Certainly unused to such courteous regard, Ainsley gave a polite nod.

Rodric's mouth curved slightly as he observed her obvious discomfiture.

"You will be honored as Lady of the Legend while here among us evil MacDonald devils. Calm your nerves, for you have nothing to fear from us, my lady."

"My Lord Ian has been waiting eagerly for your safe return, Lord Rodric. Shall I awaken him with the good tidings?"

"I must see him first. The morrow will be soon enough. Lady Ainsley is tired and in need of a good night of slumber. Her bedchamber has been prepared for her arrival, I trust?"

The men continued to speak together about the people and everyday doings of Arrandane as they led Ainsley through the darkness into an immense entrance hall. Only one candle lit the base of the wide wooden stair, but white marble tiles gleamed softly off the floor. In the gloom, cloaking the walls and ceiling, she could see the outline of pieces of massive furniture, and the occasional flash of candle glow was reflected in the gleam of a long row of large gold mirrors. It seemed a house rich in content, luxurious in furnishing, much how she had always dreamed the inside of Strathmorton Castle would be.

"Rodric! Is that you, come home?"

The feminine voice echoed endlessly up into the vaulted ceiling, and Ainsley swung around to find a lady dressed in burgundy velvet running down the stair. Unruly auburn brown curls peeked out from beneath a hastily pinned snood of gold netting. Ainsley watched with some interest as the girl flung herself into Rodric's waiting arms. So he was wed, she thought, watching the couple closely.

"I was so dreadfully worried about you!" the other young woman cried in an eager voice. "You were supposed to bring her back hours ago."

"Hush, Bree, or you'll bestir the entire household."

The girl smiled and covered her mouth with the tips of her fingers, then swiveled her full attention to Ainsley. "Oh, you must let me see your eyes!" She startled Ainsley by coming forth and staring straight into her face in a way few people other than Rodric MacDonald had ever dared before. "Oh, they're beautiful, even more so than I imagined! But look at your face! What has caused the scratches and that big bruise there on your forehead?"

Ainsley stood astounded, never having heard anyone describe her eyes as anything other than evil and ugly enough to be hidden under a black leather patch. She warmed to the other girl as Rodric introduced them.

"Lady Breanne MacDonald, allow me to present Lady Ainsley Campbell . . ."

"Oh, no, do not proclaim her as one of those blackguards!" Breanne exclaimed, highly dismayed, then colored quickly at her own rude remark. "I meant no disrespect, my lady," she added quickly, recoiling a bit from Rodric's displeased frown.

"She is our honored guest and should be treated with due respect."

Rodric's voice had steel threads running through it. Breanne smiled at Ainsley as she apologized further.

"Forgive my outburst, my lady, but I was just startled when I heard mention of Clan Campbell. They are dreaded enemies on Skye."

"I would know why I was brought here" was Ainsley's reply. "For I was brought into this enemy camp against my wishes."

Rodric and Breanne exchanged solemn glances, but it was Breanne who clasped Ainsley's hand. She squeezed her fingers warmly. "You are most welcome here, Lady Ainsley, and I do hope you will not consider us as foes much longer. Would you allow me to show you to your apartments? I would be pleased to, Rodric."

Initially Rodric did not appear agreeable to the idea, but when Arnolt mentioned Lord Ian's name again, he finally nodded consent.

"Go with Breanne, then. She will take care of your needs."

Ainsley knew she had no choice but to obey. The hour was late, though she had no inkling what time it was, and despite her brief catnap aboard the boat, the emotional events of the night had begun to take their toll. She followed the pretty girl in red on a twisting, turning journey through what seemed a hodgepodge of corridors, intersecting chambers and side stairs. The girl chatted constantly, but of nothing of much consequence.

"Are you Rodric's wife?" Ainsley finally demanded of her. For reasons she could not explain, she felt it necessary to know that answer.

The question brought Breanne to a stop in front of a small stairway enclosed by walls. She darted a glance at Ainsley, then laughed. "Oh, nay, I am but his sister. We have a cousin, Richard MacLeod, as well, though his blood kinship is quite remote. Did you not meet him?"

"Is he a handsome lad, tall with blond hair?" When Breanne nodded, Ainsley added, "Aye then, but I was told his name was Richard Lancaster and he wore the red coat of a dragoon. He sailed with us from the mainland."

"He is my brother's right-hand man," she said as a peeved look wrinkled her smooth brow. "He is probably on his way to Dunvegan. He is quite obsessed with a lady there." Breanne's voice became gruff with ill feeling about said lady, but Ainsley was more interested in Rodric's circumstances.

"And your brother? Is his wife awaiting him here in this house?"

"Rodric is not yet married," Breanne answered, observing Ainsley with a mysterious smile tipping her mouth, but went on again before Ainsley could venture more queries. "Your chambers are just up the steps. The windows afford a lovely view of the sea."

The dark-haired girl preceded her up the enclosed stair and into the large bedchamber she was to occupy that lay across the hall. Ainsley stared around the rich room with its forest-hued velvet bed hangings and beautiful tapestries covering the walls. The floor was covered with many rugs, fringed in gold and patterned with dark pink roses. The headboard of the heavy wooden bed was carved with the MacDonald crest—a gauntleted hand holding a cross. Near the foot of the bed, a fire burned brightly in the grate of a white stone fireplace. A copper kettle hung above it.

"Water for your bath is warming on the fire," Breanne told her as she lit a taper and went about lighting many others in candleholders around the hearth. "The hip bath is there at fireside behind the screen. If you need a serving girl, you need only ring the bellpull by the door." Breanne smiled as she paused at the threshold. "I must go now before I am discovered absent from my bedchamber so late. I will see you on the morrow when you meet his lordship. Sleep well, my lady."

Then she was gone, quietly closing the door behind her. Ainsley frowned when a key turned in the lock. Despite the kindness, the splendid room was still a velvet cage in which she remained captive of the MacDonalds.

Chapter Eight

Ainsley sank to her shoulders in sudsy water scented faintly with purple heather, and leaned her head against the rim of the copper hip bath. She had gone the length of her lifetime without the pleasure of a tub bath, and now had enjoyed the luxury twice in the same night. The water soothed muscles that ached from the grip of brutal fingers and her thighs which throbbed from hours atop a horse in driving rain. The soreness of her limbs began to subside, and she felt relaxed for the first time since she had climbed the abbey wall for vespers. Could that moment truly have been not yet a full day past?

Her long lashes drifted down in a thick veil as she tried not to think about all the things that had happened. The image of a certain tall, arrestingly handsome MacDonald wriggled into her mind like an escaping adder. Could she believe his fantastical explanation for her abduction? In truth, could she trust any other man who claimed the MacDonald name? Had she not been taught again and again just how deep and vicious their treachery? Had he not tricked her vilely from the very first moment she had set eyes upon him?

"You have a penchant for lounging in bathwater, I see."

Ainsley lurched at the sound of Rodric's voice, very close to her, and sent a surge of bathwater in a sloshing wave over the rim and onto Rodric's boots. He sidestepped the sudsy deluge as Ainsley snatched a towel into the water over her. He had the audacity to grin at her flushed face, and she glared at him, cursing herself for being so caught up in her thoughts that she had not heard him enter.

"How dare you enter my bedchamber without knocking first!" she cried furiously, still struggling to hide her nakedness.

Rodric made no apology for gazing down through the roiling water that did little to hide her naked legs.

"I began suffering fears that you had struck down poor Breanne in the way you laid the bottle against my own head and then ran away. So I decided to ease my mind that you were safe and sound."

Ainsley bristled at his amused smirk. "Well, you have certainly seen me, sire, so pray take your leave."

Rodric merely leaned a shoulder against the warmed stones of the fireplace. He still smiled, but at least he had the good grace to avert his stare into the darting flames.

"Forgive my intrusion, but there is a lady who

wishes to speak with you this night. Perhaps the sight of her will make you more agreeable to accepting your status here at Arrandane."

"Accept a locked room in the lair of MacDonalds? I do not think so. 'Twould sooner be agreeable to sinking in a peat bog."

"A dire wish, my lady, but please robe yourself, for you will receive a visitor here shortly."

He was gone in a thrice, and she waited until she heard the door-latch catch before rising and peeking over the screen to make sure he was not lingering about like some lecher. The room was empty, however, and she carefully patted herself dry with the soft linen towel, then drew on the soft white nightgown that had been draped across the bedpost.

A black flannel wrap lined with the bright red, green, and blue MacDonald weave had also been provided—did they leave anything unadorned of their tartan?—but finding herself unwilling to don such colors, she opted to wrap herself inside a soft knitted throw draping one of the small fireside chairs. She was warming nicely inside its soft length before the crackling logs when the door opened again. Did no one on Skye know how to tap for admittance? She turned quickly, unable to imagine what lady could possibly wish to greet her in her chamber, but most curious to find out.

What she saw at the portal sent her pressing back into the chair. Her face whitened. Her thoughts fell in a downward spiral into a fog of childhood memory. She shook her head, shut her eyes, thinking she was surely dreaming the tiny bent figure adorned in black dress and head scarf. No, surely it could not be Ellie? Ellie MacLeod, her nursemaid and comfort, had been long dead and buried!

"Ainsley? Lord Rodric told me he would bring you home, but oh, child, I feared I would never see you again."

A thrilling rush of gooseflesh spread over Ainsley's arms and legs as she recognized the soft voice—so heavy with Highland brogue, so beloved to her childish heart—as that of Ellie MacLeod. God protect her if ghostly apparitions walked the Isle of Skye as foretold in whispered wives' tales? Frightened to face the woman she knew as dead for so long, she stood and retreated behind her chair as Ellie moved closer.

"Ainsley, do you not remember me? 'Tis old Ellie. Do not fear me, I pray you. 'Twould break my heart."

Ainsley stared at her, realizing how much older she now looked. The soft wisps of hair that straggled from the white lace mobcap were now hoary with age, and the lines on her face cut deep and severe. Already old when she had rocked Ainsley in her arms, she had grown ancient from passing years, and the frail hand she lay so gently upon Ainsley's arm was blue-veined and spotted brown with the marks of old age.

"I thought you were dead." Ainsley somehow managed to force from a throat that seemed stuffed with balled bread. Pure emotion suddenly overwhelmed her.

Ellie smiled, her wide brown eyes the only feature unchanged by the march of years, still lively with the warmth and compassion that had been a healing balm applied to Ainsley's childish grievances.

Joy filled her, and she lunged forward to clutch the old woman tightly to her breast. She surprised herself by bursting into a fit of weeping, because she hated to cry and rarely allowed such emotions to escape her. But she was so happy to see the beloved old woman who had been more her mother than her nursemaid.

Ellie patted her back. "Do not cry, little one. I am alive and well. The story of my death 'twas yet another lie meant to deceive you."

Wiping away tears with her fingers, Ainsley drew back from the old woman and held her at arm's length, where she studied the craggy features she had not seen since she was eight years old. She hugged the old woman to her again and tiredly dropped her cheek upon her feeble shoulder.

"Oh, Ellie, Ellie, I can't believe you are here with me after so long." There were many unanswered questions, but she could not voice them. Another helpless sob ensued, and Ellie pressed Ainsley's head against her broad bosom and stroked her hair in the way Ainsley remembered so well.

"Hush, my child, do not cry for what is past. We are together now, and shall not be parted again until I am taken by God's hand."

After a few moments they sat down on the bed together, and Ainsley lifted Ellie's gnarled hands and kissed the backs of her fingers. "Where have you been all these years? If you have been well, why did you not come to the abbey to visit me? I was so lonely after I was taken there."

Ellie's expressive eyes shone with sorrowful lights, and Ainsley's heart quivered with regret at how long they had been separated. "I wanted to come to you but was afraid to."

"Why were you afraid?"

"Because I knew a terrible secret, one that Hugh Campbell feared I would reveal to you when you became older. He took you from me by force and commanded that I never seek you out again on penalty of death."

"Nay, that cannot be true." Ainsley shook her head to bolster her own denials. The earl was her patron lord. Why would he wish to keep Ellie away from her? Moisture pooled and glimmered inside Ellie's eyes, then dropped and rolled down her wrinkled cheek. Ainsley brushed it away, trying to make sense of everything.

"I don't understand what's happening to me, Ellie. Why am I here? Why are you living here among enemies? MacDonalds murdered my parents. The nuns told me so."

"The story I must relate to you burns like bile in my gullet."

Ellie's whisper was thick, and Ainsley was filled with foreboding as she sat motionlessly waiting, almost afraid to hear what would come next. Ellie looked so sad that Ainsley wanted to comfort her.

"I am so ashamed of the harm I have done to you, poor Ainsley."

"Tell me what happened."

Ellie leaned forward, her entire body gripped with some inner intensity. Her eyes delved into Ainsley's confused ones. "Hugh Campbell is not the man you think. He is evil and corrupt. He has performed terrible acts in his life. Awful things."

"But he is my lord and benefactor. He has always been good to me. He has arranged my marriage to . . ."

Her own words faded as Ellie took her face and held it tightly between her hands. "Listen to me, child, for Lord Rodric sent me this night to tell you the whole truth. He wants you to believe us and understand why you are here before tomorrow morn when you meet Lord Ian. He says he is convinced that you are the Lady of the MacLeods. Is that true? Do you have the gift of healing? I suspected such when you were little."

"I have no gift. I was trained in herbs and medicines and told of places to touch to relieve the pain of wounds. That's why I was called the witch of Kilchurn. But it is not of the devil or from the colors marked in my eyes. It is simply knowledge imparted from the kindest of monks."

More tears tracked down Ellie's face. "Lord Rodric related what happened with the grave diggers, and I will surely be judged by the Almighty for keeping my silence while you grew to womanhood suffering such ugly persecutions." She touched Ainsley's bruised forehead. "The Earl of Strathmorton has done such wrongs. Thank God that I finally gathered courage enough to come to

Lord Ian so that he could rectify the misdeeds of which I was a part."

"I don't understand."

"You must trust Lord Rodric and his clansmen. You will be treated kindly here. Your gift for healing will be revered upon Skye. You will be sought out by the sick, but no one will call you witch or wish to harm you."

"Do you really believe the tales about the Lady of the Legend, Ellie? That she would come to the MacLeods with her gift of healing?"

"Aye, and you will as well once you live in this place and understand what has transpired. I will tell you the truth now as I should have done many years ago."

Ainsley sat silently, fearful of the secrets Ellie was about to reveal. Already her mind churned like the wake of a great galleon. She knew not what to think, nor what she could believe.

"I attended your poor mother on the cold, rainy night you were born, dear one. From the moment Hugh Campbell learned that his daughter was with child, he banished her from Strathmorton to the lonely moors of the Dark Isle. Your mother was small of size like you, and the birthing process was so long and difficult that I feared she would surely succumb. By the grace of God you were born healthy, and I remember to this day how I held you up for your mother to gaze upon because she was so eager to see her child . . .

"You have a daughter, milady, a fine, healthy girl-child," Ellie cried as she folded the wriggling infant into the clean white quilt. She glanced worriedly at Lady Meredith, but the poor young thing did not respond, could no longer open her eyes as she struggled in the throes of childbed fever. She had succumbed to hallucinations in the last hours of her seemingly endless struggle to birth her daughter.

Ellie reached out to comfort Meredith and found the skin of the young mother's brow burning against her fingertips. Meredith writhed and kicked at the constricting sheets, her tangled blond hair spread across the sweat-dampened pillows.

Cradling the child in one arm, Ellie dipped a cloth into the basin, intending to moisten Meredith's face with cool water, then spun around as the bedchamber door was flung open with such force that it banged the wall. She clasped the newborn babe protectively against her breast when she saw Hugh of Strathmorton standing there outlined against the dark corridor. The candle affixed to the wall holder beside the door illuminated his features, hawklike in appearance and now so twisted with anger that Ellie's heartbeat rushed with dread.

As he came toward her with long, intimidating strides, Ellie instinctively backed away, clutching his daughter's newborn babe in her arms. But as Hugh stopped at the foot of the bed, she realized that he paid her no heed. His hands gripped the carved bedpost until his fingertips turned white and bloodless. He stared down at Lady Meredith and spoke to her as if the thrashing young woman could comprehend his intent. Rage, so awful, so full of anguish that chills flew up Ellie's back, came pouring from his mouth—words twisted and malevolent as poisonous serpents.

"My only living kin, my only child. I gave you everything in my power, laid all my possessions at your feet. And you repaid me by whoring with my worst enemy and spawning this puny child in the dead of night like a common trollop."

Ellie stood rigidly, gripped with horror, but Hugh was not finished. His heavily bearded jaw clamped hard, his face so tormented that he raised his face to heaven and groaned with agony. "How could you take a MacDonald into your bed when I paid so dear a price to wed you to the richest earl south of the Cheviots, with Varney's power beside us so I can solidify our alliance with the English Crown?"

Overcome by grief and disappointment, Hugh buried his face in his palms and muffled his low sob of despair. Meredith tossed in the throes of fever and when her father spoke again, his anger was colder, lethal with hard-edged determination.

"In the name of God, I'll burn in the fires of hell before I let Ian MacDonald's bastard seed destroy my life." His vow rang with steely hatred, and Ellie fought the urge to flee his presence.

"Where is the misbegotten bastard?" Hugh's eyes pinned Ellie against the shadowy wall. "Would it have strangled on its mother's cord than to be the shame of my clan!" Again fury drenched his words, but the callousness of his pronouncement was even more frightening. "The bairn is a child of shame, begotten from ungodly fornication." He stared down at the swaddled bundle Ellie held so tightly, then spoke his deadly command.

"Drown the ill-begotten bastard in the lake, Ellie MacLeod, then leave this place forever. If Meredith survives this night, she will be told her child was stillborn. If anyone ever learns otherwise, I will find you and run you through with my own claymore, with God as my witness, I swear that upon my own life."

Ellie quaked with terror as Hugh Campbell turned and left the birthing chamber without a backward glance at his dying daughter or her new born child.

Ellie's own sobs broke into the whispered story, but Ainsley could not even comfort the old woman, could only stare at Ellie with shock and outrage.

"Mary, Mother of God, forgive me for my mortal sins," Ellie was begging now, looking fearfully to heaven for redemption. "I have kept this terrible secret for all my life, but now I can only hope to cleanse my soul by telling the truth to you."

"Are you saying the man here, the one known as Ian MacDonald, is my true father? The chieftain of the MacDonalds of Skye?"

"Aye, child, he is that, but he knew not of your birth until I came to this place with Lord Rodric from Dunvegan Castle nigh a few months ago."

Ainsley's heart rose into her throat. "What of my mother?"

"Though I was forced to leave with you, I later heard rumors that she met death that very night. But I could not do such an evil thing as murdering an innocent babe, so I stole away with you and raised you with my own kin on the Kyle of Tongue. I kept you hidden there for near eight years before Hugh Campbell learned of my whereabouts and found you alive. His men tore you from my arms, an innocent crying bairn, but he did not take you away and kill you as I feared. God's grace saved you from harm and put you safely in the abbey."

"Yet you waited all these years to tell this tale to Ian MacDonald."

"I was afraid and I didn't know where you'd been taken, until I heard about the witch of Kilchurn and how the countryside lived in fear of her evil eye. When its unusual coloring was described to me, I knew then that you were she, and I could not die with such sins blackening my soul. That's when I went to my kin among the MacLeods of Dunvegan of Skye. It was Lord Rodric who heard the story and brought the truth to the MacDonald. I feared for my very life at your father's hands, but he received me with kindness and was grateful that I came to him with the truth."

"And that is when he sent Rodric to abduct me?"

"Aye. Now that you are here, you will meet your father and take your rightful place as wife to his heir."

"They brought me here to marry?"

For the first time Ellie looked happy. "Aye, you are already wed in law, and as your husband Lord Rodric will assume the title of chieftain from Lord Ian and pledge his honor to protect you from any revenge countered by Strathmorton. That is Lord Ian's greatest concern. But you have naught to fear because Lord Rodric is a good and honorable man. He is most eager for you to accept him as husband. That is why he sent me to you with the truth."

"I cannot be married to him! I am promised to an Englishman, the Earl of Varney. We were to wed within the year!"

"Your father and Lord Rodric have entered into a legal contract of marriage. Both the betrothal and transfer of power was accomplished and sealed weeks ago."

"But he tricked me, Ellie, and brought me here to this MacDonald stronghold against my will."

"*You* are a MacDonald" was Ellie's quiet reminder, "by your father's bloodline, and he has claimed your patrimony with great pleasure. You must accept your fate, Ainsley, because you have no choice. You will learn to care for Rodric and his clansmen. You must trust me now, for I am finally speaking the truth."

Overwhelmed by ragged, conflicting emotions, Ainsley lay her head against Ellie's breast and let her nursemaid comfort her. The past revealed to her had been full of sorrow and betrayal and lies, but what of the future? How could it be any different as long as Campbells and MacDonalds bloodied their swords and cursed the other? Once

Hugh Campbell learned of her whereabouts and that she was wed to a MacDonald instead of going to England as wife to Randolph of Varney, there would be more fighting, more spilled blood, more tragedy, and she would be the cause of it, for she was naught but a pawn in the hands of warring Highland chieftains, just as her mother had been before her.

Chapter Nine

If not for the white silk wedding gown that Ainsley discovered draped by some unknown hand across the foot of her bed when she awoke the next morning, she would have surely dismissed her abduction from the abbey, the appearance of her long-lost nursemaid, and the story of Ainsley's marriage to Rodric MacDonald as some preposterous dream.

Now as she lay thinking of all that had happened with the light of dawn slowly invading the heavy velvet draperies drawn against the encroachment of day, the misdeeds shared between Hugh Campbell and Ian MacDonald seemed frighteningly sinister, and she a helpless, unwilling pawn tossed between them.

After all, Ainsley had neither seen nor heard from Ellie in many years, and her old nursemaid was a member of Clan MacLeod. Could she be lying to hide ulterior motives for the supposed wedding? It seemed inconceivable that the great Earl of Strathmorton could be so cruel as to order the murder of an innocent babe, much less his own granddaughter, if the impossible notion of her close kinship to Hugh Campbell was to be believed.

Sweeping back her warm coverlet, she crossed quickly to the window, parted the drapes, and unlatched the heavy wooden shutters. Sunlight flooded the dusky room with a great wash of light, and she gasped at the sheer beauty of the first glimpse of the Isle of Skye. The firth shone glittering blue under the sweeping rays of the rising sun. Great dark-colored mountains ringed three sides of the fortress, rising steeply and foreboding behind tall grassy hills, and far across the water she knew the mainland of Scotland lay out of sight. With no sure reason why and no method of escape, she was a captive here in this strange island, where magic was purported to be commonplace, where fairies supposedly intermingled with mortals. Was she merely a prize of war held tightly in the grip of the MacDonalds?

Prone to believe the bizarre tale of her birth was fabricated for Rodric MacDonald's own agenda, she could not bring herself to be so tractable as to simply don the wedding gown and repeat vows as he no doubt expected her to do. She would flee the place now while most slept, if for no reason but to give her time to decide what to believe. Whatever the truth, events were happening much too fast and mysteriously for her to comprehend.

Dressing hastily in one of the plain gowns that she found hanging in a large wardrobe in the corner—a lovely azure blue wool that fit her reasonably well—she took a moment to brush and braid her hair into a loose queue down her back. The door handle turned easily, and it surprised her that the chamber was unlocked. Peeking furtively outside, she found the corridors still and inactive. The narrow hallways were deserted with no sign of even a single servant scurrying in answer to breakfast summons.

Relieved that no one would impede her flight, she hurried toward the back of the house, anxious to find her way out of the maze of corridors, to breathe fresh air and decide what she should do. The back stair up which Breanne had led her the previous night was no problem to locate, but she fought growing trepidation as she tiptoed down the worn stone treads. Near the bottom landing, she drew up abruptly in alarm when she heard two women talking together in the hallway below.

"Is it true what Lady Breanne has said? That Lord Rodric brought his bride here in the dead of night?" The first voice was girlish and held a note of excitement.

"Aye," replied her female companion, "already wed by proxy they are, but she'll be joined to him in the eyes of God this very day." She chuckled then amid the rattle of a tin pail and splashing sounds, as if she wrung out a rag over the bucket of water. "And she be a lucky lass for all the household ladies will mourne that one's saying of nuptials. Many a lass will weep herself to sleep with loneliness here at Arrandane, and inside the walls of Dunvegan as well, if the tales of Lord Rodric's prowess are true ones."

"Old Ellie says his bride is specially blessed with healing arts."

"I have heard such as well, though none have seen her yet. 'Tis said she bears the mark of the Lady of the MacLeods in her eyes, and that the heathen Campbells accused her of being help-meet to the devil."

The women continued to discuss her as they moved off, and Ainsley considered their words once they were gone, especially the part about this being her wedding day. Rodric MacDonald wasted no time. She sneaked around the corner and headed down the hall in the opposite direction. The great manor seemed to have been built piece-meal with many additional wings, and from what she could see from the windows facing the large interior courtyard, the majority of the place was constructed around a central keep enclosed by crenelated battlements with square corner towers facing each direction.

The more she observed the more she realized how futile was any hope to escape. No wonder she was left unguarded. Perhaps, though, with a great deal of luck she could make her way back to the quay, where they had stepped ashore the previous night. If she offered a hefty recompense from the Earl of Strathmorton's purse for anyone who helped her, she might find a villager greedy enough to transport her back to the mainland. A great many *ifs* involved in that plan, she realized with her usual practicality, but such attempts

were better than just pliantly accepting a fate over
which she had no control.

Eventually the central hall turned at right
angles into a narrower side corridor, and she ran
down its length, until she espied a wide oaken
door affixed with one small pane of glass protected
by brass bars. She raised herself to her toes and
peered outside, more than pleased to find the portal exiting into a small walled garden.

The moment she stepped outside, the salty tang
of the sea assailed her nostrils, and she inhaled
deeply in the crisp morning air. Her determination
to evade the wedding being forced upon her was
uppermost in her mind as she rapidly tred the
shell-covered path in search of a gate. All around
her trees and flowers were beginning to bud in
the slowly awakening springtime.

Even in her haste, she hesitated when she saw
the rare bloom of the pink lupine, with which
Brother Alfonse had taught her to soothe upset
stomachs. She paused to make sure it was such,
then saw against another wall a stand of lavender
catmint, which she had often given as a remedy
for fever. A quick perusal showed many other rare
plants she had come to use, some brought home
from afar and planted in the abbey gardens after
Brother Alfonse's many journeys abroad. She wondered who tended this medicinal garden, Breanne
or an apothecary apprentice. In any case she
would have enjoyed examining each leaf and bulb
herself, but could not take the time for fear of
detection.

An arched door at the end of the walk led to a

cobbled rear courtyard where activity abounded. Servants busied themselves with various tasks around the smokehouses and buttery, and the metallic clang of a blacksmith's hammer carried to her in the quiet air. Other young men worked in a field of barley, and the happy voices of children playing at some game drifted to her ears.

Once she stepped outside, she could see the stables as well, a series of long, airy buildings with sloping mansard roofs. Many stalls lined the courtyard side, and Ainsley was reminded of Jeremy when she saw stable boys inside patiently wielding grooming brushes upon their equine charges. Her hopes of stealing a mount dwindled, and she gauged the length of the walk that would take her high atop the hills rising at the base of the taller peaks. She was drawn to the higher elevations somehow, especially one where she could see stone ruins, and she eased toward the open meadows lying at the base of the first steep foothill.

The children were the first to notice her presence, but paid her little heed until one overthrew the small red leather ball they tossed about in their game. She kept walking as the ball rolled past her, bringing a small girl dashing in pursuit.

"Good morrow," Ainsley murmured as the child stopped in her tracks and stared at her out of enormous blue eyes.

"I be Rachel, the carter's daughter," she murmured in her childish speech, her face solemn as she examined Ainsley's face. "You got eyes like the Lady of the Legend, the one Lord Rodric marries this day. Are you she, my lady? The one who was stole away from us by the wicked Campbells when she was a little bairn?"

Astonished that even the tiniest babe of Arrandane knew every detail about her, she turned and hurried away as the other children scampered forth to see what kept little Rachel.

"Rachel found Lord Rodric's new bride!" an older boy yelled loudly enough to make Ainsley cringe. "My lord, my lord, your bride is running away!"

Ainsley stopped in chagrin, then turned to search the surroundings for the man calling himself her husband. Rodric was easy to spot by his great height alone. He stood near a saddled horse, but she was surprised to find him now holding little Rachel perched atop one arm. The little girl pointed a chubby finger in Ainsley's direction, and when Rodric turned and found her place at the edge of the cobblestones, she was struck motionless for one awful moment of indecision. Then, as he put down the child and reached for the reins of his mount, she lifted her skirts and fled at top speed across the open pasture rising into the mountains.

Attaining the length of the field, she stopped to draw her breath. When she looked behind her, Rodric was riding slowly through the high grasses after her. She accelerated her pace and steadily climbed the gradual rise, fully aware that in spurring his horse, he could overtake her progress. She ran on until she was breathless and found that Rodric patiently walked his horse a few yards behind her. Idly holding the reins in his right hand, his left resting casually on his thigh, he drew up and smiled at her.

Feeling the sharp prick of silent mockery, she trudged haughtily on, the morning dew wetting her hem. Every time she stopped to rest, Rodric did so as well until finally she sought the only course available to her pride. Ignore him, and let him follow if he must. She would just as soon he keep his distance.

The hill was high, and by the time she reached the stone tower toward which she had striven, she was compelled to sink to the grass to rest. It was only then that Rodric kicked his mount to faster gait and overtook her. Once his horse stood directly in front of her, he leaned indolently across the low saddle horn.

" 'Tis a lovely morning you chose for a walk, my lady."

Ainsley looked up at him and found his grin less than endearing. She looked away as he dismounted and stood a few feet from her. He wore a full white shirt, and for the first time she saw him in the belted plaid of his clan, the bright red, blue, green tartan of the MacDonalds that reached well to mid-calf. Boots of soft tanned leather laced tightly to his knees, and she could not fail to notice the great broadsword strapped across his back. The brace of pearl-handled pistols, which had saved her life the night before, were in their place in his wide brown leather belt.

"You heap shame upon me, you must ken, by causing me to give chase to my bride on the day of our nuptials. And under the watchful eyes of my clansmen."

"You heap shame upon me by forcing me to wed you, a man I hardly know, a man who tricked me, abducted me . . ."

"Saved your life and lovely eyes?" he finished for her.

Ainsley frowned at his blunt reminder that she was certainly indebted to him, and Rodric dropped his reins and squatted on his haunches close beside her. "I had hoped Ellie MacLeod could lessen your displeasure over the way we met. Did you not trust her words as truthful?"

"You truly expect me to believe that a great lord like Hugh Campbell would murder his only grandchild?" she spat in response. "I daresay that is nothing but a far-fetched tale that you have created for your own machinations. I am more interested in why you would go to such trouble to force me to become your wife."

In response he released a long-drawn sigh, then lounged beside her in the grass, stretching out his long legs beside her, much too close for her comfort. She inched away a bit, but she was so aware of his size, of the sheer power of his masculine body, that she almost shivered.

"You are right, of course, Hugh's treachery is hard to fathom. I, too, was hard-pressed to believe such perfidy could exist, even in a villain like Hugh Campbell."

Startled that he admitted such, Ainsley dared a glance and found his face serious. For an instant as their eyes met, she thought he meant to reach out to her. He seemed to reconsider, however, for he did not touch her.

"Perhaps after you have met your father, you will lean more toward the truth as we tell it."

"I do not think so."

Rodric did extend his hand then, lifting her heavy braid where it hung against her back. He caressed the silky curls at the end. "I like it better worn loose and free over your shoulders as it was when first I met you."

When Ainsley jerked her head away, he braced his elbow upon bent knee and gazed steadily upon her face until she burned under his rude scrutiny. "But I am most pleased to see you adorned in lady's attire rather than leather trews and baggy servant's shirt."

She said naught but bent her gaze upon the sparkling firth in the distance. The winds blew fierce so high upon the hill, and she let the breezes touch her upraised face and flutter the unfettered hem of her skirt and undergown.

"Is it so terrible a fate I implore of you, Ainsley?" he murmured softly after a lengthy silence had settled between them. "To live here in this beautiful place? To be lady to the lord of the isle? I swear I will treat you with all manner of respect due a beloved wife. I will consider your every need and wish as my sole purpose. I will even pledge no intimacy between us as man and wife until you feel yourself ready for me to claim my right as your legal husband." His grin was a wry one. "Though that vow, my lady, is one which comes much harder than any other."

Surprised by his unexpected offer, Ainsley eyed him with a sidelong glance that held not a little suspicion. "And if I am never ready to call you husband and allow such intimacy?"

Rodric answered with a knowing, supremely self-confident smile, and again Ainsley felt he wordlessly mocked her. "I will take my chances upon that unfortunate result. Though I do not purport to vow never to entice you to me. 'Tis sons I want for the future of my bloodline, like any other man of means. And daughters to comfort us in our old age, as well, lovely golden-haired lassies who look like you."

The visualization of the two of them begetting sons and daughters welled inside Ainsley's mind in a wealth of alarmingly vivid detail and sent a rush of color up her slender neck. Cheeks pink and hot with embarrassment at the intimate bent of their discourse, she plucked a stalk of grass and fixed her eyes on the great house below, so she wouldn't have to meet his disconcerting stare.

" 'Tis more than a decade you spent inside the bleak walls of the nunnery, Ainsley. Is that the life you prefer to one here with me and your true clan? Dismal cells and endless prayers prefer you to this glorious isle with its waterfalls and hidden glens? Have you never longed for a husband's protection? For bairns to nurture at your breast? Have you never had the womanly longings to have a man to take you in his arms and love you?"

Ainsley had indeed experienced each and every one of the longings he mentioned, regrettably the last one since she had first laid her eyes on Rodric

MacDonald. "I will have all those things. I am pledged to another, an Englishman, Randolph of Varney."

"Not any longer. You are mine now."

His statements were so totally proprietary that she was incensed. "I am not yours to use like common chattel. You brought me here by force. Will you make me accept you as husband in the same cowardly way?"

"We are wed by law. This very night we will add God's blessing to our union and the well wishes of the people of Arrandane. And they welcome you as my lady and the lady of the MacLeods."

When he gazed toward the house below, Ainsley could not help but speak the question hovering in her mind. She brushed the grass from her open palm. "No one here seems to fear my eyes. Not even the children harbor misgivings for me to look upon them."

"That is because we consider you gifted, not cursed. No ignorant men will chase you down to plunge hot brands to your flesh, not while I draw breath and lift sword to stop them."

"Why are you willing to give up your own choice of a MacDonald wife or a MacLeod heiress in order to wed me, a stranger you had never met?"

Rodric gave a soft laugh, as if her remark bordered upon absurd. "Why would you think you would not be my first choice among all other womenkind?"

His honeyed words did not disarm her. "Perhaps you are swayed a good deal by the fact that

you have become chieftain now that you have wed
the daughter of the present MacDonald. Perhaps
you covet the title of lord of the isle and all these
beautiful lands that Lord Ian MacDonald gives
over to you?"

"I wed you to please my Lord Ian, I do not
quibble with that, but you are a bonny enough
lass to please the king himself. Any man would
covet your affection, and I am no different."

Fingers of unimpeded pleasure seeped into the
dam of anger Ainsley had built up inside her
breast, unwanted, unacceptable, yet in her heart
she wondered if he was not right. Would not a
life spent here among people who did not fear her
be a far sight better than what she had experienced until now? Never had she wished to leave
her beloved Scotland for faraway England, only
the abbey did she long to leave far behind; but
until now she had felt she had little choice in the
matter. Had she not dreamed of a place such as
Skye where she wouldn't be persecuted, where
she could have a husband and family? If Rodric
was willing to allow her a period of adjustment as
he decreed, could she learn to be happy?

"Come with me and greet your father. Poor Ian
has been up since before sunrise awaiting your
acquaintance. Refrain in your decision until then,
but believe me when I say that I will not touch
you as wife until you are ready for me to do so.
'Tis not in my nature to have a woman who would
resist me."

Ainsley felt sure there would be few women in
that category, probably her alone, if the real truth

be known, and even she could think of worse men than Rodric with whom to pledge one's troth. "I will meet this man who claims to be my father, and I will listen to what he says. I will make no further promise."

Rodric's smile was so openly triumphant that Ainsley briefly considered reassessing her decision and might have done so if he had given her time to renege. But he rose too quickly and pulled her up by her hands. "You have not misplaced your trust, my love, I vow that upon my heart and soul. You have made the right decision."

"I do not trust you, nor any other MacDonald," she reiterated with no lack of feeling, but he merely laughed as he lifted her onto his saddle. He climbed up behind her and gathered her close into his embrace.

"But you're beginning to, are you not, my bride?" he whispered against her hair, his lips nibbling at her delicate ear and the hollow just beneath in a way that sent shivers shooting into her breast. She sat upright in front of him, but she appalled herself by inner longings that encouraged her to lean back against the solid muscles of his chest and close her eyes beneath the lovely feeling of his mouth gently nuzzling at her earlobe.

Chapter Ten

A blaze of sunshine slanted through the tall and mullioned stained-glass windows in the great hall, spilling the shape of a giant Celtic cross in glorious rectangles of ruby, emerald, and lapis lazuli across the spacious stone floor. Beneath the cavernous dimensions of the rafter-vaulted ceiling, Lord Ian MacDonald sat in a high-backed carved chair, every nerve on edge, awaiting the arrival of a daughter he had never before seen.

Both Rodric and Breanne had discouraged him from leaving his chamber, but he adamantly refused to greet his only child propped against pillows in a sickbed. He had learned to live with pain since the day nigh three years ago when a broadsword had ripped through his thigh muscle from hip to knee in a skirmish with Campbells, and he would meet the daughter he sired from his beloved Meredith standing firmly upon his own two feet. And he would wear the four eagle feathers in his bonnet of the chieftain of Arrandane for the last time, for he would give them,

and the power they symbolized, over to Rodric
before the day was done.

What was keeping them? he thought, frowning
with impatience, a trait uncharacteristic to his nature. Rodric had sworn to fetch the child to him
the moment she was up and garbed for the day.
In some discomfort now, after so long in the same
sitting position, he picked up his leg and positioned it straight, his foot propped on a low stool.
He fixed his eyes on a smaller arched window
across from him, one that faced the Sea of Hebrides. Very far from shore he could see how a play
of flitting shadows crossed the water's surface as
swift-scurrying clouds fled from winds kicked up
from the stormy night just passed.

The day was washed clean, the sky brilliant blue
and the air sparkling clear, but even the beauty
of the morning could not rid his mind of constant
thoughts of Meredith. He dwelled on the way she
had looked the last time he had seen her. The
memories, so bittersweet and painful, had monop-
olized all his waking thoughts since the day Rodric
had returned to Arrandane from Dunvegan with
Ellie MacLeod at his side.

Reverently, as if it were a saint's relic, he found
the chain around his neck and pulled it out of his
quilted scarlet tunic. He cradled the round silver
locket in his palm. He had carried the locket
against his heart for nearly two full decades, and
his thumb smoothed lovingly over the familiar surface, then pressed the ridge of the clasp. The lid
sprang open to reveal the image of the only
woman he had ever truly loved.

"Your daughter has come home, my love," he whispered in very low tones as he stared sadly at his beloved wife's image. Inconceivable agony hit him, for her loss seemed as unbearable in that moment as it had the day he found her gone. Fingers of sorrow squeezed around his heart, and his spot under the colorful windows seemed to darken under the weight of leaden grief.

Years of grieving had not alleviated his pain. He still thought of Meredith every day, mourned for her every day. Would the girl-child she bore him in secrecy resemble her? Would she have the same pale tresses, so softly curled, the lovely warm hue of honey gleaming in the sun? Would her smile melt away his pain and anger, and bring him the kind of joy that her mother's had?

A daughter, he thought, his mind spinning, a flesh-and-blood child begotten from the love of his life. Ellie MacLeod's story had been shocking, but Ian had believed her from the first night she had come to him and wept out her heartache for her part in Hugh Campbell's web of lies. His bearded jaw jutted as anger shook through him. He grasped the arms of his chair to control the rage building inside him.

The sheer perfidy of Strathmorton's acts were enough reason for Ian to wish him dead. Though their clans had been bitter enemies for generations, with wars and duels of savagery that had left both MacDonalds and Campbells rotting in their graves, never in Ian's memory had a Highlander perpetrated such treachery upon his own child in order to destroy an enemy.

How Meredith must have suffered after her father had discovered their elopement! They had met in Edinburgh—she a lassie of sixteen years on a visit with her uncle; Ian sent there to purchase stained glass for the very window under which he now sat, a commemoration of his older brother's wedding. One look at her fair face was all it had taken to smite him with abiding love for her. He had been absolutely mad about her, had convinced her to wed him in secret despite the war between their clans.

Meredith had begged him to let her go back to her father, to persuade him to agree to the union, and Ian could not say no, though his reservations troubled him greatly. Then she had not shown up at their tryst. His brow crumpled as he remembered how she had disappeared without a trace. He never saw her again. Never knew what had happened to her. It had been as if the sea had swallowed up her very existence.

Hugh Campbell, damn his soul, would not reveal her whereabouts, would not believe they had been wed, and though Ian had searched the length and breadth of Scotland, had even hired men to find her, no one could tell him her fate. A year passed before rumors of her death began to appear. Hints of her demise and burial in some foreign nunnery were whispered in hushed tones in drawing rooms of the Edinburgh elite, but he had never attained real proof of her end. And, never, not until the day Ellie MacLeod arrived at Arrandane, had he even suspected that Meredith had borne him a child.

More furrows dug into Ian's forehead, weathered creases of never-ending grief. The melancholy quickly dissolved into helplessness and rage, and he sought to quell the fury gnawing his soul into strips of raw flesh with the same sharp, vicious pecks of vultures upon carrion. He had his daughter back now, and he had Rodric to thank for that blessing. Rodric had never failed him, never once since they had met when Rodric was little more than a boy. He would be a suitable heir, a valiant chieftain, and he was proud to give his blood daughter in marriage to a man he considered a son. Together they would carry on his name, and if her eyes were truly as all described them, the Legend of the Lady would live through her as well.

The sound of boots upon the tiles rang through the spacious hall, and he turned quickly toward the sound. Almost in dread at first, and then gripped by a great eagerness, he came to his feet, bracing one hand upon the back of his chair.

Rodric walked toward him down the long length of the hall, a girl at his side. Ian's eyes ventured nowhere but upon her face. She was wearing a dress of blue and appeared tiny indeed alongside Rodric's great height. Meredith had been so small and fragile boned that Ian had been able to touch his fingertips around her waist. His breath caught when the girl stepped from the shadows and into the bejeweled river of light flowing through the colored glass.

Oh, God help him, she was the very image of her mother. He felt awash with pain, so harsh and

physical that he almost staggered. Just looking at
her transcended the present and sped him back
into the quiet gardens behind the Campbell estate
on the outskirts of Edinburgh. There, hidden
within cool, leafy bowers, they secretly met and
loved, lying upon his MacDonald cape of red tartan so detested by her family, surrounded by sheltering green fronds and flowers. Those had been
the happiest days of his life, and he found his
throat closing up until it seemed he could never
draw breath again. He fought the clenching hold
on his jaw and struggled with burgeoning, debili-
tating emotions, grateful when Rodric sensed his
inner turmoil and lay a comforting hand upon
his shoulder.

"My Lord Ian, I am honored to present to you
the Lady Ainsley MacDonald, your daughter and
my wife."

The girl looked startled by the introduction, and
acutely wary, with perhaps a tiny glint of resentment in her eyes, but so lovely, so much like Meredith. He could not take his eyes off her as she
dipped into a graceful curtsy before him.

"You look so like her . . ." He was forced to
stop, his voice quavering like an adolescent swain.
"You are very beautiful, as was she."

"I thank you, my lord." Her voice was little
more than a murmur, and she glanced several
times at Rodric, as if he bolstered her courage.
When Rodric smiled reassuringly at her, his eyes
lingered just long enough for Ian to wonder if he
was already smitten by her beauty. His feelings
for Meredith on that long-ago day had struck him

like a thunderbolt. Perhaps Rodric had been hit the same way. Ian's heart warmed to think of the gift that thought gave to him. If the young couple could find some of the happiness that Hugh had stolen away from Meredith and him, he would find pleasure in their joy. Had Rodric already won her heart, even in so short a space?

Few of the fair ladies of Arrandane had been able to resist the handsome young warrior since he had become old enough for the wenching that eased his manly desires. Rodric had courted many women, but he had shown no inclination to wed. Now he looked at Ainsley with banked fires glowing deep in his gray eyes, a burning flame that Ian understood all too well.

"Would you care to gaze upon your mother's face?" Ian held out the locket still cradled in his palm for his daughter to inspect.

Ainsley met his regard, and as he gazed deeply into her striking eyes, he found the final proof that she was born from his own seed. Her eyes shone with the same azure brilliance of his own, with only a small spot of brown to mar the limpid irises. Meredith's eyes had been as black as the midnight hour, but as large and expressive as the young woman who stood before him.

"I was told my mother and father were killed by MacDonald raiders." She raised her chin, her expression hinting defiance. " 'Tis strange that your tale bears such a different slant, one that makes my Campbell kin of so villainous and cruel a nature."

So accepting their kinship did not come easily

to her heart. Hugh Campbell had done his job well, seen to it that her mind was poisoned against MacDonalds for too long and too well. He proffered the locket with outstretched arm, praying the miniature would help convince her of the truth. He observed her face as she bent her gaze upon the tiny painting of her mother, and the stunned disbelief that overcame her features did not surprise him. Her incredible eyes darted back to him.

"This portrait could have been done in my own likeness."

"Does that not make the truth of my revelation easier to accept, my child?"

"I do not know."

"I will tell you of your mother, if you would hear of her."

"I would gladly listen," she replied softly.

Rodric immediately stepped back. He bowed respectfully. "I will provide you a private audience with your daughter, my lord."

Ian nodded at the younger man, albeit absently, and as Rodric departed toward the back of the hall, his mind was enslaved totally by the girl standing before him. Ian swallowed down a thick lump of pain as the sunlight touched her hair, setting aglow a halo as bright as a pure gold crown. He longed to touch one particular tendril that had slipped free from the loosely bound plait at her nape, where it curled prettily in front of her ear, but did not dare. She was openly guarded and distrustful of him, and by the Holy Grail, he would give her no reason to reject him as her sire.

Ian led his daughter to a bench with a carved back and softened with black velvet cushions, and watched Ainsley seat herself there with the same graceful femininity that her mother had possessed. Ian stared down at her silently, awe-inspired that this beautiful young woman was his child. That she had been carried by Meredith. He no longer had any doubt, none whatsoever. She wore her mother's visage and gazed at him out of his own eyes.

"Has Ellie revealed to you what happened on the night of your birth?"

Her face reacted to his question, almost a flinch. "Aye, and 'tis a cruel tale she told. I am sorry, but I find it hard to fathom that a grandfather could be so heartless to his own flesh and blood."

Although Ian endeavored to temper his loathing, glimpses of his hatred could be heard in his cold tone. "Hugh Campbell has never considered honor a virtue. The heart beating inside his breast is crusted black with his mortal sins."

Ainsley appeared faintly startled, then veiled her eyes with long thick eyelashes and focused her attention upon her hands folded atop her lap.

"I have no wish to offend you, dear daughter." Heaving a long, drawn-out sigh, he took a place beside her, wondering if she would ever fully accept the truth. She was legal wife to Rodric now, and therefore a MacDonald by matrimony, but would she accept him as husband after having had no say in choosing the match, after being abducted against her will to join them in her rightful place as lady of Arrandane? If she had inherited her mother's stubborn independence, he feared she would not.

"This is very strange and unsettling to you, I realize, daughter. I wish there had been another way to right the terrible wrong done us without resorting to the subterfuge we used to bring you home to Skye. Do you think you will ever be able to forgive us for stealing you away from all you've known thus far in your life?"

Ainsley suffered his hopeful scrutiny for a moment. Her response, though earnestly stated, was openly troubled. "I do not know what to think. I would you had asked me here to meet with you so that you could tell me the story."

"Hugh would never have allowed you to come here. He did not suffer you to have visitors at the abbey, did he? Did poor Ellie not tell you she feared for her life at the hands of that villain?"

She nodded. Sadness haunted her eyes like a barely invisible wraith.

"You were wed to Lord Rodric MacDonald by proxy a fortnight past. A legal contract of marital union was written and sealed by my hand as your true father before a magistrate. This night the same vows will be read before God for all to hear. 'Twas necessary to do so as soon as we knew of your existence, do you not see? So that Hugh Campbell could never legally marry you to another before we could bring you home to Skye. After this night, he will have no right to take you from us." He paused and drew in breath. "And there are other reasons for such extreme haste. I am growing old and will not live on this earth forever. When Rodric took you as his bride, he swore to me upon his life that he would protect you against Hugh Campbell and any other enemy who might try to take you off Skye."

"Yet I had no choice. I still have none."

"It is the duty of a father to select a suitable husband for his daughter, an honorable man he chooses with care who will keep her safe from harm. There is no finer man walking this earth than Rodric MacDonald. Your marriage to him will provide you with the love and protection of all Clan MacDonald, and fashion the children the two of you beget as legal heirs to all my lands and wealth."

"And you will give all of this to me with no real proof of my birthright other than my resemblance to the woman in the locket?"

"Aye." Ian's voice cracked. Embarrassed by how close his emotions swam to the surface, he spent a moment clearing his throat.

"I see her in your face, I hear her in your voice, and I feel her in the graceful way you move. You are the embodiment of my Meredith. You will make me happy again in the last days of my life. Perhaps with you here I will grieve less for days gone by and love lost. Perhaps now I can derive pleasure in making my daughter as happy as I would have made her mother, if she had not been taken from me."

Ainsley remained silent, and Ian took her hand and gently closed her fingers around the small locket. "Take it with you, my child, look upon

Meredith's face and in time you will know in your heart that she is truly your mother. And I, your father. Now go and prepare for your wedding, for the feast is to be held this very night."

As Ainsley rose and walked slowly away from him, Ian knew he had done the right thing by bringing her here. It was imperative to make her accept Rodric as her husband, to have him consummate the marriage, perhaps even get her with child before the Campbells learned of her whereabouts. There would be clan warfare over her abduction, of course; there could be no other outcome. But a centuries-old battle had waged between Clan MacDonald and Clan Campbell. Even his own great love for Meredith Campbell had not been able to bridge the gap between their families. Now he longed to fight them with his own sword before his wound took his ability to walk, before age took the strength from his sword arm and prevented him from thrusting his blade deep into Hugh Campbell's vicious heart. That was the only way to exact his revenge for taking Meredith from him, and he relished the day he could strike his nemesis dead.

Later that same evening, a few minutes before the mantel clock chimed the hour of eight o'clock, Ainsley stood before a cheval glass and allowed two chattering chambermaids to fuss over the fit of her wedding gown. Breanne flitted about as well, leaning this way and that, clucking and supervising every stitch and tuck, with great excitement. Ainsley said little, reluctantly having resigned herself to the strange events now forging her life.

What other choice did she have? She was already married to the man—legally and soon in the eyes of the church. She had nowhere to run, nor to hide. She had exacted Rodric's willing promise not to force himself upon her, but she certainly did not share Breanne's giddy enthusiasm about the ceremony.

She waited patiently while Rhetta and Ana, the two female servants, spread out the voluminous satin train while Breanne tucked small sprigs of purple heather—which Breanne proudly informed her to be the sacred plant of Clan MacDonald and therefore carried at the forefront when their clansmen marched into battle—into the thick coils they had twisted and braided into a blond crown at the top of her head.

The dress was fashioned from the softest fabric she had ever worn, so smooth and silky she could not help brushing the tips of her fingers across the sumptuous weave. Hued of fresh churned cream and sewn with white ribbons and seed pearls, the bodice had been fitted tightly to her waistline that very afternoon and the long tight sleeves tightened to flare gracefully at her elbow in a flowing swath of silk. The neckline was modest, but even so tenfold more scandalous as the staid novice gowns she had worn hitherto this day.

"You are such a beautiful bride. Rodric will lie down and die when he sees you."

Ainsley couldn't help but smile at Breanne's odd choice of words. But she did not share her senti-

ment. "He will care little about my appearance
one way or another. He only married me to secure
his rise as chieftain of Clan MacDonald. I daresay
he would marry anyone at all for such a presti-
gious prize." Annoyance nipped at Ainsley when
she remembered that he had readily admitted the
truth of his motives, blithely, to her face.

"Aye, that is truly the way of it. He would do
nearly anything to honor Lord Ian, but he is
pleased with you as well. I can tell by the way he
stares at you, as if his eyes are tied to your face.
He has already developed a certain fondness for
you, I truly sense it."

"After only one day of acquaintance? I think
not. 'Tis the mantle of power he covets from this
day of nuptials."

The quick denial came easily to Ainsley's lips,
but she wondered if he did stare at her in the way
Breanne had described. He had been kind
enough, and he had saved her life, she would
never forget that. For that reason alone, she could
not bring herself to hate him. She shuddered,
thinking how the splintered log had scraped her
back and how the knife glowed red-hot.

On the other hand she knew as well as he that
the consummation of their vows was the only true
validation of the marriage. She wondered how
long his promised reprieve would last once they
had been pronounced as man and wife before the
people of his clan. Rodric MacDonald was not a
patient man. That was one of the first things she
had noticed about him during the first moments

she had observed him in the chapel the night he came for her.

"And now for the most beautiful garment of all," Breanne murmured, reverently lifting a flowing length of lace from a casket lined with rich red satin. She had carried the box into the room earlier but had not opened it until now. "Rodric sent this to you. 'Twas the veil worn by our mother, and her mother before her. Look very closely in the threads, and you will find lilacs embroidered upon the lace. My great-grandmother knotted her veil by hand, because my great-grandfather presented her with a lilac bush brought from the Acropolis of Athens on the very day he asked for her hand in marriage. She said that whoever wears the veil will enjoy a long and fruitful marriage to the man she loves. That's why Rodric wishes you to wear it. You will do it for him, won't you? He will be dreadfully disappointed, if you do not."

Breanne beamed at her, so friendly and amiable, that it made it hard for Ainsley to refuse. Rodric's sister looked lovely in her forest-hued gown and crown of pink heather entwined in her shiny auburn curls. She was to stand with Ainsley as maiden of honor, and Ainsley was pleased that at least there was a girl her own age to keep her company in the coming days. She missed Myrna very much and hoped her friend had made it back to the abbey. If she had, the abbess would have already alerted Strathmorton of the MacDonald crimes against him. Then the war would commence, but Ainsley did not want to think about that.

"I pray my own wedding day will be performed in the warmth of summertide," Breanne murmured, giving a wistful-sounding sigh that caused Ainsley to look at her.

"Are you betrothed, then?" Ainsley inquired of her as the maids fluffed her flowing train by lifting it by the edge and billowing it downward with a whoosh of fabric.

"Nay, but I wish to be given to Richard in wedlock, though he barely knows that I exist. It is Leona of Dunvegan that he adores."

"Dunvegan?"

"Aye. The castle of the MacLeods that lies on the shore north of us. 'Tis the clansmen of our mother's family. Her name was Penelope MacLeod, and Richard is our cousin, born of the MacLeods of Lewis. Richard will return to Dunvegan soon after the feast is done, and to see her, I fear."

"Richard is a handsome man. You would make a fine couple."

Breanne lost all manner of melancholy and began to beam at her again. "Do you really think so? Did he mention my name to you on your sojourn from the mainland?"

"I did not see him but briefly when he was disguised in the garb of an English dragoon. Rodric said he was emissary to the Earl of Strathmorton. 'Twas quite a dangerous hoax they played so deep within Campbell territory."

"My brother has always been bold of nature.

He likes danger, I fear. All the ladies think he is quite dashing and handsome, and will be jealous that he now takes you as his wife. Many have set their cap for him in the past, but only Leona did he consider as a possible wife."

The last remark piqued Ainsley's interest. "He thought to wed Leona of Dunvegan?"

"Aye. I fear that now that Rodric has been wed to you, she will take my Richard as her betrothed. She is very beautiful."

They both turned as the maid, Ana, rushed into the room. "The bridegroom is anxious. He paces like a lion at the bottom of the stair. He sent me posthaste to fetch his bride, for he wearies of the wait."

Ainsley took a deep breath and followed Breanne out into the hall. There she could see that Rodric was indeed eager. He had climbed the steps and stood a short distance from the top landing. He was no longer pacing as Ana had described, but leaned his back indolently against the wall as if he were as calm as a priest at prayer. He wore the dress tartan of the MacDonald, both a belted kilt and red plaid draped over his shoulder. A large brooch with emeralds fastened it at his shoulder, and a sporran hung at his waist. He smiled when she appeared at the top of the stair, then slowly ascended the steps to meet her. His eyes never wavered from her face.

Bending deeply from the waist, he extended his hand and smiled broadly. "My lady, my wedded wife, you are more beautiful than I could have ever dreamed."

A curious mixture of embarrassment and pleasure added darker spots of color to Ainsley's high
cheekbones. She placed her fingertips very lightly
atop his palm, and he quickly took her hand and
placed it in the crook of his arm, then led her
slowly down the steps and into the banquet hall,
where most members of the clan had already
gathered to meet her. She could see Lord Ian—
her father?—at the far end of the room beside a
priest in flowing black robe. Ellie stood nearby
them as well, smiling happily when she saw
Ainsley.

A hush descended over the assemblage. Ainsley's knees trembled just a little as she walked
forward at Rodric's side, grateful for his strong
arm on which to lean. When they reached the
end where the great cross-shaped window stood
dark and tall, she stopped before the man who
claimed to be her sire.

No warmth of familial kinship flooded through
her when she looked at him, but there was no
denying that she resembled the woman he
claimed to have loved. If the awful story told to
her was true, she was now at home with her family of Arrandane, safely away from the grandfather
who had ordered her murder. If they told her lies,
she had become a dangerous pawn in the hands
of avowed enemies, no doubt to be used as their
weapon to wreak vengeance on Strathmorton.

The priest began to chant, and she listened to
the vows as if sleepwalking through an extraordi-
narily bizarre dream scape. She heard from afar
Rodric's deep voice promising to cherish her and

protect her. Holy Mother of God, what was she doing standing at his side and allowing this to happen? she thought in sudden mindless panic. Why hadn't she run away when she had half the chance?

But other thoughts soon calmed her dread, for would she truly have preferred to remain at the convent, suffering the fear and ridicule of all? Or be sent to England, where the very same could happen? Regardless of all else, she was safe here on the Isle of Skye. No one would chase her and threaten to strike out her eye. She was being treated with utmost kindness and respect. Could she learn to adapt and forget all the hatred drilled into her from childhood? If they had not murdered her parents as she had been told, what other grievance did she harbor against them?

Then she found herself murmuring words of acceptance, words that everyone waited to hear from her lips, and soon the vows were done and she was Rodric MacDonald's wife. Rodric was smiling, pressing his lips to the backs of her hands, and she was shivering from his kisses and the possessive way he was gazing down at her.

The skirl of bagpipes began at the hands of pipers, a dozen strong, from somewhere high above in the tiers of an upper balcony. The music floated over them, as if it flowed to earth from the heavenly hosts, and Rodric led her to a dais where two high-backed chairs had been placed. Ainsley could not help but smile at the ebullience with which the dancers began to whirl and sing in time to the songs of the pipers, accompanied by the lively beat of tabors and the sweet notes of flutes. She enjoyed it mightily, for there had been no dancing at the nunnery, no laughter, no happy songs.

"You are my wedded wife now, Ainsley, for all to see, and I will not stop until you are as eager to share my bed as I am to claim you as my own."

Rodric leaned close, his lips touching her temple, brushing gentle kisses, lingering and disturbing. His voice was husky with a different sound, low-pitched and intimate, one she had not heard before from him but that even she, in her maidenly innocence, recognized as unanswered desire.

"You said you would not force yourself upon me if I would stand beside you at the ceremony," she reminded him, suddenly afraid and finding it impossible to keep her voice as steady as she wanted. "Is your word of honor so carelessly given, my lord?"

"I stand by my promise, my true love. 'Tis you who will have to invite me into your bed."

He took a decanter of wine and carefully filled a silver goblet, setting it on the table in front of her. "Drink a toast and enjoy yourself, because you are now Lady Ainsley MacDonald and in your rightful place between your father and your husband."

Ainsley drank indeed, more to bolster her courage, to resist his dazzling smile than to salute her new station. She had not often imbibed of liquor—the only libations of the abbey being barley water, goat's milk, and occasionally a sneaked mug of apple cider—but the ruby-red brew now filling her cup had a sweet, heady flavor. Rodric refilled her goblet with eager regularity until a group of his friends gathered around and enticed him away with them to be honored with a congratulatory toast to his nuptials.

The evening progressed with hours of jigs and gambols, and all manner of happy frolicking to the beat of the music. Ainsley watched all the conviviality with solemn demeanor, not sure how she should feel. She knew none of these people, who claimed to be blood kin. She felt out of place, though it was pleasant that the serving maids would replenish her plate and cup, look straight into her eyes, and not recoil in horror as had so many others in her past. She found her toe tapping in spry fashion to such snappy tunes, even as she hummed along, and felt gloriously happy for Breanne when she saw the man named Richard smilingly swing the auburn-curled girl onto the floor among the other dancers.

"Come, love, and dance with me before your slippers tap your feet off this platform!"

Rodric was back, pulling her to her feet, laughing, and Ainsley found herself being lifted high into the air then down onto the dance floor. Though she knew not the steps, it did not matter for the dancers merely joined hands and made two rings, one within the other. The pipers' song grew faster and faster until the pace and the wine within her lightened inside her head and made her brain spin in the same dizzying circles in which the dancers rushed with such abandon.

When she drew up suddenly in an unsuccessful attempt to steady her staggered vertigo, Rodric took advantage of her fuzzy condition and swung her bodily into his arms. He carried her down the length of the hall with all manner of lusty cheers and bawdy cries from well-wishers following them from the gathering.

To Ainsley's surprise he did not set her on her feet, but took the steps two at a time until he reached the upper floor. He carried her into his own bedchamber, kicked the door shut behind them, then tossed her onto the softness of the deep feather bed. She stared blearily up at him, blinking hard a few times to right her thoughts as he stood above her, gripping a bedpost with one hand as he unpinned his plaid at his shoulder and let it fall down over his belt. Had he already forgotten his promise? Did he intend to ravish her? Now that she was so weak from wine, could she resist him if he did?

Chapter Eleven

"You promised you would not . . ." Ainsley moved her head from side to side, weakly denying his advances, but could not seem to pluck away the sticky strands of intoxication coating her mind. She had drunk far too much wine, she realized with belated regret, but her breathless protestations died dangerously when her new husband leaned so close that his breath fanned a swath of her hair and cooled her heated cheek.

"Aye, and 'tis a fool I am for vowing so recklessly. I will keep my promise to you, though I cannot think of a more arduous task to petition a bridegroom on the night of his wedding. Especially when wed to a lady with a face worn by angels in heaven."

Ainsley relaxed considerably and nestled her head deeper into the softly contoured depths of a feather-filled satin pillow, baffled by the perversity of her emotions. Pleasure battled in equal portion to disappointment, and though she knew with every kind of certainty that she should look anywhere but at the man—at her unwanted, stranger of a husband—standing so tall and imposing beside the bed, her attention rested squarely, wide-eyed and unwavering, upon Rodric MacDonald as he unfolded his neck cloth and tossed it carelessly upon the fireside chair. Now he was loosening his full-sleeved white shirt at the throat, baring a glimpse of dark chest hair. Then he moved swiftly, unexpectedly, stunning her with what he did next.

While she watched, he jerked back the heavy red velvet bedcover until it quite hung off the end of the bed in a rumpled heap, then mightily ruffled up the linens beneath. His last act was to pull askew the bed hanging adorning the corner post. She blinked in some disbelief.

"For the benefit of Rhetta and Ana, so they can spread the word of our nuptial bliss throughout the castle and save me embarrassments I would rather not suffer," he explained with a cocked brow that pulled an amused curve to Ainsley's lips.

He smiled, too, then lounged down on the length of his side inches from her. The stiffness that held her spine so straight melted away as her fear of him took a similar course.

"I don't suppose I have yet plied you with wine enough to relinquish me of the damnable restraint you forced upon my honor?"

Ainsley shook her head, but he laughed when a fragile hiccup escaped her. Sheepishly she found herself joining him in his enjoyment, and wondered again if she was indeed slightly drunk as he picked up a decanter from the bedside table and poured more wine into two crystal goblets.

"I believe you wish me inebriated so that you can . . . do, I mean . . . lie alongside me as a husband."

His grin broadened at her rather inarticulate accusation, but still a sense of happiness and well-being enveloped her. Whether from the spirits or all the merriment in the hall below, nothing seemed to dampen her own elevated mood. Rodric was not attempting to hurt her or force her into anything she did not wish to do. In faith, he was being so very pleasant that she could not prevent the soft smile she presented to him. Though she did not know him well at all, she trusted his word, at least on this particular matter. Besides, his charming mien was hard to resist when he sat so near that their bodies nearly touched and when he smiled so sweetly into her eyes.

"You wound me, wife, with such hard expectations from me. In truth, I only wish to toast the beauty of my bride and the good fortune and great joy to be wed and have her at my side at long last." With such extravagantly honeyed words he raised a glass, clinked it softly against hers, then sipped from his. As she drank along with him, their eyes locked, his mirthful expression gradually fading to a serious stare.

Ainsley's heartbeat began to quicken with increasing awareness of just how masculine he was, sprawling there so close beside her, and she felt an extreme need to throw open the casement windows and heave in great, cleansing gulps of the cool, spring night air. Not sure she could negotiate the distance of the room with a steady step, she wrapped the fingers of both hands around the fragile glass and held it as if it were the Holy Grail.

Nerves jumping like baby rabbits at play, she took another taste of wine as he unfolded his long limbs into an even more comfortable position, as if he meant to stay there the length of the night. To her wonder, his legs stretched nearly the length of the bed just this side of the ornately rendered pastoral scenes carved so intricately into the mahogany bedposts.

"You surely do not intend to pass the night here with me in this chamber, my lord? Certainly not in this bed, not with me in it, too?" Ainsley thought it a reasonable query, if delivered with slightly less than silver-tongued eloquence.

"That I do, lass, or 'tis an awful burden of ridicule my men will heap atop my head come the crown of dawn, even with the bed hangings ripped and torn."

It occurred to Ainsley with no little amount of shock that she was actually pleased he intended to remain the night with her. In puzzlement, she dinted her brows in consternation, trying to think why she would feel that way after all she had been through because of him.

"I trust you will find it in your heart to allow me to retain that one shred of pride before the eyes of my clansmen, will you not, dear Ainsley, my love?"

My love, her mind repeated, the unexpected endearment cajoling her to grant him that one wish. Especially since he had given her his word not to bother her. "You are welcome here as long as you hold to your vow to leave me be."

"You mention my folly too often, dear wife. As a fitting reminder that you find your husband repugnant, mayhaps?"

Ainsley took a moment before answering that, and openly admired his fine dark hair and the way his lean cheeks creased with deep indentations at the corners of his mouth when he smiled so broadly at her. Husband. Was it possible that the extraordinary man beside her was truly such? Her gaze lowered and lingered upon his firm mouth until strong white teeth flashed and she remembered herself. Quickly she glanced elsewhere but found his agreeable image again in a large standing mirror set not far from the foot of the bed. In it, he watched her with just as much intensity.

"Did you enjoy the wedding feast?" he inquired at length as they continued to watch their reflections.

An inordinately safer subject to pursue, she decided as she answered, "Oh, aye, 'twas a lovely celebration. The first time I've seen such dancing and playing of the pipes. The abbey was quite staid and somber, as you no doubt noticed."

Her voice had held a note of sadness at the end, and she watched Rodric turn toward her, then saw him reach for her with fingers that felt warm and strong as he took her hand and entwined his long fingers with hers. His words were low but filled with compassion that she could not help but detect.

"Hugh of Strathmorton sentenced you there to a sorry life with his self-serving lies. You should have been here with Ian and Meredith, and with me to fall in love with you as you grew up before my eyes." His tone had become so soft that she felt compelled to turn her face and meet his gaze. "I can make you happy here on Skye, Ainsley. From this moment on that will be my quest, to make you feel as much a part of us as if you had been here all along."

Ainsley was touched by such words, and she believed him. How could she possibly not do so with earnestness so evident in his silvery eyes? For the first time she could ever remember, she felt completely safe, protected, and aye, even beloved, though they knew each other not well at all.

When she offered no reply, he proffered more wine, but she placed her fingers across the rim to refrain him. "Accustomed to such heavy drink, I am not. Perhaps 'twould be wise if I drank no more this night."

"The wine is watered with honey. 'Twill act to calm your nerves and help slumber embrace you."

She wondered if it truly was slumber with which he intended to embrace her, or his own muscular limbs? That idea sent her pulse to jumping, and rippling shivers trod her spine. Unwillingly she moved her eyes to the opened neckline of his shirt and fought the inclination to slide her fingertips inside the fine white cambric and tease the texture of the dark masculine fur hidden there.

With that scandalous thought she imbibed readily from her cup after all, just to brake that overwhelming inclination. Then the steel-hewn curve of his thigh brushed her hip, and all manner of sensations took hold. She quickly set the glass aside for fear she would need her senses about her. Rodric MacDonald had a way about him, one that robbed her of reason. "I am done with drink, my lord."

Rodric had no objection to her decision and merely replaced her goblet, and his as well, upon the marble-topped table. He relaxed back full length, then effortlessly caught her attention.

"Tell me, Ainsley, do you have any inclination to accept that Ian is truly sire to you? Or do you still suspect yourself to be the object of some elaborate ruse we've designed to trick you?"

Ainsley found herself more hesitant to cast blame than she had only hours before, yet she did not say as much. "I do not know what to believe. So much has happened and in so short a span that my mind cannot stop spinning."

"I had hoped that Ellie's account would convince you. She has no reason to tell you lies."

"I know not what moves Ellie. I have not seen her in many years."

Rodric gave one long sigh edged with weary acceptance, then changed the subject. "Would you like to know more of your father?"

Ainsley responded to his request with a slight nod, but her thoughts delved more into how much his eyes looked like molten silver under the flickering and fluttering of the candles and how his dark brows slanted together each time he smiled. He was handsome beyond any man she had seen, and virile of body, if her overheard comments of the servants were true. He was chieftain of Clan MacDonald now, her husband, and her avowed protector. But would her contract of betrothal to the Englishman negate the vows they had just taken?

"Lord Ian is the finest man I have met in my life. I first became acquainted with him years ago when I was but a lad with the MacDonalds of Balluchulish. My father was a chief there until he was killed in battle with the Campbells of Argyll. My mother was with child then and died in the birthing when Breanne came early." He reached out and stroked a forefinger over a strand of Ainsley's hair that lay curled upon the pillow. "So at twelve I was left to fend for myself and a baby sister. Ian brought us home to foster at Arrandane and has treated me as son, Breanne as daughter. Now he has given over to me the reins of his power. I would give my life for him." He paused, serious now, all humor gone from his eyes. "And now I would do the same for you."

So tender was his tone that Ainsley was greatly touched by his pledge, but she attempted to tamp down the affection beginning to bud to full-blown flower inside her breast.

"You hardly know me, nor I, you" was her soft reminder. "What reason have you to vow such allegiance to me?"

"I have loved you, I think, since I was that small orphaned lad Ian brought home with him to Skye eighteen years ago."

Startled, Ainsley stared at him as he turned upon his side and braced his head atop an open palm. He kept tight hold on her fingers with his other hand. "The locket you now wear was opened to me in those long gone days, and when I looked upon Meredith's likeness, I truly thought her the most beautiful lady I had ever beheld. Ian told me many times of her grace and gentle ways, and I fear I fell in love with the woman he described. Now I see her again, in the flesh, and as my wife." He turned her hand and pressed his mouth to the sensitive point where her pulse beat an erratic pattern on the inside of her wrist.

Ainsley's long lashes drifted together with burgeoning pleasure at the romantic notion, but as his lips moved slowly up her bare arm, she returned to reason and snatched her hand from his grasp, realizing what he was about with his sweet words.

"I am not my mother. I am myself and known only to you for a single day."

Her reply had pleased him. She saw that clearly in his expression. When he spoke again, she discovered why he was triumphant.

"If you accept her as mother, then you must also feel the kinship of father with Lord Ian as well."

"Aye, I mean, nay. I don't know. You turn my words around and feed me spirits to befuddle me."

"I fell in love with your face long ago. Now I

am ready to adore the woman you are, if you'll but give me that pleasure."

If he was affecting a seduction, 'twas certainly having a positive effect upon her senses, she determined, but why would he not woo with consummate skill? He no doubt had much practice with the Lady Leona, whom Breanne had mentioned, and countless others thunderstruck by his good looks and fine manly physique. She would have to keep her wits about her, she vowed, for she was learning quickly that it would be an easy thing to melt into such strong arms and do his bidding, and whatever else he might ask of her. She moved slightly away from him to strengthen her resolve, and fixed her gaze on the night where it pressed against the windowpanes like a preening black cat.

"I've angered you?" Half question, half statement, he sat up and propped an elbow on his bent knee so that he could look down at her. When he took her hand again, she sought to pull it away, but though his pressure was gentle, he refused to release her fingers. He pressed a warm kiss upon her bent knuckles.

"Do not fear me, Ainsley. I would never hurt you, I swear it. You draw away now. Are you afraid to let me touch you?"

Yes, yes, yes, her mind screamed, but only one whispered word escaped her lips.

"Nay."

"That pleases me almost as much as this sight of you in my bed."

Rodric lifted his other hand and caressed a

loosened tendril that brushed her temple, then slid his fingers into the winding coils of her coiffure. Slowly, his eyes intent upon his task, he began to pull the combs and ribbons free, one at a time, until her heavy tresses began to fall around her shoulders in loose silken-sheened waves.

"One time long ago," he murmured, testing with his hand the heaviness of her hair, then watching the soft strands sift through his spread fingers, "Ian described your mother's hair to me, spun of gold he said, shiny and so soft it did not seem of the earth. Yours is exactly the same, silky fine and beautiful."

His eyes warmed with a heated perusal, hers increasingly wary as he wrapped a long strand around his forefinger and gently tugged it until she was forced closer to him. He did not speak again until their faces were but a handsbreadth apart. "I hunger to taste the sweetness of your lips. Allow me that on my wedding night, lovely Ainsley, one kiss is little for you to part with, just one touch of your husband's mouth upon your own."

So enthralled was she by the husky desire underlying his whisper that she could not deny him. His handsome face came closer, so near their lips almost touched, but she drew back when she realized how much her body yearned to press up close against him. He did not force the kiss but moved unexpectedly, clasping her shoulders and moving her bodily before she could resist, and she found herself sitting between his legs, her back pressed against his chest. Gasping, she tried to extricate herself, but his arm lay heavily across her chest, holding her firmly and intimately between heaving breasts.

Imprisoned in his arms, she watched Rodric in the mirror and found his eyes upon her, banked with fires she was beginning to comprehend. She was alarmingly aroused both in mind and body, and by just observing the intimacy of their entwined pose. Suddenly all things about him took on a tingling, rivetingly vivid intensity that she had not experienced before, and she became aware of every nuance of him, the solidity and weight of the muscular arm pinning her back against him, the faint clean scent of soap that lingered in his hair—of fragrant forest pine—as he rested his chin atop her head.

"Relax, my love. You lie tense and wary against me. Trust me when I say I will not have you this night. I gave you my word, and I will honor it. I will neither hurt you nor force you to do anything you do not want to do."

Ainsley tried to obey his request but trembled inside, though Rodric only sat still with his arms loosely holding her in front of him. After some moments thus, she leaned her head back against his shoulder and watched the smile her capitulation engendered from him.

Rodric began to stroke her hair with his palm, dipping his fingers into it, caressing the texture between his thumb and fingertips, and she watched him at such tasks through the mirror until her lips parted with breathless wonder. She had never been held in such a way, never in her

life, not by mother, father, sister, lover, no one
other than old Ellie when Ainsley was hardly old
enough to remember the sensations. It felt wonderful. It felt as if she were a part of someone
else, not alone in the world, not the witch of
Kilchurn ostracized by everyone. His gaze captured her eyes until she closed them to hide her
teary feelings, then his lips pressed, warm and
tender, against the throb of her temple.

"I have loved you from the moment I saw your
face in the locket." Soothing was his admission,
uttered softly as he nuzzled her head aside so that
he could press a kiss on the side of her throat,
beneath her ear, then in the sensitive hollow of
her ear, where he whispered more soft words.
"Never did I think myself fortunate enough to find
a woman like you. You are my destiny. We are
meant to be together as one, to love each other
as man and wife, and I will prove that to you if
it takes the rest of my days."

A tingling sensation was born, flared hotly, then
streaked like a white-tailed comet down into her
body, deep into her virginal core. Unnerved, her
teeth caught at her bottom lip as all manner of
thrills and goose bumps rioted over her flesh.
When she opened her eyes she could see him in
the mirror, watched with parted lips as he slid his
palms slowly up and down her arms.

A soft sigh of contentment escaped her, and
she shifted her body under the awakening of her
womanly needs. His hard thighs tightened around
her hips, and for the first time in her life she felt
the part of a man that desired a woman. One

convulsive swallow went down hard, as if her throat had shriveled to the size of a reed, and she became fearful about what she did not know. His arms tightened when she attempted to extricate herself from his embrace.

"Don't leave me, love. At least let me hold you. I'm not hurting you, am I?"

Ainsley felt dizzy, overwhelmed by the unaccustomed sensual responses washing through her mind and body, but she wasn't sure whether she was in danger or not. She trusted his word until she felt his fingers working at the fastenings of her gown and the bodice suddenly loosened at the neckline. She caught the gown tightly against her breast and stared at one bare shoulder in the glass as if the image belonged to another woman. Her skin appeared as pale as the ivory dress she clutched so tightly in front of her, and when Rodric rested his palms atop her shoulders, his fingers looked long and brown against her naked white flesh. He began to knead her tension-tight muscles, slowly, gently, forcing her to relax.

"It's not so horrible a fate to share a bed with one's husband," he murmured very low, and she found she could not drag her eyes away from him. "I can make you feel love such as you've never known before, Ainsley. 'Tis my right now as your wedded husband to touch you this way, to hold you and kiss you, to adore you as my woman."

"I'm afraid," she admitted, voice atremble.

"Of something as sweet as this?" he asked in a murmur, turning her face toward him. For the first time he captured her mouth, fully, possessively, and she began to tremble as his lips touched hers, softly, tenderly—not with the wet, clammy feel of Jeremy's, nothing like that—but firm, warm, knowing, as if he tasted the most delicious of culinary delights, nibbling at her lower lip, then suckling at her entire mouth with gentle expertise.

She moaned when the tip of his tongue traced the line of her lips, dipped into the corners, then parted her mouth and found her own. She heard a sound, from somewhere deep in his throat, and before she knew what happened, he had turned her swiftly until she lay flat against his length, belly to belly, breast to breast, both breathless as their mouths caught together. His lips twisted and subjugated her will until she curled her fingers over his shoulders and squeezed hard as she strained up against him in quivering wonder, and her mouth finally opened beneath the insistent quest of his tongue.

Rodric groaned aloud when she finally stopped all vestige of resistance, her arms clinging tightly around his neck, his own desire leaping with the unquenchable fires burning in his blood. He fought against taking her then and there, against rending the thin silk gown asunder, where it lay already half unfastened and making her his wife in every way. But could he risk it, could he? he wondered as he kissed her, over and over, both hands tangled in her hair as she seemed caught up in a frenzy of awakened sensations, arching her body and moaning beneath his mouth.

God, he had never experienced torture until this

moment, and he could not last much longer with his heart pounding through his temples. But he could not use her like some tavern tart. He wanted more between them, did not want to alienate her, or make her resentful that he had not kept the vow she had demanded from him.

Her innocent passion pleased him greatly, but it made her vulnerable to his wealth of experience. He wanted her as a wife, a woman to hold him to her breast and love him, to stand proudly at his side before the world. He hungered for her respect, for her belief. For her love. That was what he really wanted, he realized with a faint wave of inner shock, he wanted her to love him.

Taking her now in the heat of the moment would be a mistake, a deadly error that could end their relationship before they could grow to care about each other. Before he broke his promise and spent himself on her, he forced himself to thrust her aside and lunged to his feet, struggling against his own overwhelming needs. His voice was hoarse, unfamiliar. He had not often denied himself a willing woman.

"Sleep well, my love, and when you wake on the morrow remember that I have kept my promise to you this night."

Tousle-haired, confusion riddling her face, Ainsley pushed upright and braced herself on her hands as he crossed the room to the portal of the adjoining chamber. He stopped and looked back, and every fiber of his manhood screamed for him to rush back to her. But if he did she would shun him before the dawn broke in the eastern sky, and her anger would be justified, her scorn righteous. If he left her now, perhaps in time she would want him to stay of her own accord. They had the rest of their lives together, did they not?

Heaving a deep, fortifying draw of air, he entered the adjoining bedchamber. He shut the door and leaned against it, then dropped his head and massaged his forehead with his fingers. God help him get through this night. He had known many women in his life, had more lovers than he could remember, experienced women, a few not so, but none of them, past or present, had gotten into his blood the way that Ainsley already had.

From the first moment he had looked into her extraordinary eyes, he had craved her, body and soul, with such strong yearning that he still felt shaken. He felt a need to protect her from the ignorant of the world who had so wrongly persecuted her, to keep her safely with him, happy and smiling, and tapping her toes to music as she had done earlier during the wedding feast.

Even now, he longed to return to her, to take her in his arms, even if it was only to hold her. Perhaps he could do that much, because God help him, he feared it would take a miracle to survive this night in the cold, empty bed before him, when knowing full well that Ainsley, beautiful, soft, warm, silken-skinned Ainsley, his lawful wife, lay just beyond the door in his own bed, awakened to the passion of love, and only a few footfalls away.

Chapter Twelve

❦

Shreds of slumber weighted Ainsley's eyelids like heavy gold coins. She forced them open at last, feeling her way back to the light of day like a stumbling blind man. For several drowsy moments she was unaware of her surroundings, not until her bleary vision began to focus upon the black whiskers forming Rodric MacDonald's beard, mere inches from her nose.

Her entire body became rigid, muscles tensed with surprise that escalated swiftly into outright shock as she realized she was curled intimately alongside his long lean form. Nay, she was pinned securely there, beneath one heavy muscular sword arm, her cheek resting against the smooth skin of his naked brown shoulder, his fingers threaded loosely in her wavy tresses.

Sweet sainted Mary, she had been alone before she slept, hadn't she? She garnered her scattered thoughts, searching for those last moments before she had succumbed wearily to sleep, fighting emotions still heated from Rodric's devastating touch.

But he had left her alone; she was sure of it. Yet now he still slept in peaceful oblivion to her dilemma, his broad chest rising and falling with slow, easy breaths.

When had he removed his shirt? He had still had it on when he held her to him, kissing and caressing her. She recalled vividly the feel of his hands upon her skin, his mouth upon hers, and shivered uncontrollably. And when had he returned? she wondered, and had he compromised her further while she slept despite his assurances that he would not?

Her fears were soon in abeyance when she realized he still wore his belted plaid and she, her wedding gown. Though the bodice was loosened at the back, and the skirt hunched up alarmingly around her bare thighs, the dress still wrapped her with modesty and her undergarments were in order. He had kept his promise, but would he if he awoke with both of them half-naked and so scandalously entwined?

She watched him at rest for a few moments, revisiting the powerful if fuzzy memories of his sweetly uttered words and gentle touches the night before. Debating her chances of easing out of his arms and obtaining the safety of her own room without disturbing him, she decided to try, craving time alone to think about what had transpired. She could not in good conscience blame Rodric for the encounter, for she had certainly lain as a willing accomplice in his arms and let him do to her what he would, in truth, enjoying every minute of it.

As the rise of the sun brought forth sounds of employment behind the door of her adjoining bed-chamber, her courage was bolstered considerably for fear of intrusion by the servants, and she inched with supreme care away from the handsome stranger who was now her husband. Rodric's arm tightened around her, as if he sensed and deployed her departure even as he slept. His dark eyelashes lay long and straight against his cheeks, and she watched them gradually flutter open. He stared upward at the tapestried canopy. Only an instant passed before he remembered her. He jerked his head sideways and found her watching him, then softened her heart considerably with the most tender smile he had yet to bestow upon her.

"It is good finding you here with me in my bed when the sun floods through the windows. I hope you are not angry that I came back to you after you slept." He gave a sheepish shrug. "I couldn't seem to stay away."

Words meant to please. So husky, so warm. Sentiments from a master of seduction. He meant to disarm her, and thus far he had succeeded in doing so with admirable ease. As her own accusation left her lips, the words were less convincing in her own mind, for she knew all the blame did not fall upon his shoulders. Still, she felt the need to utter them. "The promise you made meant little once we were abed. Your honor seems not to be the virtue you purported."

Rodric looked visibly startled, but his surprise turned rapidly into displeasure, openly revealed to her by the downward pitch to his eyebrows. He raised himself upon one elbow and kept her in place with a spread palm upon her shoulder. To her own chagrin, she thought more of his sword-callused fingers touching her bare skin than his forthcoming denial.

"I compromised you not, through no hard effort on my needs as a man. You are an innocent lass indeed if you think anything else went between us." Suddenly his face lost all trace of annoyance, and he smiled as if pleased by his own revelation. "It is good that you are so chaste. Such virtue in a wife pleases a man well."

Ainsley blushed, for she was indeed an innocent; her sheltered life had naught to do with males and their physical wants or needs, but she was not so naive that she did not know something quite extraordinary had happened between them. It seemed impossible that anything more pleasurable could be forthcoming.

Rodric relaxed back against the pillows, then drew her down beside him. Unresistingly Ainsley went, shocking herself by wanting to press a kiss against the hard, broad expanse of his chest.

"It is not so heinous a crime to share a mild intimacy or two on the nuptial night, my love. If you did not wear your innocence so charmingly, you would know that I showed nearly inhuman restraint . . ."

"A few mild intimacies? Is that all they were to you?" she exclaimed, coming up on an elbow with chagrin showing in her face until she saw his knowing grin.

"You have much to learn in the art of lovemaking, fair Ainsley, and I can only console myself with the pleasures that we will share once you welcome my embrace to the fullest."

Suspicion narrowed Ainsley's eyes, and Rodric sought to reassure her.

"You are a virgin lass still, through no small sacrifice on my heart. We've only begun our journey together as man and wife. Alas, I cannot even claim you as my own of yet, though only the two of us will know you have denied me my heart's desire."

Tenderly he brushed back a cascade of wavy golden tresses behind her ear. When she ascertained the bent of his gaze, she found that her unbound bodice had left her breast undraped for his viewing. Quickly she pulled the silk up into a semblance of order. Rodric cocked a brow at her modesty, then sobered as he fingered a silky curl.

"I kept my word to you, Ainsley, as I will always do. You do me wrong by tossing my eagerness to love you back into my face on this first day of our married life. As I vowed, I have not taken you to wife yet and I will not, until you take me to husband with willing accord."

"But 'twas so wondrous . . ." Ainsley faltered for want of an acceptable description and wondered about the details of what other intimacies transpired between a man and a woman. She now wished she had been privy to discussions concerning the carnal act whispered among the other girls at the abbey, but she had been shunned from their group because of the color of her eyes.

Myrna had been her one true companion, and she had known even less about the marriage bed than Ainsley had.

At seeing her obvious confusion, Rodric ran a forefinger down her cheek and caressed her bottom lip. Their eyes met, and he drew out a painful sigh. "I best be up and away from you before I lose the better part of my intentions. But I have made plans for us to spend the day together. Be up and about your ablutions, and garb yourself in the new black riding outfit that now hangs in your wardrobe. I have a wedding present that I wish to present to you before the morning is done."

Tossing off the covers, he rose and stood at the side of the bed, tall, broad-shouldered, lithe and long of limb. She watched a band of muscles stretch with sinewy power as he reached for a black linen dressing gown he had discarded on the floor. He turned as he drew it over his torso, and before she could follow him from the bed, he scooped her up with one arm as if she were but a wisp of thistledown and held her tightly against his chest. He kissed her thoroughly, not so much with the gentle exploration of the night past but with confident masculine proprietorship. When he suddenly let her go, she was so weak-kneed, she had to grasp onto the bedpost for support.

"Hasten then with your toilette, for I already miss the feel of you close against my heart."

Ainsley watched him stride away to his dressing chamber in search of his manservant, then wilted onto the bed, her body riddled with all manner of fluttery anticipation.

Within the hour, however, she was bathed and garbed in the black velvet riding suit that he had described. The two servant girls, Rhetta and Ana, had helped her dress, and she had colored warmly and often under their knowing smiles and veiled remarks about her sleep-deprived eyes and rumpled wedding gown.

Even now Rhetta was giggling as she gathered up the strewn bedclothing that Rodric had tossed about in his destruction of the marriage bed. Her face flamed to a rosy hue when Ana discovered the torn bed hanging and turned wide eyes upon her. At that point Ainsley fled her husband's bedchamber in pure mortification.

"Lord Rodric awaits you at the stables," Ana called as Ainsley heard their trills of laughter chasing her down the hallway.

Ainsley was happy enough to find deserted hallways, not particularly eager to face the other inhabitants of the castle, feeling almost as if she wore some badge upon her breast heralding her new intimacy with Rodric. A blush rose in heated surges until her face felt warm, and she ran down the back stair and through the herb garden until she found Rodric waiting where foretold. He smiled broadly when he saw her and walked forth leading the most beautiful white mare Ainsley had ever beheld.

"I chose this beauty because her coat is similar to that of your Saracen." He patted the graceful curve of the horse's neck, admiring the animal even as he spoke. "She is from the sands of Arabia and the prize of Skye."

"Yet you present her to me?"

"Aye, a husband's gift. To do with as you will."

Ainsley trailed her fingers down the mare's velvety nose. "She is truly beautiful. I am grateful for your generosity."

Rodric's eyes shone, could it truly be with such unveiled pleasure? Still Ainsley knew well his motives. Yet another ploy to make her content with her abduction and forced marriage. In truth, she was happier here thus far than had she ever been at the abbey, except that she missed Myrna's company. Would she be so content, though, once the Campbells raised their battle pennons and sounded the trumpets of war?

"I would have thought you not a man to waste your time wooing a captured Campbell bride."

"A MacDonald bride," he corrected with affable good nature, "as you well know. Someday you will know me better and will no longer pose such insults." His reply seemed casually dismissive rather than a forceful rebuke, and his ensuing grin designed to charm. "May I help you in mounting, my lady?"

When she nodded, Rodric assisted her onto the mounting step, and Ainsley paused there to eye with consternation the uncomfortable-looking leather sidesaddle. She had not mastered such a contraption; in truth, in her stolen rides upon Saracen, she had ridden no way other than bareback astraddle in the way a man would.

"I daresay the velvet of your habit, though more than becoming to your person, will confine you more than the tight leather trews that caused me such dangerous stirrings on the day we met." His whisper was low, meant for her alone, and not the pair of stable boys working nearby.

"I daresay I could bribe similar garb from yonder lads, my lord, if you'll give me leave; the trews are surely preferable to me as well."

"I think not, unless we are of a mind to cause scandal in the village of our destination. The seamstresses work hard on your new wardrobe even as we speak. More wedding gifts to you from your true and loyal kinsmen."

Rodric took hold of her waist and lifted her to mount, and she allowed him to hook her knee securely around the triangular horn of the saddle. His hands were large and strong, and lingered overly long upon her thigh, and she remembered with some quivering discomfiture the way the same hand had invaded her clothing the night before.

A rash of tormenting sensations swept her body, and she concentrated with undue necessity on arranging the soft folds of velvet around her hips. He stood looking up at her, and she wondered if he too thought of their shared kisses as he caught her gaze. The heated hunger inside his gray eyes indicated that her conjecture was most assuredly the right one.

"You should not gaze at a man so, wife, or you will sabotage the chambermaid's chore to right our bed before she has made the last tuck and fold." His words and the way he looked at her brought more immodest thoughts rising like steam off a hot griddle. Her dilemma was, she realized with not a small degree of misgiving, that she felt a delicious yearning for his hands and lips upon her again, soft, gentle, caressing her until she shuddered and shivered in quite a shameless fashion.

Rodric's mount was a black stallion, equally beautiful as the white mare, regal of head and powerful of limb. He swung into the saddle with practiced ease, then turned the horse toward the lane that led downhill toward the sea. Ainsley urged her mare to a sedate walk that would take her abreast of Rodric, and to a point where she could observe him out of the corner of her eye.

He was kilted in MacDonald tartan once again, as she sensed would be the garment he preferred. This was not the formal plaid he had worn at the wedding celebration, but one of a darker hue to facilitate the hunt. She could glimpse one steel-muscled thigh at the point where the fabric had caught above the leather boots hugging his calves. He handled the reins easily in his right hand, his left resting on his hip where the movement of his mount caused the double emeralds of his signet ring to sparkle in the sun. The tail of the red plaid was pinned where it draped over his shoulder with a bejeweled Celtic cross.

It seemed strange to see the bright scarlet tartan so often, for she was used to the blue and green of the Campbells, and every time she saw the red color, she was reminded of the circumstances that brought her to the Isle of Skye. Could it really be that he was already her legal husband as he had said? And not the Englishman Varney whom she had considered her betrothed for so long?

If only this handsome Highlander had treated her with ridicule and disrespect—as the abducted enemy—then she would have found him an easy object for her continued hatred. Yet not only had he saved her life from horrible men, now he treated her as a cherished part of his life. He minced no words when he decreed her his wife and that he intended to keep her with him as such.

Still basking under the warmth of his kindness, and that of the other members of Clan MacDonald, she wondered if it would be such a terrible sentence to live with them at Arrandane. At any count, Rodric vowed to be a kind husband who would protect and care for her. She had never laid eyes on Randolph of Varney, who was her betrothed. He had never once seen fit to visit her at the abbey, though the date of their wedding was not a year away. Nor had any Campbell visited her for that matter, not even Hugh of Strathmorton, her purported benefactor, and if Rodric and Ian were to be believed, her own grandfather.

As they eventually left the looming shadow of the great keep behind them, the nervous fear that had plagued her since she had been thrust into her new world began to subside. She felt immense relief just being outside the castle and its sprawling outbuildings, and able to breathe the fresh sea air. She gazed wistfully out across the open fields to the west and longed to race across them as she had in her breakneck return for vespers the night she had met Rodric. Only a few nights past, it now seemed much longer, as did every aspect of their short acquaintance.

"I thought you would enjoy seeing the hamlets nearest to Arrandane. Your father built a small hospice nearby. I assumed you would like to visit, since you are interested in the healing arts."

There was something questioning in his voice, and in his eyes as well. Was he suspicious of her? Somewhere deep inside did he secretly fear her as the witch of Kilchurn?

"A messenger brought word of an accident early this morning," he said, his brow furrowed with concern. " 'Twas the wee lassie you met yesterday morn, little Rachel. She slipped beneath a wagon wheel and lies severely injured."

"The little girl with the ball?" Ainsley's heart twisted at the thought of the child's suffering.

Somber-faced, Rodric nodded, then looked at her. "Her mother is your distant cousin."

Again he spoke of her as a MacDonald, expecting her to accept his story at will, but she did not debate his remarks, for her heart went out to the poor baby.

"It's particularly sad because she's not expected to live, and her mother is widowed but for the bairn. She's a bonny little lassie, if you'll remember. Sweet and kind-natured to all around her." He eyed her speculatively. "Do you think you could help her with your remedies?"

"I would gladly try," she answered without hesitation. They rode in silence after that exchange, but Ainsley had noted how he had watched her intently when he mentioned her cures, as if he knew more than she had told him. Did he? How could he even guess the secret she had kept for so long?

Chapter Thirteen

The village of Arrandane lay a scant three miles from the castle on a winding road that meandered along the edge of the shore. The ocean vista was awe-inspiring, but Ainsley was more interested in the village they were approaching. Small in size, it was surrounded by whitewashed crofts with pitched roofs covered with thatch, habitations of farm families who tilled the land as well as fishermen who plied the sea. Perhaps a dozen quaint structures made up the town proper.

Many of the villagers, some busily at work in the fields of oats, others driving carts, all took a moment to greet their popular new chieftain with bows and respectful salutations. To Ainsley's surprise, Rodric called most everyone by name as they slowed their mounts and walked down the dirt street. Such ready interaction between ruler and subjects seemed strange to Ainsley, for many crofters on Hugh Campbell's lands resented his camaraderie with the foreign English dragoons.

On the Isle of Skye, however, Rodric MacDonald was beloved among his clansmen, and though the villagers gazed curiously at her, they doffed their caps and called for a happy lifetime for the newlyweds. If they knew of her reputation as the witch of Kilchurn, or noted her different-colored eyes, neither open repugnance nor fear was revealed in the faces of anyone they encountered. Indeed so welcomed did she feel that she began to wonder if she could live here among them as any normal wife and mother, free of accusations of witchcraft, free of fear.

The hospice was a larger structure than the other buildings she had seen since they left the immediate surroundings of Arrandane Castle. Built of quarried yellow stone, it rose two floors from the ground. Once they dismounted and were inside the entrance, Ainsley's wariness returned when they encountered a nun wearing a white wimple. She cast down her gaze before the sister could see her eyes.

"Is wee Rachel faring better this day, sister?"

"No, sire, she lingers on this earth still but has yet to awaken. Her injuries are internal, and we fear she will not survive them, God preserve her little soul."

Rodric, not bothering to hide the distress caused him by the bad news, shook his head with sorrow. "I hate to hear such unhappy tidings. And what of her poor mother? Ginnie does dote mightily on that dear child."

Ainsley fought an internal battle. Most likely she could help the child, but to do so would break a vow made long ago in the sight of God. Yet how could she stand by and allow a wee babe to suffer agony, possibly even perish before her eyes? If she helped Rachel, rumors about her would abound again as they had in the villages around the abbey. Persecution and fear would soon follow, until the crofters of Skye, so friendly and obliging in their present welcome, would wish to burn out her evil eye. Nay, she could not take that chance. Not even for little Rachel.

"Would you like to come with me to visit Rachel?"

In answer to Rodric's query she gave a silent nod, then followed him down the corridor, up a flight of wooden steps to where one large room composed the sick ward for the surroundings of Arrandane. By her flaxen curls alone, Ainsley found the injured child, where she lay in a small cot near an open window facing the ocean.

As still and white as a carved ivory icon, her skin looked pale, pasty gray, and so lifeless in her repose that Ainsley sought at once for signs of her breathing and found a slight rise and fall in the contours of her thin chest. An openly distraught woman leaned her head upon the bedsheets and wept, quietly but so full of maternal agony that Ainsley wasn't sure she could bear to witness such all-encompassing mourning.

"Ginnie, I am sore distressed about Rachel's plight." Rodric curled a comforting hand upon the mother's heaving shoulder.

As his low voice penetrated her grief-stricken fog, Ginnie slowly rose to stand, her face red and blotchy and absent of hope. "Aye, milord, 'tain't fair that my baby be taken before even her third year. She is a good little lassie, so sweet and never a cause of mischief to me."

Rodric murmured soothingly to the inconsolable woman, and Ainsley rounded the side of the bed until she stood very close to the child. The woman had given herself over to a sobbing wail, terrible in its low-pitched keening. A silky strand of pale yellow lay across Rachel's white cheek, half hiding the horrible black mark where the wagon wheel had struck her down. The awful bruises faded in yellowish-purple discolorations from her temple to the point of her jaw. Her left eye was closed and blackened with grotesque swelling, but even her horrific injuries did not mar the cherubic innocence of the child's face.

"She is so beautiful," Ainsley murmured as she brushed the lock away so she could examine the bruise at closer range.

"You are most kind, milady," Ginnie muttered, but her voice broke pitifully, and she kept dabbing at her tears with the white towel that she had used to bathe her child's face.

"My wife is skilled as a healer." Rodric's tone was hushed, but his mention of their marital status shocked Ainsley as he continued in a comforting tone. "With your permission, she has agreed to try to help Rachel."

Ginnie could only nod, her face ravaged by tears and exhaustion, but even so she managed to summon a look of hope, so eagerly that Ainsley felt she should temper any unrealistic expectations. "I work with herbal potions and massages that often act to relieve pain, but I am not sure that I can bring relief to so severe an injury as this one suffered by Rachel."

"I beg only that you try to help her, milady. She is all I have and so wee and innocent."

Ainsley glanced at Rodric, who stood silently waiting, then looked again at the mother who continually wrung her fingers with open anxiety. Her regard shifted to the beautiful little girl. Could she ever forgive herself if Rachel died, without Ainsley even trying to help ease her pain? There was truly only one answer to such a question.

"Would you allow me to hold her in my arms, Ginnie? Just for a moment?"

Tears brimmed, and rolled like raindrops down Ginnie's face until she wiped at them with the damp towel. "I wanted to rock her, but they told me she should not be moved."

"I would be very gentle."

With some reluctance the woman stepped back and allowed Ainsley to gather her dying daughter's frail body into her arms. Rachel felt limp, almost boneless in her unconscious state, and Ainsley seated herself in the simple wood chair beside the bed. She gazed tenderly into Rachel's horribly bruised face.

"I have prayed to heaven since the day she was struck down and lit candles at the altar, my lord," the mother told Rodric brokenly.

"Perhaps God will work His will for one so innocent in this life," Rodric answered quietly.

Ainsley looked down at the frail body cradled in her arms and knew she must try to help her.

She hesitated for a moment, well aware that both
Rodric and Ginnie watched her every move. If she
did what she contemplated, she would put herself
in danger. If she did not, the bairn would surely
die. Did she have any real choice?

With a sigh of resignation, she knew she did
not. Very carefully she cupped the back of the
child's head in the open palm of her left hand,
then gently lifted Rachel's eyelids with her finger
in the way Brother Alfonse had taught her long
ago. The pupils were huge and black, nearly oblit-
erating the cornflower-blue irises. Rachel's breathing was dangerously shallow, the rapid rasping of
one clinging to life by a thread of will, and Ainsley
held her right palm downward over the side of her
face disfigured the most by the swelling.

Spreading her fingers wide, she slowly dragged
her fingertips down the child's face and torso, not
quite touching her skin as she tried to ascertain
the extent of the inflammations. When the tips
of her fingers began to tingle, she formed rapid
concentric circles around the darkest part of the
facial bruise. Instinctively, in the way she had
known since she was not much older than the
bairn she held, she knew the place where the poi-
sons festered.

"I will pray over her," she murmured, but she
did not pray. She closed her eyes and felt the heat
undulate up from deep inside her, the familiar
wave that she had banished from her life since
Alfonse had died. Slowly, effortlessly the flood of
heat permeated her hands and flowed from her
fingertips into the child's damaged flesh. She

began to sense the blockage, could veritably feel the sluggish flow of blood through the child's brain. She moved her fingers along the slowly pulsating artery at the side of Rachel's throat, then breathing deeply herself she held her thumb there until the beat began to quiver, first tremulously then with more force as blood flowed in faster surges.

"That's the way, little sweet one," she whispered in the lilting syllables of Gaelic, the ancient tongue of all Highlanders, "fight for your life. You are too young to die."

Pleased by the success of her ministrations, she opened her eyes and spoke somberly to the suffering mother.

"I fear there is nothing more I can do to help her, but I will come here and pray for her recovery again if you would like me to."

"I am grateful, my lady."

Ainsley avoided Rodric's eyes as she rose and gently placed the sick child upon the bed. Ginnie took the child's hand and gazed tenderly down at her. She gasped. "Oh, sweet Mary, did you not see her eye flutter just now as you fixed her head upon the pillow? She has not twitched even an eyelash since the wagon overran her. 'Tis surely a good sign that God will be merciful."

" 'Twas told to me by a skilled healer that if one speaks often to a sick one caught in unnatural sleep, the angels will hear and more readily grant your prayers."

"God bless you, my lady," Ginnie murmured, taking Ainsley's hand and kissing her fingers.

Embarrassed by her eager gratitude, Ainsley nodded, then moved quickly out of the sickroom. She was upset by the child's pain and the mother's grief. She did not know if she had been of help and would not know for some time to come. She could only pray for divine intervention as she had promised. She had done all she knew how to do.

"You did more than just pray over her. Can you truthfully say you did not, Ainsley?"

Ainsley's heart stopped at Rodric's thoughtful query. Did he suspect her of witchcraft? She could almost feel the color draining from her face at that thought. "Nay. I did nothing. I simply held her to please her mother. There is no herbal remedy I know for one hurt so severely."

Rodric searched her face until she felt he could see her every thought. She averted her gaze and sought to put a distance between them, glad when they were safely out of the hospice, mounted, and on their way once more. She should not have held the child, should not have touched her in full view of others, especially Rodric. But if Rachel survived, wouldn't the result of such risks be well taken?

As they reached a curve in the road that took them upward into the interior of the island, she sought to alleviate the internal stress building up inside her.

"I would like to gallop for a time, if I may?" She fully expected Rodric to deny her request.

"If you feel you have the expertise to curb the mare—"

Ainsley didn't wait for him to finish but spurred

her mount into a headlong run that took her up an adjacent hill and through a field spotted by rowans and patches of cedar. A surprised yell drifted somewhere behind her but was spun away by the wind rushing over her face. The muffled pound of the mare's hoofbeats were comforting, allaying all the fears that plagued her in this new place, and though she sat the sidesaddle awkwardly for a time, she secured her seat by leaning close over the mare's neck.

Within minutes Rodric had overtaken her stride, and she heard his laugh as he flew past her. On Saracen she might have given him a fine race, stallion for stallion, but her exhilaration was still unbounded as she galloped hard and close in his tracks.

After a breakneck romp through narrow, gradually rising trees, Rodric veered into an open meadow, a windblown field high atop a cliff overlooking a shining silver sea. He slowed and swung down from his saddle as she brought the mare to a prancing halt.

"You ride well, milady. More proof that you are a MacDonald born." A wide grin fashioned his admiration as he grasped a tight hold upon the mare's bit and held her horse with firm hand. "Pray tell me where you learned to ride like a warrior into battle? Surely not a pursuit encouraged by the abbess and her cane?"

"I have borne bruises that prove 'tis not," she answered with a happy smile she could not prevent, but his face sobered instantly. He reached up to lift her to the ground, and with his hands upon her, she found her breathing growing more shallow as thoughts of his lips upon her skin gained custody of her mind. He held her a moment longer than perhaps he needed to, but not for so very long. For that she was embarrassingly disappointed as he secured both their mounts to a low-draping branch.

"I brought you here because I want to show you something." He gestured to the stone ruins that rose on the hill above them. "This is a holy spot for those of my mother's clan. The MacLeods of Dunvegan worshiped here for centuries before the place was destroyed."

"Was it a church then?" Ainsley allowed herself the luxury of observing his strong profile as he gazed at the crumbling stones.

"Aye. Come, let me help you, for the footing is treacherous in places."

Ainsley put out her hand, and he smiled as he threaded his fingers through hers. He adjusted his longer stride to hers as they climbed upward on a walk of paved flagstones. The spot was deserted so high upon the windswept mount, but the sea spread out a beautiful royal blue beneath the azure sky. He led her among half-toppled walls into what must have been the nave, and Ainsley looked up, trying to imagine the church as it had been when MacLeods knelt in prayer beneath its roof.

"What happened here?" she asked curiously, envisioning pews and windows of stained glass among the walls now choked with weeds and crumbling debris.

" 'Twas sacked by raiding MacDonalds."

Ainsley jerked around, not having expected such an explanation. Rodric smiled at her astonishment.

"Aye, they came with sword and fire, with near three hundred proud MacLeods at prayer inside these walls. A bloody massacre it was, with only three survivors to tell the tale before their kin at Dunvegan could rush to their rescue."

"Was it your own clan who wielded the swords?"

Rodric sat down on a toppled pillar and watched her try to catch her hair as the high winds blew it around her face. "I am half MacDonald born, and half MacLeod, so this place holds a special grief in my heart."

"Then, why do you come here?"

"To remind myself that the clans must unite and stop such unnecessary bloodletting as occurred here. We fight each other and kill Scot sons when we should fight the English, who wish to grind us beneath their heel as they did our Welsh brethren."

"Yet you kidnap me from Clan Campbell for your own political purpose."

"Is that the thought you harbor?"

"Is that not true?"

He was gracious enough not to deny it. "Our marriage unites the MacLeods and MacDonalds of Skye and ends the worry for tragedies such as the one that afflicted my family here on these bloodstained stones. If the feuds continue, all the

Highlands, nay, all of Scotland will lie in ruins such as these."

"Yet our marriage will give rise to the clan warfare you deplore."

She wasn't surprised when he dodged her reasoning. "You are my destiny. Thus our marriage was meant to be."

Something in the way he said the words gave her pause. She studied him intently and saw the determination molding his expression. "How can you believe that? Or expect me to? When we both know you came to me only because you needed my hand in marriage to rule as chieftain and bring Ian's people into your camp?"

"Do you see the white marble stone where the altar used to stand?" Obviously a change of subject was his intention. "Go there and look upon the floor pavings. I heard words of Gaelic leave your lips not an hour past. Read the ancient words you find written there by my ancestors, then convince me that we are not entwined by God's hand."

Puzzled by the request, Ainsley made her way the length of the interior to the white portion of the floor. At first she almost missed the black onyx stone set beneath where the altar had once stood. She knelt, brushing away the dirt and letters worn smooth by decades of wind and sea salt.

"Every fourscore a lady of Skye will be born, her gaze mismatched in hue, sent by the angels to heal the sick and forlorn. A warrior of the bull she will wed, a man of peace will unite the clan of red."

Ainsley emitted a startled gasp as she finished, then turned to face Rodric, unable to hide her shock. "You quoth part of this to me upon the ship."

Rodric's face reflected his intensity, though his mouth tipped up with a tender smile. "You are she, Ainsley of Arrandane, the lady of the MacLeod legend. Every man, woman, and child on Skye knows of you. They will welcome you as such. One healer of the legend died in this church the day of the massacre."

"I don't believe you."

"You do not believe, though it is etched in stone before your eyes."

His reason was undeniable and brought forth an intensified frown of confusion.

"The first moment I saw your eyes, I knew you were she. I knew our marriage was meant to be."

"Whose words are these, carved here for all to see? And for what reason are they written beneath a church's altar?"

"The answers you seek lie, too, in the tales of the ancient bards. 'Tis said a MacLeod of old saved a fairy princess who had made her way to earth from the Dark World." He smiled slightly. "And though she fell in love with him for saving her life, she was only allowed to stay with him in the land of mortals but for a score of years. She was purported to have borne a child with such eyes as yours and the inner gift to heal, and 'twas said her seed still flourishes here on Skye, appearing every hundred years or so."

"You speak nonsense. I am not even a MacLeod."

"You are the issue of Ian MacDonald, the lord of the isle before I assumed that honor. There are MacLeods in your ancestry, as well. You are the lady. I watched you today with Rachel. You also have the God-given gift of healing, do you not, Ainsley? Is that what you try so hard to hide from me and from others who might call you devil-possessed?"

Ainsley began to shake her head even before his words were out of his mouth. "No, I am not she. I only prayed for the poor baby, just as anyone would, be they blessed with a heart's compassion."

"I know you have the power to heal. Ellie told me how you discovered your gift when you were a little girl. You fell from the well and broke your wrist. Yet you healed the broken bone without even knowing you could, by gripping it tightly with your other hand until the pain went away."

"Nay," she breathed, "I did not. I am not this lady of the legend. I am not sure even that I am a MacDonald. There is no proof except my resemblance to the woman in the locket."

"The Campbells have worked great ill upon you to make you deny and fear a gift so wondrous as that you possess. Healing is not the work of the devil, nor of any evil eye, especially none as beautiful as yours. That's what you really fear, is it not, Ainsley? That each time you heal the sick, you relinquish a little more of your soul into Satan's keeping?"

No one, in her entire life, had voiced her basest fears aloud, and she stared at him with such horror that he rose and took a step toward her. She shook her head and held out open palms to fend him off.

To her relief he stopped and gazed out over the sea for several moments before he spoke again. "In time you will believe what I know is true, and then you will find happiness, here on Skye as my wife." He held out his hand. "Now come, you've seen the stone bearing the MacLeod legend and know it not to be a figment of my own imagination. Let us go back to Arrandane. Your father has invited us to dine with him this night."

Ainsley walked with him, but her mind whirled with the things he had told her. Even after he had helped her to mount, she stared at his broad back as he preceded her down the slope into a wide valley below, more confused than ever and full of new fears she could not understand.

Chapter Fourteen

Nearly a fortnight later Rodric rode once more with Ainsley through the glens of his beloved Skye, more than ever convinced that she was indeed the lady of the MacLeod legend. Without question, she had to be. As he had told her, he had known as much the very first time he had glimpsed her incredible eyes.

Now, at long last, she was his wife, heiress of Arrandane, and the woman who would stand at his side when the clans of Skye rallied together as one people, as Scots who loved their country and the Highlander way of life. He feared now, however, that convincing Ainsley of that fact would be the bane of his life. She seemed determined never to accept the truth.

Glancing back at her, he was initially thunderstruck, as he always was and always would be, by the sheer perfection of her beauty. She sat the spirited mare with grace, the regal quality of her poise underlining her consummate skill as equestrienne. Wife, he thought, pride making him wish to roll the word longer on his tongue. But still, after what seemed an eternity, they were wed in name only.

He had not visited her bed again since that first night of the wedding feast. Neither had he coerced, nor encouraged her to come to him, though he had spent many wakeful hours hoping for a midnight knock upon the door connecting their sleeping chambers. Unfortunately that moment had never come.

So he had taken the last few weeks to single-mindedly court her with the respect that she deserved and which he had not been able to give her before their wedding was performed. He had accompanied her daily upon long rides in the hills around Arrandane, presenting to her all the beauty of the Isle of Skye—the cascading waterfalls falling over craggy rocks, the green-carpeted glens, and shining lochs. He had spent time sitting with her in the herbal garden she seemed to enjoy so thoroughly, watching her collect roots and leaves and listening to the melody of her voice as she told him about Brother Alfonse and his remedies. He had taken pleasure when she applied ointment to the knife wound in his side and decreed it healing nicely as she wrapped it with clean white gauze. They had visited little Rachel many times, though she still lay unconscious, but Ainsley continued to hold her, to comfort her mother, and to pray for the child's recovery.

No longer did he wish to rush her into his arms, nor prod her emotions in any way, not after he had realized just how important she had become to him. He had taken his time getting to know the person she was—finding her strong and true of character, despite her loveless upbringing—and he had striven to earn her trust, but he had never stopped wanting her in his bed with an excruciating inner ache that never left him.

Now, however, the hour was at hand. The time had come to consummate their vows, and he would not leave the peaceful valley to which he now took her, not until she lay in his embrace, his in every way. If it took a year of wooing her alongside the cobalt waters of the mountain loch, he would do so. For she would bear him many sons and daughters; 'twas only a matter of time and gentle courting.

More than softly trembling kisses and cries born from love's pleasures would he take from her before their tryst ended. They would join together in conjugal union, and their coupling would put at end any further claim upon her by Hugh Campbell and the English fop to which he had betrothed her against the laws of man and God.

Crucial was it that their marriage be legally inviolate, that he knew only too well, and as soon as possible, in order to keep her safely with him upon Skye and at the same time, to cement the new alliance between the MacLeods and the Mac-Donalds. Despite his promise to her, his greater duty lay in making sure she yielded to him as wife to husband, and with no further delay. She wanted him as much as he wanted her, for her innocent, though hotly passionate, response on their wedding night had been as gratifying as surprising from a woman so young and so long sheltered in a nunnery.

All too well he knew how easily he could have seduced her in the marriage bed, had come closer to it than he would ever acknowledge, and God knew how much he had wanted her. Such betrayal at his hands would have driven her away from him and robbed him of the eager acceptance of his touch that he so coveted. If he had gone ahead with his masculine wants, had broken his vow to her with arrogant disregard, she would not be riding so readily at his side this moment, nor would she turn to him and bestow the angelic smile that now spread across her face when he looked at her.

She looked so beautiful and so happy to be in his company that sexual desire hit him hard. It was a full-blown, overpowering, sheer gut-wrenching need of her. Smiling back as if his teeth were not clenched tight with self-control, he chastised himself in no uncertain terms. *Forbearance, man, forbearance, patience, and you shall have the greatest prize of all.*

"Skye is such a beautiful place that I never get tired of our rides," she called out to him, apparently quite ignorant of his own plight as he shifted in his saddle, his masculinity hard with needs held unassuaged for much too long.

"Not at all as eerie and frightening as I had heard it told to be," she finished on a cheery note.

Glad he was that she was finding his home so greatly to her liking. "Aye, and I am taking you to my favorite spot upon this beautiful isle. A secret place that I wish to share with you."

Again her smile seemed to flow across the space that separated them, born in heaven by the gossamer stroke of angel wings, and a kind of warmth in her two-toned eyes that grabbed at his heart in a way no other ever had.

"Is this lovely place nearby, my lord?"

Enjoying the title of respect from her lips, Rodric pulled up and flung an open-armed gesture toward the valley floor. "A hunting lodge lies on the far end of yonder loch, where a creek pours over boulders to replenish its depths. You can see the line of its roof if you sharpen your gaze."

"Do you often take parties there to hunt?" A raised slender forearm shielded her eyes from the glaring sun and gave him better view of her womanly figure, one he enjoyed hungrily for an instant before she looked back at him in quest of his answer.

"More often I come here to be alone." She looked surprised, so he shifted the reins and told her the truth. "I thought it best to deliver you from prying eyes at the castle and the expectations of others toward a newlywed couple."

"We will be completely alone here?" She glanced the length of the valley, and he recognized her expression as one of alarm as she added, "Tis an isolated place, is it not? And unprotected from those who might wish us harm?"

She was afraid, no doubt of men like the loutish fools of Ingott who tried to maim her beautiful eyes. A sour wash of nausea spiraled down his throat and into the floor of his stomach when he remembered how close they had come to succeeding in that evil deed.

"You need never fear the people of Skye. None bear you animosity. On my life, I have sworn to be your protector, and I will do so. The lodge is comfortable and the valley a peaceful place. I hope you will agree that it will be a good place to build our house when we are ready to fill it with our sons and daughters."

Rodric could not tell if she was pleased or displeased with the idea, and when she made no answer, he continued hopefully. "And I will confess that I wished time alone with you so that we could become comfortable with each other at our leisure."

Impassiveness cloaked her usually expressive brow, alerting Rodric that her naivete did not prevent her from realizing the import of their physical union. Perhaps that was the very reason she exacted the pledge from him? To keep herself pure for the Englishman who claimed her through Hugh Campbell's designs? If that were the case, she would surely also now suspect his real intentions for transporting her here.

A short ride through a thick wood of rowans brought them into view of the structure handhewn of log and granite stone. The place had been his retreat and refuge since Ian had granted him deed to the valley nearly a decade before. "You can glimpse the lodge from here, love," he told her, surprising himself at how easily now came such endearments. They had not met so long ago, yet he felt they had known each other for many years. Again a sense of preordination gripped him, giving him pause before he finished his remarks. "There it lies, Ainsley, just where the creek bends into the meadow. Near a year of felling logs and working them into place with bare hands brought the structure rising up from the ground into the only place I call mine alone."

"You are very proud of this place you built." Her inflection branded it more statement than question, but he was pleased when she exclaimed further over the rippling waters in the swift-flowing creek bed.

"Aye, I am proud. Hard labor is a virtuous endeavor among the clans of the Hebrides."

"It is not a large house."

"Nay, not yet. 'Twas only for me until I laid my eyes on you, and knew you must belong to me."

She dipped her chin, her expression coy, her eyes shying away from his intense gaze to concentrate on her reins.

"MacLeod lands lie to the north, MacDonald holdings southward, with less than a day's ride to either fortress. With the isle clans united upon the saying of our vows, we shall have little need to keep our children locked behind ugly granite walls and hidden in castle keeps. Someday we will live in an estate in this valley such as the English nobility enjoy, with vast tended lawns extending down to the loch, cultured gardens for your medicinal herbs, and cobblestone highways leading both to Dunvegan and Arrandane for when we wish to visit our kith and kin."

"You have made many plans."

"I have had many years to conjecture what I wish the future to hold for the people I protect."

"Peace among clans never lasts for long among Highlanders. 'Tis our way to fight and shed blood."

At first he thought she mocked his visions, but her face mirrored shades of sorrow quite perceptibly, and the same melancholy clouded her eyes.

"You are safe here with me, Ainsley. You will live here at my side, and I will defend you from any who might wish you harm. I swear so upon my father's honor and my mother's virtue."

"Unless I am kidnapped back by Strathmorton and his soldiers?"

Did therein lie her fear? he wondered, the notion striking him with some dread. "No one will take you from me. Every MacDonald and every MacLeod warrior will rally around you with swords drawn and hearts brave."

"Yet you took me from Campbell protection by trickery and subterfuge."

" 'Twas an act of justice. They stole away your birthright and blackened your regard of your Mac-Donald forebears. You belong here upon Skye, God willing. You always have, you always will."

"Yet I am used as a pawn to fuel the hatred between chieftains and war between their clans."

"An heiress's fate is to unite families and strengthen alliances. Your father had the right to choose the man to have you. Lord Ian did so as was his duty, and in turn I will choose a husband for my sister, a man who can keep Breanne and protect her from harm. You are a MacDonald, heiress to one of the greatest of all chieftains and should be proud to hold so coveted a title as wife and mother to the first chief born in the brotherhood of the clans of the isle." He whetted her humor with a lighter note, wishing to hear her laugh and see the happiness light her face. "You belong with me, 'tis destined by God so you might as well love me and be done with it."

Ainsley did not yield up to him the response he wished from her. "You had little knowledge of me when you came to steal a bride. You coveted only the alliance our wedding would secure."

Rodric regretted that he could not deny her accusation, one which obviously had pricked her sensibilities. He had wanted the union enough to risk the consequences of her abduction, but he would not insult her intelligence with lies meant to honey her aversion to his act.

"Aye, a marriage between the two of us was of utmost importance to me. I am ambitious, both for myself and for the security of my clans. I will tell you, however, with God as my jduge, I have wanted you from the first moment I laid eyes on your face, both as my wife and as a woman to hold in my heart and to bear my children."

The frankness of his words seemed to bring surprise to her face. "And if I were not heiress of Arrandane, and not Ian MacDonald's daughter? If another held such birthright and tonic of your ambition, would then I be the woman to hold in your heart? The lady of the MacLeod legend who is your ultimate destiny?"

Her questions were threaded with innate wisdom but unfair for her to ask of him, and she had to know as much. He had no suitable answer that would ease her heart. Thus he said nothing, and in his lack of response answered her with more eloquence than his words would have shown to her. She was silenced, and the exchange of civility between them thus far that day, one he had hoped to bear such promise, had ultimately ended up tarnishing their budding attachment.

A sudden realization hit him, the insight that he did crave friendship from her, a relationship strong and true in which they could talk and be of mutual support in all they accomplished together. And they would share their hearts, he vowed with new determination, for he meant to entreat her well until she knew he wanted her as his own as much as he needed her.

When they reached the lodge, he dismounted and lifted Ainsley to the ground. She immediately walked past him to the edge of the wide shallow creek, then gazed downstream past the quiet pool where the gurgling, cold spring water fed in falls over flat rocky inclines of different heights before emptying into the loch.

"You have chosen a lovely place for your home," she said with one long sigh that held so much wistfulness even he felt sad for her.

"For our home. And for that reason it is glad I am to find this glen to your liking."

"Will we stay here long?"

"As long as you wish. Forever, if you so decree."

He was triumphant when his remark won a soft

chuckle from her. "But how can we? I have no garb other than this riding suit I wear."

"Do you think me so shortsighted in my plans? I ordered all we would need brought here yesterday while we spent the day afield with Breanne and Richard."

She smiled at the thoroughness of his planning as he took the key from his sporran and allowed her to precede him inside. Though the place was rough of character and fit more for a man's comfort than the pleasure of a woman's eye, he was proud to show her the immense stone fireplace he had labored to construct at the far end of the long, rectangular room. The couches, covered with animal skins, and the long oak table and chairs stood ready for their first meal together there as man and wife, and behind it, the buttery was well stocked for a long stay.

"The bedchamber is up the stair. Would you like a time there to rest and freshen yourself until we sup?"

"Aye. I am not used to such a long ride, I fear." She grinned, rather sheepishly he thought. "Especially with my knee crooked impossibly upon this lady's saddle."

Rodric watched her climb the wide steps he had fashioned himself from an ancient oak that had stood for centuries near the falls. The giant trunk stood there still with its girth the size of a man's arm span. Soon, Ainsley of Arrandane, he thought, soon I will hold you in my arms and make you mine, and you will love me back.

*   *   *

Later that evening when Ainsley awoke from a much more peaceful nap than she would have expected under the circumstances, she freshened up by washing her hands and face from the pitcher and bowl she found on a chest of drawers overlooking the upper end of the creek. As Rodric had mentioned, a chest of her new clothing was set at the foot of the bed, and she chose a lovely dress of burgundy linen with a white lace collar.

Dressed and ready for supper, she stopped by the end of the great bed made from logs with a rack of great stag antlers hanging above it and picked up the warm flannel plaid of red tartan that Rodric must have draped over her while she slept. In the cabin she found the MacDonald red everywhere, and still she could not bring herself to identify with colors she had cursed as those of her enemy for her entire life. How peculiar to now live among MacDonalds! Even stranger was to think they treated her as family, and the Mac-Leods, another clan abhorred by the people of Strathmorton, honored her further as the lady of their legends.

When she wandered down the steps in search of Rodric, she found him reclining upon the cushions of an oversize divan that stood at right angle to the fireplace. Outside, darkness had fallen like a heavy blanket once the sun sank out of sight behind the mountains. She stopped on the stair, yet Rodric continued to contemplate the crackling logs, seemingly lost in his thoughts.

While she watched him, she could not help but wonder if all the tales of legends he had told her during the last few weeks had been true or simply manufactured to win her loyalty? Could he truly have developed feelings for her after so short a time? Even more disconcerting, had she? The way he kissed and touched her that first night had sent her into helpless, mindless submission, even now she went shivery and cold with the memory. Still, he had not forced himself upon her, had not even made another attempt, which, if the truth be admitted, would have taken very little to win her accord, with her so eager to experience the very sensations that his touch seemed to bring alive inside her body.

There was little doubt as to why he had brought her to such an isolated place. He meant to consummate their vows and bind her to him forever. She did not know if she wanted that, or even what to expect from the act of coupling between a man and a woman. The abbess had frowned and hissed to the heiresses awaiting nuptials that the physical union was excruciatingly painful, a burden to endure so that a child could be conceived and for no other reason.

Ainsley looked at Rodric, so big and strong, with muscles heavy from sword and toil and the handling of reins. She shivered, then reminded herself that he had been most kind thus far, had not hurt her, not even when she had run from him and caused his own injury in her rescue.

Those thoughts were heartening, and she slowly descended to the great room. When he heard her step upon the stair, he came to his feet at once, and she saw that he held a tankard of ale.

"Are you hungry, my lady?"

Grinning, Rodric gestured expansively to a low wooden table he had set before the warmth of the hearth. Draped loosely with yet another length of red tartan, Ainsley had to smile, too, for it seemed Rodric was determined that she not forget what clan of which she was now a part. The fare arranged for their repast was hearty, a dish of cold mutton pie, goat cheese and ale, and even a bowl of oranges from the latest ship at port. She took a place at the other end of the table as Rodric poured her a cup of ale.

Ainsley drank sparingly of that libation, having enjoyed little in the way of spirits since her wedding feast, but eagerly partook of the bounteous meal, realizing she had borne little hunger since her arrival on the island. He watched her closely, though he made a valiant attempt to make it appear just the opposite, and she duly conjectured about what manner of life he had experienced before this night when they sat together as veritable strangers yet husband and wife.

"I know little of you, my lord, other than that you are my husband and have brought me to this lovely place for your own reasons."

Rodric chuckled and relaxed back into the soft cushions. He, too, had changed his travel-stained attire, and washed the smell of horses from him. He propped his foot on his opposite knee and casually rested his mug on the wide arm of the couch.

"I hold no mysteries apart from my wife. What do you wish to know about me, my love?"

Ainsley sipped her brew and canted her head to observe him closely. "Have you always lived here on Skye?"

"Nay, but for a goodly portion of my manhood I have enjoyed the wild beauty of the garden isle."

"You were not born here?"

"I was born to the MacDonalds of Balluchulish near where Loch Leven joins Loch Linnhe. My mother was a MacLeod of Skye, an heiress such as yourself, who married my father in the hopes of an alliance between their clans. As I told you, my father was killed when I was hardly more than a lad, and my uncle took his place as chieftain of Balluchulish."

"So you have spent your life here on Skye?"

Rodric nodded. "Mostly, though Ian sent me to England for a time to be schooled. That was when I saw with my own eyes the way the redcoats hunger to rule all the world. They have robbed the Welsh of their culture, have set down their rule upon the colonials in the Americas, and they will take the liberty of the Scots if we do not stop the petty wars within our own ranks and unite with alliances which will make us strong, such as this one that you and I will solidify."

Ainsley basked in the warm glow of his eyes, silver, deep, afire now with his passionate beliefs. "And now you intend to woo me to your bed so that the deed be done and our marriage safe from annulment?"

"Aye, I confess that is my dearest cause and will be till my dying day, I fear."

"Yet you gave me your word you would not force me?"

"And keep the pledge I will, though you tempt me greatly with the sweet fragrance of your golden honey hair and that smile you wear that robs mortal men of reason."

"You have resorted to flattery, my lord."

"I am ready to resort to any manner of words or actions or deeds or even coin that will win to me your undying affection."

Ainsley had to laugh at him but somber emotions followed closely, for the matter was too serious to make light of and both of them knew that. "You could have had me already, every night since we repeated our vows, as was your husbandly right. I expected such from you, if I tell the truth, just as I would have expected in the bed of my English husband if he had come for me at the abbey before you stole me away. Why do you hesitate to claim what you purport to want so desperately?"

"Do you think MacDonalds such animals that we rut like stags when the season is on? We of Arrandane respect our women, and truthfully, the same holds throughout the Isle of Skye. I respect your wishes on my honor. I will wait if you deny me."

Even as he said such words, he reached out and took her hand and lifted the back of it quickly to his mouth, his lips teasing the softness of her skin and flooding Ainsley with exquisite moments she remembered only too well. She swallowed once, then moistened lips that had become dry, but still the distrust of MacDonalds that she had lived with so long came back to haunt her like wispy apparitions peeking through windowpanes. Was the tale he told with such tender glances and sugared words the truth?

With more reluctance than she liked to admit, she pulled her hand from his grasp, quite aware that if she relented at all, he would seize the moment and make her forget any and all her misgivings. Though they were wed and the moment of consummation a foregone conclusion, she did need more time to adjust to all that had happened, to the way her life had changed like quicksilver, especially if he was so generous as to give her such a choice.

"If what you say is true, then you will bear me no ill for excusing myself to an early night, for much has happened in the last few weeks and I am more often weary than in the past."

"I am entitled to share your bed even here in this deserted place."

"Aye, my lord, but there is little need for you to join me there, for I am not full of spirits this night and too tired to be of much wit. I bid you good night."

Ainsley left him where he sat but turned when she reached the stair, almost guiltily, she realized, stunning herself for harboring the emotion since he was the one who kidnapped her against her will. He should be riddled with guilt, not she. Rodric stared at her with such banked desire burning that his eyes seemed to glow, and she knew that he would be hard-pressed to forget his honorable words that night, alone as they were. Turning quickly, she hurried upstairs before he followed through on the passion so easily read upon his face and took what they both knew was his to have.

Chapter Fifteen

❦

As it turned out Ainsley did lie alone in the giant antler-decorated bed, and once sleep found her, deep, restful, absent of dreams, she awoke refreshed and without a good deal of the tension that had riddled her mind and body since she had been taken from the abbey. Her first inclination was to believe that Rodric had not climbed the stairs at all until she noticed the candle beside the bed stood black, burned nearly to wick's end, much farther than when she had snuffed it herself. Again he had come when she lay unaware in her slumber, but without disturbing her rest.

Touched by his sensitivity to her wants, she performed her morning ablutions, realizing it was rather late by the slant of the sunlight across the loch. The white linen gown was plain of decoration and soft against her skin, so she donned it, listening all the while for sounds of Rodric's doings below. She heard nothing but the nearby and joyous warbling of birdsong on a branch outside her open window, and farther away, the soothing rush of water pouring over the falls.

Downstairs the great room where they had supped lay deserted, everything orderly and in place, but still no sign of Rodric's presence. The tall hearthstone was cold, only the banked glow of embers in the ashes. Disappointed at first, her second reaction came with an increase in heartbeat. Surely he had not been so chagrined with her stubbornness that he would leave her in the valley alone. Fear touched her heart, though she could not imagine him doing so after his pretty words vowing protection to her.

To her relief their mounts still stood in the stalls of the lean-to stable, so she redoubled her attempts to seek out her companion. A few steps from the low porch gave her a glimpse of him where he waded midstream near where the falls cascaded over rocks to a deeper pool. He wore no shirt and most likely little else, and she felt herself react to his nudity in a fashion that was becoming all too familiar to her.

After intimacies such as they had shared, though scoffed by him as little enough before what was to come, had brought her acute feelings that the sight of him only intensified. Now his long black hair, wet, slicked back from his angular face, made her shudder with emotions she feared to identify. The truth was, and with all her attraction to his manliness aside, she simply liked him a great deal, enjoyed being in his company here in the beautiful valley.

She strolled along the bank toward him, envying

him his freedoms as a man, of casually bathing outside in the light of day with no care who might see him disrobed. A smile came unbidden to rest upon her lips when he saw her and waved an eager arm to bring her closer. She obeyed his summons until she reached the spot where he had discarded his belted plaid and a clean doe-brown shirt. Leather boots lay nearby, having fallen where he tossed them.

"Did you pass a restful night?"

Ainsley shyly averted her eyes from his nakedness as he waded toward her, but found herself looking back almost at once. Crisp dark hair matted muscles molded like steel chest armor and trailed downward in a thin line over his belly and beneath the waterline as he stopped waist-deep a few yards from the bank. She could not determine even a trace of embarrassment in his face for appearing before her so immodestly.

"Aye. I was very tired. Did you sleep easy, my lord?"

"I will not pass a decent night until you lay contented in my arms, as wife and helpmeet. 'Tis my vow this day to see that happen, and this very night, I hope."

His grin acted contagiously and could not fail to charm her, thus she could not call herself unaffected by his sweet words. Still she sought to change the course of their conversation to something safer. "Is the water not very cold for bathing so early in the morn?"

"Aye but refreshing to a bridegroom after so lonely a night as I suffered through."

Still she tried to distract him for his obvious mind-set. "It seems indecent to bathe in the light of day."

"Indecent? With no one around for many miles. Join me, love, and see how good the river feels."

Scandalized at even the idea that he suggested such a thing, Ainsley was quick to shake her head. "Such public bathing was deemed evil by the abbess."

"And what was not denied to you in that nightmarish hole? I remind you, madam, that I have given you freedom to do whatever you wish."

Not exactly true, she thought as he gestured to the bank, for he would not agree to sending her home if that was her desire. But was it?

"Then sit there and dangle your lovely toes into the creek bed. Surely that does not equate with any cardinal sin."

"Nay, but 'tis hardly a modest act of a lady."

"A lady wed, with only her husband to see her do so. Believe me when I tell you that I am little offended by the sight of your bare skin."

Ainsley laughed at the way he raised a brow with the most lascivious expression imaginable. "I daresay not."

"Come, Ainsley, there is no one to scold you anymore, to punish you, no one even to see. Enjoy the freedom while no one is about to cast blame. That is the reason I brought you here so far away from the castle and its thousand eyes."

Incredibly tempted, as she was by many of his unseemly suggestions, Ainsley glanced around, an unnecessary precaution she well knew, then swelled inside herself with secret pleasure as she realized he spoke the truth. For the first time in her life, she was free to do just about whatever she pleased. How many times had she watched from the high south wall of the abbey and envied the village boys who swam like slick-coated young otters in the shallows of Loch Awe?

Choosing a flat rock padded by soft green moss, she sat down and took care in unbuckling her black slippers. Modestly, most self-conscious that Rodric's eyes never left her, she reached beneath the skirt of her gown to pluck loose the ribbons holding her white stockings. She unrolled her hose one leg at a time, and managed to pull them off out of sight of the man in the water, then swung her feet into the calm water.

"You said it wasn't cold," she accused him with a shiver as the water shocked her warm skin.

"And it is not, after you grow accustomed to it." Rodric moved yet closer, and she felt his fingers wrap around her bare instep. Before she could contemplate his plan, he was dragging her resisting off the bank, with no care that she was fully dressed.

"Stop, Rodric," she cried but laughed at the sheer absurdity of what he was doing, "please release me! No, I beg you!" Her cries went unheeded, and he laughed at her gasp when she finally plunged to her waist in the water, her full skirts billowing out around them both as he kept a firm grip upon her waist.

"I cannot swim, Rodric, I will drown, I tell you.

I have never been in such deep water. Rodric, please."

"I like the sound of my name upon your lips," he whispered, holding her gaze in the inexplicable way he had about him. "But I covet the taste of them so much more."

His mouth took what he craved but the kiss was brief, fleeting in a way that disappointed her, and she squealed and held tight to his shoulders as he took her swirling deeper into the water until her white skirt floating atop the water gave her the look of a great snowy-feathered swan.

"Stop this, I tell you," she cried again but more laughter was forced from her as he clutched her securely and moved deeper into the water.

"I will teach you to swim so that I will never worry about losing you to a watery grave. It is a simple enough feat, merely kick your feet and flail your arms like a windmill."

"That does not sound like something a well-bred lady should do. In fact, it sounds completely unladylike . . ." her words faltered as she looked down and caught sight of how the thin fabric was plastered against her chest, the cold water revealing the erect tips of her breasts as if she wore nothing at all.

Rodric's eyes followed her attention alerted by her quick gasp of dismay. "Aye, now that, my lady, is a sight that a man would pay any ransom to feast his eyes upon."

Blushing with embarrassment at the way his hot gaze latched upon her wet dress, Ainsley realized her feet now touched bottom, though the depth of the water was well nigh to her shoulders.

"Shall I demonstrate the technique, my love?" Rodric performed a backstroke for a few yards. "I vow that you shall not leave this pool before you are more adept at unladylike pursuits."

Ainsley shook her head first, but she knew she would try. She wanted to know if she could perfect the skill others used so well. "Will you not let me go under if I try?"

"Have I not sworn to protect you, my lady? From whatever might cause you fear?"

Ainsley kicked her feet but only managed to thrash her legs into a gigantic realm of her soggy skirt, nearly sinking in the ensuing tangle. No wonder women did not swim in rivers, she decided, as Rodric grabbed her arms and towed her in securely against his chest.

"I have saved your life for the second time, my lady. What do you intend to give me as reward?"

Glad for his supporting embrace, she relaxed enough to loop her arms around his neck, all the while thinking he was so extremely hard to resist that she was rather tired of trying to do so. Especially when he seemed to savor her willingness to be held so close to him.

"Now this, my lady, is a reward I have spent long nights dreaming about" was his whisper, one that engendered new tenderness in her eyes.

"Did my ears fail me or did you not insist that you enjoyed no sleep for want of my company, my lord?"

"You are in my thoughts, awake or in slumber,

my lady. My vow to keep myself away from you has brought me to my knees like nothing else in my life. Release me from such folly and make me the happiest man in all of Scotland."

"Do you intend to tempt me to you in your every waking moment?"

"Aye, that I do, for the reward is worth the trouble."

"Would a token of friendship do instead?"

He did not look particularly thrilled with her offer. "What token, my lady?"

"A kiss, mayhaps?" Immediately embarrassed by her own flirtatious words, for such boldness she was certainly not accustomed to, Rodric gave her little time to regret her proposal.

"A kiss would be welcome indeed, a fit beginning for what a man and wife should share," he murmured even as his mouth found her cold lips, then quickly robbed her of any other idea of denial.

The embrace had not the brevity of the last but was hard and with an eagerness that even Ainsley recognized as a man hungry for a woman. He pressed himself tightly against her, his palms going down her back and forcing her hips against his loins as he followed her head backward whenever she attempted to escape his mouth.

His soft, nibbling kisses slowly gave way to more as his tongue invaded her mouth gently but so insistently that she knew he would not be turned away in his intent. She was first shaken by the quick rush of excitement, then totally aroused as her body reacted with a wave of heat that made her forget the coldness of the water. Moaning incoherently as he held her head tightly, he kissed her again and again with such unbridled passion that her breath was robbed from her.

"That is indeed a fair token of affection," he murmured, not unaffected himself it seemed. His eyes delved into her own. "And a mere token of what awaits you when you invite me into your arms this night."

"I do not think . . ." she began, but her own denial sounded so weak and unsteady that it brought his knowing chuckle.

"Come, it's time we broke our fast on this beautiful morn. I will take you afield this day and show you the ruins of an ancient Norse temple just over yonder hill."

She turned her back as he climbed from the stream and waited patiently for him to don his clothes, but when she did turn around he wore only a linen towel wrapped tightly around his hips. Instead of donning his plaid, he held it as a wrap for her as she waded shivering from the stream. Quickly he slung it around her shoulders and wrapped her snugly in its length.

"Next time we will swim here unclad and unembarrassed, and make love on the grass because we cannot wait to reach our bed."

Ainsley had no reply to that, in truth could think of no words in answer to such a shocking remark, but she was beginning to think he foretold the future only too well. Each time he kissed her lips so fully, she was more affected, and she had a feeling his seduction of her was well on its way to fruition. Even she could see how her defenses were slowly crumbling, one stone at a time.

The rest of the day was spent walking along the loch and picking bouquets of the myriad wildflowers dotting the meadows. They sat awhile and watched a deer cautiously approach the loch, and Ainsley told him about the herd she had scattered into the wood upon her wild ride on Saracen just before she had found him awaiting her in the vespers chapel. To her surprise Rodric did not touch her again that day. Nor the next, or even the next after that. He allowed her leave to retire to bed alone after their long, peaceful days spent together in happy pursuits until she began to wonder if he had lost the inclination to overturn the pledge she had wrung from him.

After a week together at the valley lodge, Ainsley sat on the bank of the river watching as Rodric demonstrated with expertise the casting of line into the loch. Though she was clumsy in her attempt at such sport, he caught a good-size mess of fish for their evening meal. Later after they returned to the lodge, sunburned and tired, he grilled the fresh salmon steaks over the coals. They ate with gusto sharpened by a day spent in the fresh air, then sat side by side on the wide couch before the fire, enjoying a companionable silence.

"I have told you much about myself since we wed. Now I would have you talk about your life." Rodric took her hand and kissed the backs of her fingers one at a time in the way he was wont to do. She waited for him to pull her close for another thrilling kiss, but in vain for he seemed content only to talk. "Was there nothing at all good for you during your years at the nunnery?"

"I miss Myrna very much," she murmured with a sigh, "although I am finding this valley a lovely place."

Her compliment pleased him, she could see it in his eyes. "Aye, the red-haired lass who got away from Richard."

"I wish she had not. She would have liked it here as well. And there was Brother Alfonse. He taught me much and gave me fatherly affection that I had never known."

"He was the herbalist you mentioned who taught you how to mix your salves and remedies?"

Ainsley nodded. "He was kind and good-hearted and never believed the accusations of witchcraft or stories about my eyes. He would gaze straight into the spot of brown and tell me they were not ugly but very special." She paused, for Rodric had done much the same.

Rodric took her chin in his thumb and forefinger. "You have beautiful eyes, Ainsley, eyes that beguile and transfix."

"Do they beguile you, my lord?"

"Aye, more each time I look into them."

Still he did not touch her in any other way. She wanted to ask him why he had changed in that regard but could not bring herself to be so forward. Finally she simply blurted it out, appalling herself. "You have shown little interest in me as wife these past days. Have I done something amiss that has offended you?"

Coloring furiously, she hated her own propensity to do so as his gaze dropped to her lips, which made her moisten them nervously. When he leaned forward, she prepared herself for the kiss she hoped was forthcoming by closing her eyes, but instead he drew her into his arms until she sat between his legs with her back pressed intimately across his chest, much as he had held her that very first night.

Her heart raced as one strong sunbrowned finger trailed down her cheek, then under the fragile line of her jaw and forced her chin back. She looked up into his face as he pressed a kiss against her brow, then she closed her eyes, a muffled moan escaping her as warm lips touched her temple. She sighed when his mouth found the vulnerable cord of her throat, and barely knew it when his hands slipped into the front of her low bodice, but tensed to rigidity as his fingertip touched the soft mound of her naked breast. She felt her nipple spring to life, and she began to tremble with anticipation.

Her chest began to rise and fall with her rapid breathing, and her lips fell apart as he grasped a gentle handful of her hair and held her head trapped against his shoulder as his other hand intruded deeper into the folds of her dress. She could not move, gripped with some terrible, awful, lovely powerlessness. Every fiber of her body tensed as his fingertips caught the bud of her

breast and caressed it until it was hard, erect, un-
believably sensitive.

"Please, please . . ." she managed somehow
without knowing for sure of what she begged,
then forgot when he cupped the fullness of her
breast. Her protests transformed into weak
breaths of pleasure, and her hips writhed with
every kind of sensation, the most private parts of
her burning up with the unfamiliar response to
the touch of a man.

"I am your husband. Yield to me, Ainsley, let
me love you."

Ainsley shook her head, afraid of what he
meant, in her innocence not sure exactly what
else he wanted to do, but so aware that he had
set her body on fire with the gentle exploring of
his fingers. She could not think anymore, could
garner no righteous protestations, and she felt
limp and malleable as a piece of clay under the
stroking fingers of a talented sculptor.

When he turned her suddenly, so that her back
lay across his arm, she stared upon his countenance. Now he was serious, and the silver in his
eyes gleamed with a kind of intensity she had not
seen before. He turned her more, and she
watched his hand catch the soft silk fabric of her
apple-green skirt and slide it up her thigh until
he found soft bare skin. She watched him as if
she lay in a dream, as if she were observing another couple entwined on the couch. His fingers
trailed upward farther toward her hip, but she was
distracted by the way his other hand had delved

into the fullness of her bosom, caressing her breast until she wanted to squirm with pleasure.

Somehow the ribbons of her shift gave way, and she squeezed shut her eyes as his hand slid over the flat plane of her bare stomach and into soft curls below. Then he was touching her at the very core of her womanhood, and she came quickly to her senses, struggling to extricate herself, in sudden fear of the unknown. He stopped touching her but held her tightly against him.

"Let me give you pleasure, let me show you how it is to love a man."

"Ohhh" was her response as the top of his finger slid lower into the soft flesh between her legs. She jerked bodily when he touched her, then arched upward toward his hand. When his fingertip began to stroke her, she dropped her head against his chest as the most exquisite of sensations began to stir down deep inside her, so deep she felt the quivering could never rise to the surface of awareness. He murmured sweet words she could barely hear as she writhed against his hand, other fingers teasing her nipples, and she forgot everything, forgot herself as he took her past conscious thought, past pleasure, past endurance. Her body seemed to contract in upon itself, over and over, with such powerful unspeakable waves of pure pleasure that a shocked cry was forced from her lips.

Rodric knew the moment he found success. She closed tightly around his finger and cried aloud. He forced down the uncontrollable desire gripping his own experienced body, and it took every ounce of his will not to rip away the dress half clinging to her body and feast his eyes on the beautiful body he was exploring so intimately.

Oh, God, help him to control himself. He was hard and hot, throbbing with a passion he had never known, but he could not pleasure himself, not without breaking his vow. He could not betray her, and he had not meant to go quite so far so fast. He had intended only to introduce her to the pleasures of lovemaking, to show her that he did care, but he had meant to go slowly, with only enough pleasure that she would long for his touch when again night fell over the valley. God help him, what a price he was paying to honor her wishes.

After a moment she collapsed weakly against him, and he smiled at the quick eagerness of her newly awakened passion. He lowered her to the cushions. Her eyes were half closed, and her breasts, half exposed by the unfastened bodice. He found the hardened tip of her breast with his mouth, felt her jerk as he suckled gently until she brought her hands up into his hair and clutched him tightly with her fingers. She smelled like flowers, tasted like them, too. He wanted her desperately; he had never wanted a woman with such blinding need.

"Oh, Rodric . . ."

Ainsley's low moan brought Rodric close to what he desired most, and he caressed her with his fingertips until another low cry was forced from her lips. When his mouth came back to her trembling lips, her body was aquiver from his touch, but she accepted the gentle probing of his tongue and set his loins afire with unquenchable longing. Still, he held back.

Never would he make a mistake that could not be righted, that would haunt him as he tried to make a life with the woman in his arms, so he fought himself and then Ainsley, too, as her hands held him against her with growing insistence. He could have her now, this moment so alive with the passion they shared, without one more second of tortuous self-control. He could rend the silk of her gown to shreds and feast his hungry eyes on her naked body the way he had dreamed of doing every night since he had stolen her from the damnable abbey.

He wanted to make her his wife in the most intimate way a man could, and by the saints she was ready to have him do so. She writhed beneath him, overcome by awakened desire, but he steeled his resolve, only devouring her lips with draining kisses that left her in a frenzy of new sensations and him on the verge of forgetting his vows. He groaned as she arched up against him and moaned against his mouth.

"God help me, wife, but I cannot keep my promise long if you pull me upon you this way," he muttered, his voice a hoarse rendition of its usual timber, his heart heaving his chest with need. He had accomplished what he had set out to do. He had introduced her to the act of love, and now that she had tasted the pleasures they would share, perhaps she would be less inclined to shun him from her bed.

With more willpower than he ever thought himself capable, he pushed himself off her and stood on shaky legs beside the couch. Ainsley half righted herself and gazed up at him with parted kiss-swollen lips and eyes so clouded with desire that he could not resist her sweet entreaty to return; her outstretched arms welcomed him back against her breast. Was not that the very act he had hungered from her?

Going back to her, he lay atop her body, bracing his weight on his elbows and snarling silken curls of soft honey-blond hair, muttering with pleasure when he felt her hands upon him beneath the plaid, gripping the back of his thighs in her eager innocence.

The triumph of her surrender was more fleeting than gratifying, after the physical torment of corralling blood running rampant with need. He wanted her with a kind of desire he had not experienced before, never this unquenchable, mindless absorption that left him as jittery as a lad with his first wench. Even then when he was young, he had never felt this joy in a woman.

He rose to his knees and swept up her gown and wet his lips when he saw her long lithe legs, naked, soft, the color of pale ivory, his to touch, to possess. He unbuckled his belt and the plaid fell on the floor behind him, and he was pleased when Ainsley's face held no trace of maidenly fear but a loving expression that warmed him even more. Though the long coveted moment was at hand now, he did not wish to rush into his pleasure. She was pure, unknown except by his hand.

He had known as much from the first moment he had touched her body. He had to be gentle; he had to remember how fragile her innocence was.

Easing down atop her he shut his eyes as his chest flattened against the softness of her breasts, and he braced himself and inquired one last time. "Are you sure you wish this coupling, sweet Ainsley? You have forbidden me this moment for longer than I thought I could stand, but I do not want to hurt you or betray your trust in me. I am your husband. I respect you too much."

Her answer was a mere whisper, barely heard beneath his own harsh breathing. "I will yield to your gentleness, to your kindness. You have been patient with a wife who did not yet know the kind of man you were."

Warmth, true affection pooled like warm water around his heart, and he knew in that instant that he loved this woman who looked at him out of her incredible, enchanted eyes. No witch, she, but angel born of the earth, and soon his in every way.

"I dread that I must hurt you to make you mine," he murmured against her lips, cupping her cheeks gently inside his palms. " 'Twill not be an awful pain but would there be another way, I would gladly seek it."

"I am a maiden, 'tis true, but perhaps not so fragile and frightened as you fear."

Her soft answer engendered a smile from him as he lowered his lips to touch hers while he lowered his hips upon her loins. Her arms came up to lock around his bare back, her fingers upon his skin in tentative exploration. His mind was awhirl with sensation so acute, he felt his very nerve endings were on fire. He was so close now, the moment he had craved and courted and hungered for since the day he had first laid eyes upon her exquisite face. He moved down and found her ready for him, though she stiffened within his arms. He whispered low, soothing assurances until she relaxed again.

God in heaven, he could hear his heartbeat in his ears, rapid, hard, but he could not stop now. She cried out as he entered her, and he stopped, his lips muffling her pain, then moved slowly until she joined the rhythm, clutching him close, and he held her tightly, moving inside her, feeling the exquisite sensations as they moved together until the moment came in a flash of blinding light. He leaned back his head and groaned with pure, unparalleled pleasure so exquisite that he dropped down upon her, still joined as one, and clasped her tightly to him as if he would never let her go again.

Chapter Sixteen

Richard MacLeod rode behind Breanne MacDonald, watching the way her hips swayed sultrily in rhythm to the gentle gait of her mare. By Saint Columba's eyes, of late Rodric's little sister gave him pause. Ever since the night of the wedding feast, he had begun to notice her in ways he should not, and never had before.

Because of that new inclination on his part, it seemed the girl could entice him into endeavors he ordinarily would not consider—such as the one into which he now found himself. He was not at all certain that his decision to accompany her on a visit to Rodric and Ainsley at the mountain lodge a very good idea.

Still Breanne had persisted with a smile he now considered most sweet to look upon, when before he had hardly noticed it at all, and her persuasions and cajolery had continued tirelessly until he had reluctantly relented. The truth was, however, that he had other, and more pressing, reasons for undertaking the trek. The length of three

Sabbaths had come and gone since Rodric had secreted his kidnapped bride in seclusion at his mountain lair with not a single tiding forthcoming as to how they fared.

Although Richard well knew Rodric wished to court his new wife's affection in privacy and that his reasons were of incredible significance to the entire clan, alas, to the entire Isle of Skye, he still feared the recklessness of their isolation. Though Rodric was a warrior of legendary repute, and more than capable of defending himself and his own in battle, in Richard's eyes the couple was much too afar from Arrandane, or even his own Dunvegan Castle.

Hugh Campbell would find out soon enough who had Ainsley in his keep, and why, and he would rush to avenge his worst enemy. Clan Campbell would be bold to attack their strongholds upon Skye, but Rodric was acutely vulnerable, alone as he was, despite the fact that few knew just where Rodric had built his hideaway— and that handful counted only himself, Ian, and a couple more of Rodric's most trusted friends.

"Do we have a far ride ahead?" Lady Breanne queried, turning at the waist to gaze back over her shoulder at him. She gave her quick, bright smile that initiated a distinct rush of pleasure in him— now, that thoroughly confounded him!—then eagerly continued, unbeknownst of his newfound dilemma.

"I am most anxious to see Lady Ainsley again. The two of us will be dear friends, as well as sisters-in-law. I know this, here in my heart where it counts." She tapped her breastbone with one forefinger, and so happy was she at the prospect lying ahead that her dimples deepened, carving soft hollows in each rose-hued cheek.

Holy Mary, he thought, astonishment gripping him further as he observed with intense admiration just how finely her face was appointed. Why, by the gods, she was absolutely beautiful, a trait he didn't remember noticing before! Startled, then uncomfortable with the knowledge, as well as annoyed with himself, for after all, though sixteen now, she had always seemed little more than a child in his eyes. He appalled himself further by noticing how her breasts swelled with womanly curves underneath her modestly cut gold riding jacket. By thunder, what was the matter with him?

" 'Tis not a far ride for those with an ounce of patience!" he snapped when he realized she was still awaiting his reply, instantly aware that the underlying reason for his shortness was his own ridiculous, and certainly less than honorable thoughts about the girl he had always considered as his own little sister. Furthermore, her hurt expression chagrined him more than it should have.

"Well, no need to harbor so hateful a tone, Richard." Her cheeriness disintegrated rather thoroughly into a frowning regard that robbed him of the pleasure of viewing her dimpling cheeks. He scowled with black displeasure, glad they had reached the point of travel where the valley fell in gradual descent to where Rainbow Creek flowed merrily into the blue waters of the loch.

The remainder of the ride was had in total,

miffed silence, on both their parts, and he struggled with his new awareness of her, feeling rather like an idiotic adolescent eyeing a fresh-faced young maiden, when the length of a full decade separated their birth dates.

As they approached the lodge, his moods elevated somewhat as he remembered plenteous good times spent within those log-hewn walls with his cousin. He had suffered many a sore back and ruptured muscle helping Rodric fell the trees then haul them to the site overlooking the trickling waterfalls.

As they came closer to the lodge, however, his instinct for danger was pricked by the sheer desertedness of the place. Nothing moved except leaves caressed by the mild wind, no voices could be heard, no noise interrupted the warbling of a couple of nightingales perched on the edge of the roof. Rodric's horse was housed in the lean-to stable, alongside the beautiful Arabian mount he had given to Ainsley—that relieved Richard's anxiety by a degree—but as he dismounted and lifted Breanne down to the ground, trying absurdly hard not to think about her shapely waist, he was still a bit worried.

Calling Rodric by name, he waited. Nothing came back except a slight echo over the water. He tried again and received no response. As he moved toward the porch, he was brought up dead in his tracks. Somewhere faraway, behind the house, came a female scream. Jerking his broadsword from the sheath at his belt, he bade Breanne to stay where she stood and hold their mounts secure then ran around the side, fearing what he might discover. Again a deserted scene until he heard another shriek and swung around to gaze out over the meadow that hugged the bank of the stream.

At once his guard relaxed. Slowly returning his long weapon to its bed with a metallic scrape, he watched Ainsley dash wildly through the high waving grasses some distance from the house, squealing again when her husband, who was in serious pursuit, managed to catch up to her. He swung her off her feet and around, then as her laughter echoed across the field, took her bodily down with him and out of sight into the sea of high grass.

Grinning, well aware such a happy scene indicated Rodric was in good graces with his lady, he stood waiting for them to reappear. A moment passed without that happening, and he held back his shouted greeting for several more minutes before he ascertained they were engrossed in amorous pursuits deep in the soft grass.

So, cousin, by the looks of this, you have been inordinately successful in your quest, he thought, though Rodric's prowess did not surprise him, considering just how enamored Rodric had become of his reluctant bride since he had stolen her.

"What's amiss?" Breanne had come up behind him so quietly that he had been unaware of her presence. He berated himself, vowing that he would not have fared so well had it been a Campbell who had crept so close to his unprotected backside. "Was that Ainsley's voice we heard?"

"Aye, but I suspect they've gone afield, and her calls drifted from over the water. Come, let us unpack the morsels we've brought for their supper. Rodric will bring her along soon enough, no doubt."

An hour later as he sat atop his spread-out plaid on the bank overlooking the creek, he was beginning to wonder just how long Rodric intended to make love to his wife. But Richard was not unwilling to pass his time watching Breanne where she waded in the shallow water, barefoot, her skirt raised several inches above her trim ankles. He pretended he dozed lazily and paid her no mind, but he had rarely taken his eyes off her. She had become a comely lass, seemingly overnight, especially when she turned and smiled so warmly that his heartbeat jumped. Unfortunately he found a second later, he was not the recipient of her joyful expression.

"Rodric! Ainsley! Over here! We've come for a visit!"

Richard sat up and turned in time to see where Rodric and Ainsley stood near the steps of the lodge. Richard came to his feet and dusted off his trews, fully appreciative of the dark crimson hue that climbed up Ainsley's neck and stained her face, as she self-consciously straightened her skirt and furtively checked her buttons.

Rodric, in contrast, did seem a bit like a man who had realized every dream of his life, twice over, even thrice if his broad grin was an indication. As his cousin strode in their direction, Richard did not miss the affectionate way he laced his fingers through Ainsley's. The wedding trip had been a triumph, and Richard shared Rodric's elation. Now there could be no annulment at the hands of the Campbells. The alliance was cemented.

"Rodric, I do hope you aren't cross with us for coming, but it's not fair how you've kept Ainsley out here all alone when everyone at Arrandane's desperate to get to know her better." Breanne's pleased chatter continued as she hurried forth to meet Ainsley. She hugged her new friend affectionately. "You must come back soon, for no one talks of anything but you."

"What do they say about me?" Ainsley asked, a look of fear welling in her extraordinary eyes.

Richard noticed how Rodric draped a soothing arm around her shoulders.

"About your healing powers, of course!" Breanne cried excitedly. "But you do not know the wonderful news! Wee Rachel has awakened and is feeling well enough to sit up and even partake of broth. All the villagers say 'tis because she was touched by the Lady of the Legend. Is it true? Did you tend to her injury?"

Rodric was smiling, but poor Ainsley looked increasingly uncomfortable. "I but said a prayer. If she is better 'tis God's will, not mine."

"Well, everyone is so happy that she is healing and very eager to welcome you back. When are you returning to Arrandane, Rodric?"

"You are wrong to rush a couple so newly wed,

Breanne," Rodric chastised, but a smile seemed to hover constantly on his mouth. Obviously Rodric was in no mood for anger toward anyone, and Richard wondered if anything could dislodge the contented expression from his cousin's face. Was it the glow of love, perhaps? He said as much to Rodric as the two young women struck off together for the lodge, arm in arm.

"Aye. I am content at the way things have turned out."

"Content curves your lips in drastic fashion. I could say you are a bit more than content, at least at the moment."

Rodric shrugged. "What do you wish me to say? She is more than I even expected. She is an angel."

"An angel she is." Richard chuckled, shaking his head. "And she seems to opine the same of you, judging by the way she keeps glancing back at us."

"We have spent happy days here together. 'Twas a marriage meant to be, just as I always told you."

Richard nodded, pleased his cousin experienced joy in his wedlock, but there were more serious acts they must discuss. "I am glad, cousin, for your happiness but I bring tidings that are not so good, I fear."

Rodric stopped and looked at him, immediately sobered. "Strathmorton?"

"Aye. Word came two days past. Campbell soldiers attacked the villagers of Balluchulish and burned out several homes, although only a few men were killed."

"Does he know she is at Arrandane?"

"That is hard to say, but I do not believe so, or he would have come here after her."

Rodric heaved a long sigh, as if resigned to the fight that would come. He shook his head, his eyes finding Ainsley ahead of them. "Then, I fear my wedding trip is abruptly at an end. I would have my wife safe behind the walls of Arrandane before Strathmorton sails for Skye."

"Aye, Ian is of the same mind. He sent the suggestion along with me. And he longs to know his daughter. I fear he thinks you selfish with her company."

"I am," Rodric admitted readily. "And growing more so as the days go by. She is a prize to have and hold, cousin, and I will do so well and long, God willing." He grinned and heartily clapped Richard's back. "But come share a pint while the ladies enjoy a gossip and tell me what else has transpired at Arrandane in these weeks past."

Richard filled Rodric in on the everyday happenings of the clan as they walked on, but his eyes strayed continually to Breanne until he chastened himself as nothing more than a silly fool. More than that he hoped that Rodric did not notice his unhealthy interest in his little sister.

Ainsley realized she was happy. More so than she had ever been. All her life she had hungered for a husband and family, but little had she dreamed of what a bright future she would find. Even more she had longed to be safe, to lead a normal existence where people did not fear her.

She had all of those things now. Rodric had given them to her.

Though she still dutifully listened to Breanne with one ear, she smiled at Rodric where he sat on a chair by the hearth. He returned a warm one back to her, and she wondered if he, too, looked forward to evening when their visitors would leave them alone again. She immediately felt guilty because Breanne was so sweet and was trying desperately to prove herself a friend.

"I am so relieved to see that you are no longer angry with Rodric." Breanne had leaned close now and whispered conspiratorially. "That pleased-with-himself grin has not left his face since we got here."

"He has treated me kindly, and we are getting to know each other better." Ainsley couldn't help but blush, for they spent most of their days abed, making love, but it was afterward when he held her close and they talked, her cheek resting on his bare chest, that she learned the most about him.

Fortunately Breanne didn't seem to notice her discomfiture. "Well, Richard has been unkind, no matter how congenial I try to be. I was hopeful of making him take notice of me after I persuaded him to bring me here, but he acts like I am nothing but a boring child."

Ainsley glanced at Richard MacLeod, where he stood near Rodric, warming his backside at the fire, and found him staring at her sister-in-law, his expression indicating that he considered Breanne neither a bore, nor a child. Surprised, for she had not noticed such interest in his mien before that moment, she wondered what had happened.

"Surely you are wrong, Breanne. I have noticed today that he often watched you during supper, and even now, as we sit here talking."

"Truly? Or do you just hope to raise my low spirits?" Breanne asked breathlessly, but her eyes lit up as she swiveled her attention to the MacLeod. Ainsley saw then how he managed to shift his regard before Breanne could observe his keen scrutiny of her. "Nay, he is interested in Rodric's tale. I do wish he would stare at me with such devotion."

Ainsley had a feeling he would do so one day soon, but her thoughts of the other couple were distracted when Rodric came and sank down on the divan beside her. He took her hand and folded his fingers into hers, and she felt as if they fit together. Did they truly share a destiny, as Rodric believed with such conviction? She now wanted to believe so, but their future was hardly secure. Would they live forever awaiting Hugh Campbell's vengeance?

As Breanne moved toward Richard, Ainsley's morbid thoughts were quickly thrust from her mind as Rodric's lips touched her ear, his whisper eliciting a soft shiver. "Will they never leave? I want to finish what you started with me in the meadow."

"I?" she whispered very softly. "I remind you, sire, that you are the one who threw me upon the ground, then pinned me there under your weight."

"Something I intend to do again if we can rid ourselves of unwanted company."

"For shame. 'Tis your sister and cousin you shun."

"I have had them around me for as long as I can remember. You, I still savor, like a fine wine."

"And will you find my face as tiresome after looking upon it so long?"

Rodric showed a new sobriety after so many days of pleasant sparring between them. "I do not think I would grow tired of gazing upon your beauty, not if I live to be a man withered and grayed by a hundred years of hardship."

Touched, Ainsley lifted her fingertips to his cheek. They shared a tender moment, both apparently revealing their longing to deepen their embrace, for Richard suddenly cleared his throat.

"I daresay it is time for us to return to Arrandane, Bree. The afternoon will soon begin to fade of light."

"Perhaps we can leave a wreath of wildflowers at the church of the MacLeods," Breanne suggested in an imploring manner. " 'Twould please me if you'd allow it, milord."

Richard frowned greatly, and rather unnecessarily in Ainsley's opinion, for such a benign request, but then he nodded as if he relented against his better judgment. "All right, but only briefly, for I have duties awaiting me at Arrandane."

Rodric and Ainsley walked them outside and watched as they mounted. Richard sat forward in his saddle. "Ian will wish to know when you will return. He is impatient."

Rodric was not to be hurried. "Tell him we will find our way home in a day or so and remind him how beautiful I find his daughter."

Ainsley lowered her eyes, feeling shy because of

his compliment but even more pleased by it. She looked up again as Breanne called good-bye.

"Come home soon, Ainsley, for I want to give you the keys of the household. You are mistress there now. I relinquish them gladly, for I will wed someday and manage my husband's house." She peeked in sidelong fashion at Richard, whose face reddened as he fixed his gaze with undue concentration upon the waters of the loch.

Side by side, holding hands, she and Rodric watched them walk their horses down the shore. Before their visitors were at a decent distance, Rodric pulled her with him back into the house. Against the shut door he pressed her with his body, his mouth capturing hers until she could only sigh, for she had looked forward to this moment herself.

"I do not intend to waste a moment of this blissful privacy," he muttered hoarsely as he swung her lightly into his arms. "Arrandane is full of watching eyes and pressing duties, but here, you are mine every minute of the day and night."

Ainsley looped her arms around his neck as he carried her upstairs, not ready to return anymore than he, but such thoughts drifted out of her mind as he tumbled her onto the bed and came down on top of her. She threaded her fingers through the softness of his black hair and closed her eyes as his fingers found entrance to her bodice, then she moaned with pleasure when his mouth settled over her naked breast.

Chapter Seventeen

Castle Arrandane lay in the distance beside the sea like a burnished jewel washed ashore by the curling surf. Rodric halted his horse then checked the stallion's prancing as he gazed proudly down at the gray square walls of the ancient keep, his expression a study of conflicting, bittersweet emotions.

As chieftain he was honor-bound to return to his duty to the clan, and he welcomed such responsibility. But if the truth be told, he would have gladly remained in the beautiful valley with his lovely bride, indefinitely, for as long as she agreed to stay there with him.

"Does it please my lord to be home to Arrandane?" Ainsley spoke quietly from where she sat aloft upon her horse less than a yard from him.

"Aye," he answered, twisting in his leather seat and finding her fair cheeks affixed with a pink flush of health that had not been there when they had arrived weeks before. She should have donned a hat with a sheltering brim, he thought, but he knew she was not wont to cover her head; yet another idiosyncrasy he had learned about her in their days alone together. He would have to insist that she did so in the future, for her skin was so fair, softly alluring in its flawless fragility.

Mentally he had to stay his hand from dragging her from her sidesaddle onto his own mount in front of him. He enjoyed having her body pressed close against him, for he had grown to care deeply for her despite the brevity of their acquaintance. What man would not adore such a woman as Ainsley?

Aye, love her he already did, he admitted to himself with not a little surprise, for his affection for her ran with a fathomless and steady current, and not strictly because of the physical act that made him crave her mightily between the sheets. Her innocent but eager response to him had been distinctly gratifying, the sweetest of memories that warmed his heart but as wondrous as such was, a deeper, more mature relationship was what he wished most to develop between them. Ainsley pleasured him greatly in that regard as well, more than he could have ever expected. He enjoyed her wit, her pleasures at the simple tasks as when he had taught her to swim in the blue waters of the loch or how to load and shoot his pistol at a target marked upon the largest oak in the meadow.

There had been method behind that particular lesson, for well he knew there were still many who feared her enough to do her harm. The world had treated her neither fairly nor well. For the most part her past memories were gory, gaping wounds that Rodric meant to erase forever from her mind through his own kind acts and gentle care.

Smiling at her, very pleased by the happiness shining in her exquisite eyes, he asked, "How is it you feel about returning to your new home, my love? Do you look forward to assuming your position as beloved wife and mistress of Arrandane?" Awaiting her reply, he fought not to reveal his anxiety. But once she uttered her answer, he could not hide the inordinate pleasure that washed through him.

"I am content to ride at my husband's side."

Rodric reached out with a gloved hand and laid it over hers, where she rested them upon her wide flat pommel. Their smiles were softly lingering and melded with their newfound intimacy. "I cannot tell you how greatly such words please me, my lady, for more than anything upon this earth, I wish you here with me and my clansmen of Skye, happy and content with those who love you."

For a moment he was certain he saw the glimmer of moisture in her eyes, but her long lashes dropped, veiling his view. Though she seemed touched by his sentiment, it was the brightest of her smiles that she presented. "Then, let us proceed to my new home, my lord Rodric."

With such words, uttered with true sincerity, Rodric felt secure with the world and all within its domain. He urged his horse onward with his heels, now aware of no obstacle in his determination to cement the unification of his mother's and father's clans. So long had the two been enemies that time would be required to overcome some of the ingrained distrust and ill deeds performed in the past, but with Ainsley standing at his side, their problems would be more easily resolved. Soon, in the near future, it would behoove his intent to take her with him to his kin at Dunvegan and introduce her as their lady of the legend.

As it turned out, he had little need to worry about the introduction of Ainsley to Clan Mac-Leod, for as they guided their mounts down through the high grasses of the sloping foothills, they found myriad yellow leather tents dotting the pastures outside the walls of the castle. Each bright pennon fluttering in the breeze was embla zoned with the fierce black bull of the MacLeods.

At first Rodric was simply astonished to find so many of his mother's clansmen awaiting them, but familial pride soon blossomed when he and Ainsley were glimpsed and their presence heralded among the tented structures with excited shouts. Many people ran forward to greet them, and Rodric grinned at the way Ainsley blushed when the yellow-kilted warriors bowed deeply before her. There were women crowding around her as well, more than one reaching out to touch her hem while others held their children aloft in their arms to receive Ainsley's blessing.

"I would assume that tidings have traveled afar concerning Rachel and the Lady of the Legend," he told her as she laid her open palm lightly atop one small head after another.

"But I am not she," she insisted, still denying

the truth. "As I told you, I am but trained in healing arts."

Rodric felt sure there was more to her healing
skills than she professed, but he doubted she
would ever admit she owned the inexplicable,
God-given gift, not after suffering such long and
bitter persecution from the Campbells because of
it. Little did it matter. She would eventually find
it safe to display her incredible talents for the denizens of Skye, for here she would be praised, not
condemned, for the good she performed.

Once they passed through the congregated well-
wishers in the fields and courtyard, they entered
the open gate into the keep, where a contingent
of nobles, representing both MacDonalds and
MacLeods, awaited them. Rodric awknowledged
old friends and acquaintances with a smiling salute as he dismounted, then proudly lifted his wife
to the ground. Ainsley stood uncertainly at his
side until a woman determinedly pushed her way
through the crowded throng.

"I wish to thank ye, my lady, for saving my wee
Rachel from certain death. I brought the bairn
with me so all can witness the miracle."

Smilingly Ginnie held up her child, and Rodric
stared at the toddler, amazed at the rapidity of
her recovery. The terrible bruises had faded to
yellowish-brown, though still visible on the child's
pale skin. Rachel's huge blue eyes were open,
clear and lucid, as she looked around wonderingly
at all the people.

"I am very pleased that she is looking so much

better," Ainsley spoke softly and earnestly as she stroked Rachel's cheek with her fingertips.

"Would you hold her in your arms once more, milady, and give her your blessing? 'Twould mean so much to me and the bairn."

Ainsley glanced at Rodric, no doubt intimidated by the crowd, who now had begun to murmur among themselves and press closer. He nodded encouragement, then watched Ainsley assume the child carefully and cradle her in her arms. The baby laid her head on Ainsley's shoulder, and Rodric decided a bairn nestled upon his wife's breast was a pleasing sight indeed. In truth she could already have conceived his child. He grinned to himself, thinking it would be little surprise if that were so, considering the dilligence with which they had worked upon such an eventuality during their days at the hunting lodge. He hoped so, for he longed for many children.

After she had returned Rachel into Ginnie's arms, he took Ainsley's hand and led her inside the great hall. Various chieftains lined their way, and he introduced her to them one after another until they reached Ian MacDonald's place on the far end of the hall. Rodric was pleased when Ian bowed low before Ainsley.

"We welcome you home, daughter, for these walls have been an empty shell with you outside them."

Breanne stood next in line, fidgeting and excited in her usual ebullient manner. She wrapped Ainsley in an enthusiastic hug. "I am so happy you're back. I long to show you every nook and cranny of Arrandane. I've always wanted a sister, and now I have one."

"I, too, have wished for a sister."

Ainsley's voice had been low, unnatural. Rodric knew at once that something was amiss. As the guests began to disperse to long tables set up for the feast of welcome, Ainsley turned and fled the room from a side passage. Frowning, he nodded to Ian, acknowledging her father's concern before he followed his wife upstairs. He found her inside his own bedchamber, lying facedown atop the bed. She was crying, softly, as if her heart was broken.

For an instant he stood unmoving in the portal, shocked to find her in such a distraught state. His high hopes for their future together plummeted, as if caught in anchor ropes and dragged to the bottom of the sea. Warily he walked to the bed and sat hesitantly beside her.

"Are you all right, Ainsley?"

At the sound of his low voice she stiffened, her muffled weeping ceasing momentarily. He placed a gentle hand upon her back and felt her tremble.

"I don't understand, love. I thought you felt ready to accept our vows and live here among us." The next words came out hard, for the idea had become increasingly repugnant to him. "Does this mean that you wish now to return to your former life at Strathmorton?"

"No! Oh, no, you mustn't think that!"

Ainsley thrust herself up into a sitting position, tunneling spread fingers through the hair hanging forward over her face. She swiped impatiently at her tears and to his relief, leaned up against him as if she wished him to comfort her. Wrapping her inside his arms, he held her tightly and stroked her hair.

"Then, what is troubling you so? Why did you run away? Why are you crying?"

"Because . . . I . . . I mean, it's just that . . ." Hesitantly, unsure, voice breaking continually as she tried to explain. "It was like . . . like I have a family, a real one who is glad to see me." A sob caught, making her voice clogged and difficult. "I've never had that, Rodric, never had a father or sister who missed me when I was away . . ." Her voice dwindled helplessly.

Pure relief hit Rodric like a blast of glacial air, and he sagged back against the carved headboard, still grasping her against his chest. She was merely touched by the welcome she had received at Arrandane, her tears had been ones of joy. Over her head he could not prevent his pleased grin, but he made certain his delight did not reveal itself in his soothing voice.

"You are an integral part of us. You always have been, even though we didn't know you existed for so long."

"I feel that's true now. My heart tells me I belong here with you."

Sentiments he had longed to hear, nay, hungered to hear, were rolling from her lips until he stopped them by tipping her face toward his and they stared into each other's eyes. "We are going to have the most wonderful life, Ainsley. You are going to be surrounded by people who love you, and we all will make up to you all the lonely years stolen from us by Hugh Campbell."

Pleased by his pledge, Ainsley nestled even closer against his heart, and they sat quietly together, no more conversation passing between them, but for the first time, totally content with each other.

Several months after being brought to Arrandane that storm-tossed night, Ainsley sat upon her knees in the walled garden. She stopped in her weeding, brushing dirt and twigs from the roots of a freshly pulled root. She leaned back on her heels and glanced across the shell-covered path at Ellie MacLeod, who was snapping beans into a wooden bowl. The old woman was looking back at her, so she smiled and held up the root shaped in the form of a man.

"I've found a mandrake, Ellie, and a perfect specimen, too. I had to look long and hard for them when I lived at the abbey."

"Are mandrakes useful in your remedies?"

"Aye, 'tis good potion for many maladies."

"That is good, my dear."

As Ellie bent her hoary head over her work, Ainsley continued to gaze upon her, sometimes still finding it hard to believe she was really the same nurse who had rocked her to sleep when she was a babe. But she had not changed in temperament, now as kind and gentle as she had been so many years ago. Ainsley was reminded again just how fortunate it was that Ellie had come forward when she did. Otherwise Ainsley would never have been found by Rodric before she had been wedded to Randolph of Varney and taken off to England.

Though many weeks had passed since she had been deposited upon the soil of Skye, and though she had lived in terror of a retaliation from Hugh Campbell, nothing untoward had happened. She was beginning to hope that he had dismissed her as an insignificant, or at the least, not worthy of the loss of the lives of his soldiers that would be necessary to force her return to his fold.

The latter would not surprise her, for the earl knew her not, even by sight, had only kept her out of spite as the spawn of his daughter's adulterous affair with a MacDonald. She had wondered about her mother a great deal in the last weeks, had opened the locket now lodged against the base of her throat countless times to gaze upon Meredith's likeness.

"Did you love my mother, Ellie?" she asked softly, carefully placing the mandrake root into her partitioned herb apron.

Ellie returned her attention to Ainsley, sad memories ravaging the contours of her parchment-thin face and causing the furrowed lines to sink into deeper grooves in both her brow and cheeks. "Aye, my lady had the manner of an angel with her kindness and gentle voice. We all loved her. She did not deserve her terrible fate. I weep for her at times, even now, so long past."

Rearranging her wide-brimmed straw hat to cover her face—Rodric insisted on her wearing it, and she obliged him because the sun brought out all manner of freckling across her nose—she snipped a twig of rosemary to aid the unsettled stomach she was having of late. There were many questions she wished to ask about her mother, especially the one she uttered next.

"Did she tell you about her feelings for Lord Ian?"

A quick nod affirmed the question, so Ainsley pursued her curiosity about her parents. "Did you ever see them together?"

"Nay. They hid their trysts from all, for fear of Lord Campbell's wrath. But she was always so happy when she returned from his company. I can still see her smile." Ellie exhaled, a long, sad sound that told Ainsley how deeply she had cared for Meredith Campbell. Suddenly Ellie's expression changed to a happier one. "She wore the very same expression that floods your face whenever Lord Rodric appears in the great hall after a day away."

Ainsley felt hot color rise in her cheeks, but she knew of what Ellie spoke. Even at this moment so early in the afternoon, she already looked forward to the evening meal when he would return from his ride through the outlying farms of Arrandane. For the last few weeks he had been gone often, helping a survey team in its efforts to lay out a new road that would connect Arrandane and Dunvegan, one of the many plans he had for great improvements now that he had become chieftain.

"May I join you, my dear?"

Ainsley had not heard her father approach until he spoke, but when she turned, she found him standing only a few feet away. He leaned heavily upon his cane. When he rubbed his thigh as if it pained him, Ellie rose at once.

"Please, my lord, sit here, for I am due in the buttery with these beans if they are to be boiled in time for this night's fare."

"My thanks to you, Ellie. I cannot walk so easily as before, I fear."

As soon as the old servant left them alone together, an uncomfortable silence fell into place between them like a heavy, shrouding drapery. Ainsley always felt a certain shyness around the man who was her father, though she now believed that he had truly sired her. He sat down with the gingerliness of an invalid, absently massaging his leg just above the knee. She knew he was often in pain, though he rarely complained and had never asked her to nurse his injury.

"My own great-grandmother planted this herbal garden many years ago," he told her in his quiet way. Ainsley kept staring at him, wondering if her mother had thought him as wonderful as Ainsley now thought Rodric. He was still a handsome man, though his dark hair was swept with silver streaks, especially over his ears and across the top. She would not estimate him to be much over the age of forty. "She was a healer, too," Ian continued, as if he wished to join in conversation with her, "with MacLeod blood, and she took great pains in planting many of these plants for their medicinal properties. Her husband was a seafarer and often brought her plants and bushes from faraway places across the oceans."

"There are many plants here that I am not familiar with," Ainsley admitted, looking around the extensive beds containing every imaginable sort of shrub and flower. She spent a great deal of her time in the peaceful, quiet place. She felt serene when she was hidden there and safe from harm.

"There is a book in the library that deals with herbal remedies. Grandmother showed it to me long ago and told me the drawings and descriptions were by her own mother's hand. Would you like for me to show it to you someday?"

"Oh, yes, please, I would love to. Such would help me very much."

"Then, you shall have it, daughter, and anything else I can give you."

Ian had not been so bold as to call her daughter before, but Ainsley was not put off by his affectionate term. She rose slowly, placing her basket on the bench beside her, then joined him where he sat in the shade of an oleander bush.

"I have noticed how you often rub at your leg. Does it pain you overly much this day?" She remembered that Rodric had told her he had sustained the injury in battle and had suffered greatly since.

"Aye. Oft the ache heralds impending rain or squalls chasing inland off the sea."

Still hesitant, Ainsley dropped down on her knees in front of him. "At times a massage will ease the pain; if you will allow me, I will try to help you."

"Only a fool would deny the touch of the Lady of the Legend. I welcome your help."

Ian wore a belted plaid of bright red MacDonald tartan, long and loose, hanging well below his injured thigh. Ainsley lifted the edge and folded it carefully back until she could see the wound that still plagued him after so long. The mark of the Campbell broadsword had bitten deep into his flesh but was straight and wide, the scar tissue white and obvious against his hairy thigh. She touched the drawn edges of the old wound and prayed that God would help her heal him as He had helped her with Rachel and so many others before her. She let the heat of her fingers penetrate his flesh.

" 'Tis an awful wound you suffered, my lord." Still, she could not bring herself to address him as father, but he did not seem to notice.

"I am fortunate to have lived to see this day, for I lay abed for many months in the dark shadows of death. God spared me then for these days with you, I have come to believe that with all my heart."

"I, too, am pleased that I am home where I've always belonged."

Her soft admission touched him. She saw the sheen of tears, the roil of contained emotion in his eyes, so much like hers in color, before he turned his head away. "If only your mother was here to see her beautiful daughter, then all things would be well and good."

When he seemed to revert into the cobwebby corridors of his past, his gaze leaving her to focus on the back wall, his expression faraway from her and the sounds of voices and rumbling wagons filtering over the garden wall, Ainsley finished her massage and went back to her work harvesting herbs, but she looked up often to check on him, glad they had spent even this short time alone together. She wanted to get to know Ian better. She wanted to be his daughter and help lessen his suffering over her mother's untimely demise, for it seemed he mourned deeply with fresh pain as if his grief would never end.

Chapter Eighteen

Understandably Rodric was proud of the progress made on his new road to Dunvegan in the following weeks, so much so in fact, that he had arranged to take Ainsley afield so that she could see and enjoy with him his dream in the making. Out of a practicality born of necessity, he decided to bring his sister—who seemed to be growing more troublesome as she reached marriageable age—along as well, in order to meet the most zealous and persistent of her suitors, a MacKinnon of the east coast who led a contingent of his clansmen laboring with pick and shovel. Now, after partaking of her company in a picnic of kidney pie and ale, the poor fellow was already so besotted with Bree that he had deteriorated before God and man into a veritable smiling simpleton.

Even now, from where Rodric sprawled comfortably with his wife on a thick quilted blanket upon a slight rise overlooking the road gang, he shook his head as he watched young MacKinnon trailing his sister's every footfall with much the same look as a terrier pup wagging his tail so hard he knocked himself down.

"Surely you do not truly consider a betrothal contract between Neil MacKinnon and Breanne, do you, my lord?" Ainsley sat cross-legged across from him, her russet-hued skirt arranged modestly around her legs, the sunlight spinning her coiled hair into a pale gold tiara as she gazed with fixed intent at the strolling couple below. But her voice was what gave him pause; her open disapproval too prevalent to ignore. Perplexed by her condemnation, he turned all his attention upon her.

"You do not think them a good match? Neil is a good man, considerably older than she, but not too much so, and in line as chief of clan MacKinnon. Even more important, their marriage would make him a staunch ally of Arrandane. And Breanne would not live far away from us."

"All that is very well and good, my lord, and bears witness that you wish her a suitable match, but for the fact that she does not harbor love for him." She stopped, turning her gaze upon his face. A small smile developed, readily disarming his senses, but even in his receptive frame of mind, her next revelation shocked him as much as if she had sent a closed fist hard against the side of head. "For you see, the truth is . . . she cares deeply for Richard MacLeod and covets him as her wedded husband."

Stunned to absolute silence, and showing that reaction as a completely incredulous expression spread over his face, Rodric pushed himself up on one arm, then peered past the couple in question across the grassy meadow to where Richard oversaw the MacLeods working on the roadbed. Breanne, too, was gazing in his cousin's direction despite the extraordinary elaborate attentions heaped upon her by the hapless boy at her side.

Rodric huffed, a scornful dismissal, then shook his head, and finally got out. "That is absurd."

Ainsley merely smiled, the image of a smug, self-satisfied woman tolerating her husband's profound lack of intuition. "Have you asked her whom she wishes to wed?"

Rodric took umbrage to that sweetly uttered rebuke. "Of course not. The decision lies with my judgment."

"I suppose that's how you felt as to our wedded bliss?"

Rodric's consternation relaxed as did his countenance. "That was different, as well you know, but I will remind you how well our marriage has turned out. Besides, I guarantee you that Richard considers her as his little sister, and nothing more."

Glancing down at the MacLeod's position, Ainsley gave that enigmatic smile again, the one versatile enough to both enchant and irritate him, depending on the moment. "Lord Richard seems a bit distraught at being forced to observe her rites of courtship firsthand. Does he have any other reason to dislike your friend and comrade in arms, Neil MacKinnon?"

"Of course not. They are good friends, and have been for years. Neil was even fostered at Dunvegan for a time when Richard was a young lad there."

"Well, Richard does seem rather upset, though. Do you not think so?"

At her prodding Rodric did regard his cousin for signs of annoyance and found him striding back and forth near the end of construction, balled fists planted angrily on his hips, red-faced and yelling at his own belaboring men. Could Ainsley be right in her observation? Such irate behavior was totally unlike Richard, who, in truth, was usually the most affable of men, always jesting with the lads in his command. He certainly was not cheery today, however. Rodric contemplated the idea of Richard and Breanne, with not a little interest until Ainsley took his hand and brushed her lips against his knuckles with a feather-soft kiss.

"Your road to Dunvegan will bring the clans together as nothing else could," she complimented, changing the subject. "And 'tis good to see MacLeods and MacDonalds working together as one, do you not agree?"

"Aye. Once Skye is united, we will sleep safer in our beds, both from English intruders and the Lowlanders in their pay."

"Legends will be told of the things you now do," she went on as he reclined again and laid his head in her lap. She lifted a strand of his soft black hair and began weaving it tightly into a narrow plait. "And as the greatest of all chieftains, you must wear braids of power for all to see." She tied the end with a blue ribbon that she tugged from her own hair, but before she could start on another at his other temple, he stayed her hand and pressed his mouth to her small palm.

"I treasure you more than any insignia of authority, more than any deemed lands, any wealth, any power. I would give up all for the woman I love." His lips moved over the fragrant skin at the inside of her wrist as he spoke.

"Never will such be necessary, for I will always stand at your side" was what she whispered in answer.

Rodric turned on his side and propped his head in his open palm, then pulled her down until she lay upon her back. He leaned over her, kissing her, long, deep, draining kisses that neither wanted to end. When he finally rolled on his back and drew her close into his chest, she sighed contentedly and idly trailed her fingers over the muscles of his chest.

" 'Tis disgraceful to lie here as lovers entwined for others to see."

"They cannot see us from below, but little do I care for what others think. Every man of Skye knows how much you please me."

She lay quietly in the circle of his arms for a time. "Soon they will have proof of your regard, my lord."

Smiling, Rodric played with a silken lock of her hair. "There is proof inside my eyes every time I gaze upon you."

Ainsley came up on one elbow, her expression exceedingly tender as she smoothed his brow with her fingertips, then traced the lean contours of his tanned cheek. Her smile was secretive enough to provoke his curiosity. "The proof of which I speak 'tis of a different, more tangible sort."

"What proof is more so than the fact that I adore you?" he asked, pulling her to him again so that he could nibble at her lips. He didn't really care what answer she had, suddenly craving more the private sanctuary of their bedchamber.

"Your child, my lord, the son or daughter who now grows inside my womb."

Rodric's hand went still, where it idly sifted through the loosened locks at her nape. As she leaned back and gazed smilingly down into his shocked eyes, two heartbeats passed before joy began to burgeon forth in his heart, slowly rising to balloon against his chest and press into his throat until he could barely speak. "You are with child?"

"Aye, my husband. Ellie has told me there is little doubt. She predicts the birthing will be in the early spring."

"You are sure?"

At her eagerly nodded affirmation, he brought her back into his arms. He shut his eyes and clamped her close, too overcome by emotion to say more, and his speechlessness made her laugh softly into the hollow of his neck. Still, even after several moments had passed, words continued to elude him, his voice lodged tightly in his throat. He had longed for sons, for daughters, for heirs to the alliance he had worked so hard to form, and now Ainsley would give them to him.

But, oh God, now she would be at risk herself!

His blood glazed icy when he remembered his own mother's death—he became that frightened boy again, cringing in a corner, covering his ears against her long, agonizing, horrible screams as she lost her fight with life while giving birth to Breanne. Ainsley should never have made this long trip on horseback to see the road. The outcome of sitting in the saddle so long could have been devastating, still could be.

"Ainsley, why didn't you tell me sooner? I never would have allowed you to ride so far this day, and now the return journey lies ahead of us."

She cupped his chin in her palms and smiled into his eyes. "Do not worry so. I am fine and healthy. I wanted to come with you and see what's been keeping you so far from home every day. The ride will not hurt me, even Ellie says not. I am as eager as you to have this child, so I will take very good care of myself."

Relieved but still nagged by concern for her well-being, he placed a palm with the utmost gentleness upon her still-flat stomach. It seemed a miracle, unexpected, overwhelming, frightening, pleasing. He cradled her tenderly against his shoulder, and allowed the happiness to seep into his bones. For a time they sat thus, close together, quietly speaking of the future of their firstborn child, but their glow of contentment was not to be long-lasting.

Within the hour their attention was drawn to the road below, where a single rider had galloped into sight in the distance, riding hard toward the workers. Once he reached the spot where Richard stood as overseer, he lurched to a stop and jumped from his mount, unminding that the lathered horse pranced and reared in a skitterish dance. Rodric shot to his feet, alarmed, then left Ainsley and walked forth to meet Richard, who had begun to run up the hill toward them. Behind him, Ainsley rose as well, but neither expected Richard's words which rang out to them.

"The Campbells have attacked!"

Rodric was only half aware of Ainsley's horrified gasp behind him, for Richard's next pronouncement was even worse than Rodric had expected. "Maycairn's been sacked and burned! The villagers are fleeing for Arrandane, but many have already been murdered!"

A sick feeling hunched in the pit of his stomach, and Rodric turned slowly and met Ainsley's wide eyes. Her face was white, drained of color; she was terrified. He swung back to Richard, his voice quiet and controlled. "Are you certain it is Strathmorton's soldiers?"

"Aye, who else would have reason to attack us? We are now at peace with the MacLeods. Hugh's found out where Ainsley is and has come to get her back."

Rodric's worst fear materialized, and the dread that swept over him was nearly immobilizing. "Have they landed forces anywhere else on Skye?"

"None that we've had word of yet, but Ian is readying the fiery cross to summon our allies to war council at Arrandane. He wants you back there to assure the MacLeods and Clan MacKinnon." He glanced at Ainsley and lowered his voice. "And he wants Lady Ainsley safe inside the castle walls."

"Aye, as do I. Strathmorton has acted with more boldness than wisdom in attacking us in our own domain. Gather the workers and get them back to Arrandane without delay."

As Richard ran to obey orders, Rodric folded Ainsley into his arms and murmured reassurances against the top of her head, but in his heart he knew that all-out clan warfare was now unavoidable.

Many hours later Ainsley sat beside Breanne upon a cushioned bench that sat in the great hall in front of the gigantic cross of stained-glass windows. They both bent their ear in silent trepidation as Rodric and Ian, along with a council of other chieftains and surrounded by many armed clansmen, discussed the act of war perpetrated against Maycairn by Clan Campbell.

"The clans of Skye must unite and drive the invaders back to the mainland by show of force," Rodric insisted, angrily driving a fist into his open palm. "Now that we are in alliance with Clan MacLeod, we will have the force to gain victory in battle."

"Our coastal villages lie unprotected. Many innocent women and children will die before we can rally enough troops."

Ian's voice was quiet but accorded the respect due to the former, long-standing, chief of Arrandane.

"Aye. 'Twill take time to light the cross and carry it throughout the isle, then longer still to arm and mount the men necessary to quell the invasion." Richard stood as he spoke, but it was Rodric who paced agitatedly alongside the immense dimensions of the long mahogany table.

"Then, I will ride the fiery cross myself and meet with every chieftain in person. Time is of the essence, and I will not have my wife returned into Hugh's evil tutelage."

A chill passed over Ainsley's flesh at the sheer ferocity of Rodric's tone. Earlier in the day when she had told him of their baby, his words had been so soft, tender, loving, and eager. Now she was the instrument who would bring doom upon the beautiful isle in which she had found happiness and where the people had welcomed her with open arms with no repugnance for the difference of her eyes. She stood up.

" 'Tis I they desire," she said in a clear, firm voice. "In the eyes of Strathmorton, I am a Campbell. I will not be the cause of bloodshed among the innocent people of Skye. I will return if it will save MacDonald lives."

Rodric turned on her, and it took every fiber of nerve within her not to shudder beneath the black wrath exhibited so harshly on his face. The frown was so massive, so deep, his mouth set in a tight line with barely leashed fury, that she was taken aback and rendered speechless. Breanne tugged upon her sleeve to give her pause in her words, but she could not release her gaze from Rodric's cold silver stare.

"You forget your place, woman. This is a council of men. We will decide what fight for which we take up arms."

"But I will be the cause of terrible suffering . . ."

Rodric brought down his fist so hard atop the table that the map spread before him sprang from its anchors and furled with snapping sounds. Ian shot to his feet in alarm, but Rodric managed to modulate his voice before he spoke again, this time addressing the silent assemblage around him.

"Leave us, if you will, my friends. I would have a word alone with my lady."

Breanne scurried to obey without delay, obviously well acquainted with her brother's rages, though his temper was now veiled beneath calm utterances. Richard turned and followed her the length of the hall, and Ian hazarded a wary glance at his daughter before he, too, followed Richard and the other clansmen finding their way to the corridors without.

Nothing more was said for a moment, silence hanging over them as heavy as a slab of quarried marble. Husband and wife faced each other in the vast empty hall.

"Do you care so little for me that you would humiliate me before the eyes of my family and allies?" He was still angry, very much so.

"I wish only to stop bloodshed among those I now consider mine."

"And are you willing as well, Ainsley, to wed the Englishman in that pursuit when you are my wife under the tenets of our laws and now carry my child?"

Ainsley's calm demeanor began to crumble, her

voice trembled audibly. "They will kill you, don't you see? They have the English William and Mary, who will support their claims! I will not watch you die. Aye, I will do anything to keep that from happening!"

A look of pain flitted a path across Rodric's stern visage, and he turned his head away from her toward the roaring fire. When the light silhouetted his profile, she saw how his jaw worked with anger, contracting, releasing, over and over as if fighting for control. He composed himself with effort, then suddenly walked swiftly back to where she stood. She gasped in surprise when he took her by the shoulders, his fingers gripping her hard and fast, in a frightening way he had never done before, not even on the first day after she had escaped him in the wood.

"Do you think I could go on living with you wed to some Englishman you have never even laid eyes on? You are my wife now. You carry my child. I brought you here to be with me. And with me you will stay."

Ainsley fought her rising emotions. Tears burned like brands against her eyelids, but she fought against letting them fall. "What good will be done if you die to keep me here, and I am forced to wed the Englishman while your head is displayed before us atop an English pike?"

Rodric's face changed as if he now understood how and why she suffered, and he gathered her trembling body into his arms. He stroked her hair soothingly. "I will not let that happen, never, not with you here awaiting my return. The war between Ian MacDonald and Hugh Campbell is long overdue. MacDonalds will fight Strathmorton for the unwarranted death of your mother, Meredith, and for taking Ian's child away from him. Let it be fought once and won, or we will have to suffer our children to do the killing of Campbells in our stead."

"I am afraid you will not come back."

"I will be back, and then we can live together in peace. You are a MacDonald. You are finally at home with us, as you should have been from the day of your birth. Your clansmen consider it sacred duty to fight for your honor, and Ian thinks only of avenging Hugh's treachery against your mother."

"But I do not wish others to die because of me. It's wrong."

"Nay. It is the way of the Scot to fight for what is his and the honor of his beloved."

Ainsley clung to him when he kissed her because she knew that no matter how much she tried, she could not stop him. When he strode down the hall to resummon the chiefs and join the mounted soldiers awaiting them in the courtyard, she sank into the bench again, shaking with fear. He walked into danger because of her and there was nothing she could do to stop him.

Ainsley waited up late into the night, longing for Rodric's return. She paced restlessly before the windows, pausing to watch the night sky, where flames from the burning village still sent a formidable reddish glow over the dark sea. She was afraid for Rodric and for her father. She had come to care very much for them in the short time she had been at Arrandane. Rodric had filled a void inside her heart where only emptiness had been before. She loved him for giving her a home and a family.

Breanne had finally retired to her chamber and fallen asleep in utter exhaustion, but slumber was nowhere within Ainsley's grasp. She watched from her casement window and prowled the outside corridors, trod the steps down to the great hall and walked its length, then climbed back to the battlement walls to pace endlessly until she finally gave up her vigil in Rodric's bedchamber. She remembered the strangeness of her wedding night when she had been so frightened of him and the way his soft, unthreatening kisses had gradually kindled her inexperienced body to fire. Now, just as quickly as they had fallen in love, he could be taken away from her. Forever.

Overwrought with worry, she fell to her knees upon the padded prayer bench beside the window and clasped her hands together. For all those years in the abbey, she had prayed long and often for the secure and loving marriage that Rodric had given to her. Now their love could be ended in the blink of an eye, in the jab of the sword, or in the bite of a musket ball.

After what seemed an eternity, she heard footsteps entering her chamber next door. Rushing to see if Rodric had returned, she ran through the connecting portal and found him beside her bed. He turned, appearing haggard and tired, his face blackened with soot. She hurried into his arms, and he held her tightly, without speaking. His leather tunic smelled acrid with smoke and destruction.

"They killed seventeen men. One woman died in the flames," he muttered hoarsely. "The others of Maycairn escaped in time, but they fired the church and every croft within a ten-mile radius, the bloody cowards."

"Rodric, I am so sorry."

" 'Twas not your fault, so do not put the blame upon your shoulders." He released one long sigh of frustration and fatigue, then groaned slightly as he stepped back, unbuckling his sword belt.

"Are you hurt?" she asked at once.

"A mere scratch. I'm just tired. I have need of rest before we ride to Dunvegan to make our battle strategy."

"Let me help you undress," she murmured soothingly, gently tracing an angry burn that creased the side of his jaw. "I've kept water warm in the hip bath if you wish to bathe."

He disrobed, tiredly, then lowered himself into the bath. Ainsley knelt at his side and helped him to soap his back. He stopped her once in order to hold her hands tightly and kiss her mouth, but not with the passion he usually displayed. This time their lovemaking, his touch, was tender, reverent.

" 'Tis good for a man to have a woman waiting his return. I have missed much in the past, not having your gentle hands to tend me as wife when I turn weary."

Ainsley was pleased by his sentiment. "I am only happy that you've returned here unharmed, my lord."

While he dried himself and got naked into bed, she poured him a tankard of ale. He waved it away, took her hands, and drew her down underneath the coverlets with him. "I want you to lie beside me."

Gladly she obliged his wish, sliding in under the linen sheets and very close against his side. Snuggling beneath his arm, she was content to be close to the man she loved, to have him home and safe, at least for a little while before he had to return to his fight.

"They will come again, but next time we will be ready. And we will avenge our losses in turn upon the lands and chattel held by the Campbells."

Ainsley wanted to voice her despair over more loss of life, but she knew her words would be fruitless. And her own motivations were perverse, for if he did not take up his sword in her name, she would have no choice but to return to a life of misery without him.

His arms tightened around her, but he slept quickly in exhaustion. In time she closed her eyes as well, content to listen to the slow, steady beat of his heart beneath her ear until he was forced to leave her again.

Chapter Nineteen

The dark waters of a wave-restless sea was crowned by the shimmering arc of sunrise when Rodric cantered from the opened gates of the castle keep at the head of a long contingent of mounted soldiers. His chest draped vividly in the red MacDonald plaid, he had turned in the saddle and saluted Ainsley's place upon the battlement wall. Her heart had frozen over with a fear that lingered throughout the endless week that followed his departure.

Though she haunted that high, windswept wall, watchful for his return, she witnessed only periodic arrivals of military couriers dispatched from the various clan patrols with reports of continuing skirmishes on the shores of the isle, south of Arrandane. And while she and Breanne kept eyes peeled for a glimpse of pennon bearing the MacDonald cross and gauntlet, they had yet to see the two faces they longed to find among the exhausted soldiers straggling back for rest and recovery.

The wait seemed interminable, and unable to

bear the anxiety, Ainsley endeavored to concentrate her time and effort upon nursing the injured of Maycairn and the other ravaged MacDonald villages, the inhabitants of which were still being brought daily into the sanctuary of the castle. The carnage was dreadful to behold, and Ainsley's healing talents were readily sought out for the large number of burned and wounded.

Possessed by seemingly tireless energy, no doubt sustained by constant worry, she worked alongside Breanne, mixing herbal remedies with pestle and mortar and teaching the other women of Arrandane the techniques of easing pain by pressure of the fingertips. Often she secretly used her hands in the way that only she could, hoping God would intervene and heal those who suffered and fought so that she could remain with her husband on Skye.

The work was grueling, and heartbreaking, if for no other reason than the sheer number of injured and displaced families. Distress over Rodric's safety absorbed her every waking moment, but she was inordinately pleased that she could help the sick, and for the first time, here in her new home, without the awful accusations of her leagueship with the devil or of casting evil spells with demon-possessed eyes.

As the second week commenced, still with no word of Rodric, she redoubled her work in the ground-floor rooms set aside as an infirmary. One day as she sat there, absorbed upon redressing and greasing the wound of an elderly crofter felled by a flaming rafter, she was brought up short by the sound of a loud female voice whose cries fell in echoes down the hallway. Her head shot up just as Breanne came rushing helter-skelter into the banquet hall, the hem of her long yellow skirt bunched in her fists. Her face was stark white, her eyes filled with fear.

"Rodric's been struck down," she cried without a softening preamble. Ainsley's heart fell to the floor of her belly as the most terrible fear bloomed into awful reality. "And my Richard, as well!"

A sob escaped Breanne with that admission, and her emotions seemed to break through the dam of self-restraint. She lapsed into an uncontrollable fit of weeping, holding her face in her hands until Ainsley came to her feet and grabbed her by the shoulders. She gave her a swift, forceful shake. "How badly was Rodric hurt, Breanne? Are they bringing him back here to Arrandane?"

"Nay, a company of MacLeods rode in with the news only moments ago. Rodric has sent them to ride escort for you so that you can tend to his wound. Make haste, Ainsley, they wait us in the courtyard."

Somewhere in the deep recesses of her mind it occurred to her that Rodric was unlikely to summon her outside the castle walls, but then she realized he must be seriously wounded, perhaps even mortally, to request such of her. At that thought, her determination to go to him overrode every impediment of doing so. Without hesitation Ainsley gave over her bandaging tasks to the servant girl assisting her and hurried with Breanne outside into the cobbled interior courtyard.

The squad of soldiers who had brought them the ill tidings still sat astride their warhorses, heavily armed with both broadsword and battle ax, flying pennons of the long-horned black bull of Clan MacLeod. The young man riding at the forefront dismounted at once and bowed deeply and respectfully before Ainsley.

"I have orders from Lord Rodric, my lady, to bring you to him posthaste. He has fallen in a skirmish and lies near death hidden in the house of our kin."

"How is he hurt?" Her voice was barely audible as she forced the question through a tight, constricted throat so thickened by the bilious taste of fear she nearly gagged.

"He took an arrow in his shoulder and was crushed from knee to foot when his horse fell atop his leg. That is why he cannot come to you."

"Oh, dear God preserve him," she prayed under her breath, but she knew she could help such injuries if she could reach him in time. She had to get to him without delay.

"And what of Richard MacLeod?" Breanne cried, anxiously twisting her fingers together. "Is he mortally injured?"

"He took an arrow in the thigh, my lady, but the shaft pierced through without lodging in his body as did the one Lord Rodric suffered."

"I must come with you!" Breanne caught Ainsley's sleeve and wheeled her around to face her. Her brown eyes were dry now and aglow with the same fierce determination Ainsley felt. "I will not stay here and wonder if my brother and Richard are dead or alive. I can help you nurse them, Ainsley, please!"

Ainsley had no desire to argue. She only wished to reach her injured husband. "Then, order our mounts saddled for us whilst I fetch my medicinal apron."

Within the hour they were outside the keep of Arrandane, pressing hard, northward along Rodric's newly constructed road toward Dunvegan, sandwiched in the midst of a score or more of armed MacLeod soldiers. The day was bright with sunshine, mild and lovely with the chirping of birdsong, and the innocuous calm of the afternoon stillness seemed strangely unfitting for so terrible a day.

Ainsley longed to urge her horse into a fuller gallop than the steady pace to which the young MacLeod officer held the column. When she attempted to question him further about her husband's condition, he seemed unable to respond in detail and seemed more concerned with pressing on diligently with no rest stops even to water their horses.

The course they took eventually wound off the roadway and for a time brought them inland away from sheer-faced cliffs near where Rodric had shown her the ancient ruins of the MacLeod church. Memories of those happy days spent together at the hunting lodge intensified her terror at losing him. What if he succumbed to his wounds? What would she do? She could not let herself think that way. She could help him once she reached him. Why was it taking so long?

After what seemed a year of travel, the riders ahead of her veered down a winding path through a stand of tall trees bent landward from fierce ocean gusts. Below their high vantage point, she could see that an arm of the sea cut into the mountains. The bent tree limbs shielded most of the ocean vista, but as she held tightly onto her pommel, she glanced behind her, wondering that Rodric would retreat to a spot so far from Arrandane where he would be veritably trapped with the sea at his back. As they left the grove of larches that hid the beach below, she saw that a large group of men awaited them on the rocky strand.

Confused, she squinted her eyes but saw no tent to harbor wounded nor the red plaid now so familiar to her. Then she saw the lone pennon fluttering on their standard, and her heart stopped beating. The tusked boar. Disbelieving that the soldiers awaiting them could truly be of her grandfather's clan, she searched their ranks until she saw the telltale dark blue of tartan. Had a Campbell force landed? Oh, God, had they already captured Rodric?

"Wait, they are Campbells to whom you take us!" she cried to the young MacLeod, jerking back on her reins and making her horse stumble slightly. "We must flee at once before they catch sight of us!"

Her horse shied nervously as she attempted to turn its head and in the process crowded Breanne's mount farther behind. The officer grabbed her bridle and held it firmly. " 'Twas the order given to us by Lord Rodric MacDonald, my lady. We were to bring you here and give you over to these men."

"No, you lie! He'd never do that!" cried Breanne furiously, striking her whip at another soldier who was grabbing at her reins. "Run, Ainsley! It's a trap!"

As Breanne managed to break free and make a dash back up the hill toward freedom, Ainsley tried to kick her panicky mare into flight, but the man holding her horse had much too firm a grip. Frightened, she looked around frantically for help and caught sight of a ship anchored far out in the bay. Had Rodric truly turned her over to the Campbells? She could not fathom such a thing happening, but why else would the MacLeods deliver her into enemy hands?

"My husband would never send me back to Strathmorton!" she cried to the MacLeod.

"Lord Rodric is not at fault, my lady," the young captain seemed incongruously apologetic for his treachery. "I am sorry that you must be turned over like this, but Rodric is no longer in charge of our forces. He died from the wound I described to you not a full day past. Now the choice of the MacLeods is to return you to your grandfather or face the siege of Dunvegan. You will not be mistreated there, my lady."

"No, no, I don't believe you! Rodric's not dead!"

The most horrible lump of dread congealed in a thick mass that slowed the blood beating through her heart. She hardly reacted when the Campbells came for her, but as rough hands reached up to drag her from her horse, she kicked at them, struggling desperately to get away.

She was jerked to the ground, but the moment her feet touched sand, she wrenched free of their grasp and ran. Only steps away she felt a swift rush of air behind her, and the blow hit her just above the right temple. Pain shot in a white-hot flash of fire through her brain, extinguished rapidly into trailing sparks that disappeared slowly, one by one, into a deep black sea of oblivion.

Rodric glanced around the war council and studied the faces of the loyal chieftains who had pledged the aid of their clans. They had come together as a force for the first time in his lifetime, the MacDonalds and the MacLeods, and he triumphed at the accomplishment. Their alliance prompted the joining of most of the MacKinnons of the interior and a few of the smaller clans of MacCrimmons to the north.

"Then, we are of accord to wage war upon Clan Campbell of Strathmorton."

"Aye, Rodric, 'tis only the first wave of many marauders that Hugh will throw against the isle. Strathmorton has waited long for a reason to raid our shores and destroy us. I, and all my clansmen, stand with you." The vow was welcome and came from Giles MacLeod, Rodric's uncle and brother of his mother, but Rodric had never doubted their support now that he was wed to Ainsley. Richard MacLeod stood up, staunchly supporting his father's decision.

Everyone looked to Ian MacDonald as he rose

slowly at Rodric's side and propped a hand upon the broad line of his shoulder. "The Clan Mac-Donald both here and on the outer Hebrides stands firm in your stead now that you have risked all to wed my daughter and take up the chieftainship of Arrandane. Our kindred MacDonells of the mainland will fight to the man, for their hatred of Hugh Campbell's encroachment of their territory is longstanding and bitter."

Rodric nodded, then stabbed a finger down onto the map of the Scot mainland spread out on the table in front of him. His fingertip lay directly upon the Argyll peninsula. "What of the Campbells of Glenorchy and the Earl of Inveraray? Will they support their kinsman, Strathmorton, in this fight?"

"Hugh is a renegade who causes Argyll some concern, for he often disregards Campbell loyalty to Edinburgh. Some say they would welcome his demise and their resulting legal claim to his holdings on Loch Awe."

"And the English? Will they support his attack upon the Hebrides?"

"Hugh is William's lackey and lapdog. The English will support his every move, especially now that the Orangeman is demanding our verbal vows of allegiance."

"And do any of you refuse such oaths to William as king?"

Silence reigned around the table for several moments, and Rodric knew that each and every man present loathed, as any true Highlander would, the aforementioned vow of allegiance to the English king. Jacobites in their loyalty, they were, but after Robert the Bruce and the consolidation of the Crowns of England and Scotland, little could Highlanders do but acquiesce to foreign leadership of the Scots.

"As Lord of Arrandane I have sworn allegiance to King William and Queen Mary," he told them in firm, uncompromising voice.

"As have I," Ian intoned, unfledgingly support-ive of Rodric's statement.

A series of nods and low murmurs followed from the other chiefs and many of the clansmen standing behind their leaders. Rodric felt more relief than anything, for his stint of schooling in Londontown had taught him just how ruthless the English could be if the Highlanders chose to rise up against their foreign-born monarch. The English would not stop until they brought every clan under their heel or destroyed the Scot way of life completely.

"With our allegiance to the Crown, the English will not wish to anger so many clans by interced-ing in Hugh's behalf, especially if Argyll and the other Campbells do not support his war."

Giles MacLeod stood, his shaggy red hair bril-liant in the light from the flaming copper brazier. "We must first see to protect our shores and shires against further invasion, then we will con-sider attacking him on his own lands . . ."

A commotion of horses and excited shouts from outside the leather tent ended the conference, and Rodric turned, shocked when his own sister rushed into the tent. Anger came swiftly, his words ringing with ire.

"What the devil are you doing here, Bree? I told you not to leave Arrandane!"

"The Campbells have Ainsley!" Breanne's frightened words stopped Rodric's heartbeat.

En masse the chieftains came to their feet, and Ian's face blanched as Rodric frantically grabbed his sister's arms.

"What do you mean? Ainsley's safe at Arrandane!"

Breanne shook her head, tears rolling down her cheeks. "No, no, she's not anymore. Soldiers rode in this afternoon with news that you had fallen in battle! They said you wanted her to come to you, that you'd been injured and needed her! They took us to Walboran Point, and I escaped when I saw the Campbell soldiers waiting on the beach, but Ainsley couldn't get away!" She sobbed then, turning distrustful eyes upon Giles and Richard and their clansmen. "They tricked us! And they flew the black bull! 'Twas MacLeods who betrayed us!"

For an instant everyone stared at Breanne, stunned, unable to digest her accusations, then the sound of a sword scraping from its metal scabbard filled the quiet. Ian held his broadsword toward the MacLeod contingent, deep, angry lines setting his mouth. Giles MacLeod's claymore followed quickly, and the scream of steel weapons being loosed continued until every man among them held weapons at the ready. Clan turned against clan, the alliance forgotten until Rodric quickly stepped between the agitated men and put his hand upon Ian's trembling arm.

"Wait, Ian, do not fall prey to Hugh's purpose. He means to divide us asunder by this crafty ruse. I am willing to swear on my father's grave that the MacLeods performed no such treachery against me. 'Tis a trick to divide us against each other."

Both sides held their warring stances, swords gripped tightly in gauntleted hands. "Did we not lose a company of Clan MacLeod three days past, massacred on patrol?" he reminded them. "The pennon was stolen and could easily have been flown by the enemy."

Still the men glared at each other with suspicion until Rodric lost hold of his temper.

"This is my wife who has been taken by the enemy. By God, I will have her back no matter what the cost. Do you stand with me, or nay? I have no time to play the intermediary for those stubborn of pride."

His words penetrated Ian's wrath, and Ainsley's father slowly lowered his blade. "We must rescue Ainsley before Hugh kills her or banishes her from us forever as he did to Meredith. I wish only to save my child."

At his words, cold fear swept in waves up Rodric's spine, but rage came swiftly in its wake, cold, black, lethal. Viciously he drew his dirk and brought the sharp point down hard into the map and left it quivering dead center in Campbell territory.

"Then, it is done. Strathmorton's acts leave us no choice. All-out war to the last man."

"I am with you." Ian's knife dug into the table

followed quickly by Giles MacLeod's bull-crested dagger.

"Aye, to the last MacLeod."

"And I."

Rodric looked as a half dozen more dirks came down hard into the heart of the Argyll peninsula. He would not rest until his dagger lay not in the map of Hugh Campbell's estates but deep inside his black heart.

"Then, let us prepare to march. My wife lies captive to Campbell swine."

Chapter Twenty

"Ainsley? Ainsley, can you hear me?"

Someone called her insistently and would not stop shaking her shoulder. From the deep dregs of her muddled mind, Ainsley heard the voice and tried to think who it was. Had Rodric returned at last from the war council? No, the voice was softer, the words of a woman, and Breanne's face floated to mind. Groggily she forced open heavy eyelids and tried to focus on the face close above her, but it was wavery, distorted as if Ainsley peered up through a calm pool of water.

"Oh, thank the Holy Saints, you are awake. I've been so worried."

Ainsley blinked hard, trying to decide what had happened. She was confused, and her head ached horribly. As a cool cloth touched her temple, her vision cleared a bit and she recognized the woman tending her. "Myrna? What are you doing here?"

Her red-haired friend nodded, her smile broad and happy, and for one awful moment Ainsley feared that she was still in the abbey, that the past few months with Rodric had been nothing more than a wonderful dream. She shut her eyes again, and heard the sound of rain falling, softly, steadily. She looked again, found the window across the room and focused on the blurry panes. It wasn't the abbey, she thought, then the truth rushed through her mind like a cold, devastating winter wind.

"Rodric's not dead! I don't believe it!" were her first words, as she sat up angrily then paid a terrible price when her temples exploded again as if squeezed tightly in an iron vise. She put her fingers there, wincing when she found a lump as big as a guinea egg. One of the Campbells had clubbed her on the beach, but Breanne had escaped. Had she reached Rodric with the news of her abduction?

"Oh, Ainsley, I've never seen such a bump. Does it hurt terribly? I've bathed it throughout the night with cool water and vinegar. Hugh was quite furious when he found out his man had struck you . . ."

Ainsley cut short her words of concern, demanding curtly, "Where am I? Where have you brought me?"

"Why, this is Strathmorton Castle on the loch. Your grandfather sent soldiers to find out your whereabouts the moment I related your kidnapping at the hands of the MacDonald devils."

Ainsley felt shocked by Myrna's vilification of Rodric's clansmen, yet she had done the same until she had lived upon Skye. Now her hatred seemed incomprehensible. How could she have

been so filled with hatred toward people she had
never even met?

"I am a MacDonald now, Myrna, and proud I
am of it." The utterance showed so, and hot tears
born in a maelstrom of emotions swirled out of
control until dried by her rising anger.

Shaking her head in disbelief, Myrna took her
hands and squeezed them as if consoling her.
"Don't say such things. You are a Campbell, and
such vowed allegiance to our enemies 'twill only
enrage his lordship. He bears them a violent hatred." She shuddered. "I knew not how much
until he found out that they had kidnapped you
from the abbey. He's sworn to destroy them; man,
woman, and child."

She had to get away, Ainsley decided, fighting
a vicious spiral of vertigo as she swung her feet
over the side of the bed. She stood up, and her
brain careened side to side in an erratic dance
until she was forced to brace her palms against
the dressing table beside the bed. She stared at
herself in the heavy gold-framed mirror and found
a yellowish discoloration swelling upward from
the corner of her eye. She dipped one of the
folded towels into the basin of water, wrung it
slightly, then pressed it against the ugly raised
bruise.

Behind her the bedchamber was reflected in all
its grandeur, and for the first time she noticed
how extravagantly lavish it was. The crimson
hangings on the post beside her were embroidered
with gold thread in the Campbell boar. An oval
marble table stood across the room just beneath

the splendidly draped, velvet-cloaked casement windows.

Myrna saw her interest, and said, " 'Tis a beautiful room, is it not? It was your mother's bedchamber. His lordship has touched it not at all since she left here so long ago."

"My mother's?" Ainsley thought of the blond-haired woman in Ian's locket and tried to picture her standing in the midst of the luxurious Arabian carpets and gilt-edged furniture, perhaps staring out over Loch Awe. Did they take her from this very room when they imprisoned her on the moors to give birth in shame like a gallows criminal?

Ainsley put her palm against her own belly. What if Hugh found out about her child? Would he do the same to her? Would he order her baby drowned because Rodric was the sire? Fear came again, swiftly escalating to terror for her unborn child. Her grandfather could never know she was pregnant, never! She had to get away before he found out. She found her hands were shaking, and she moved slowly toward the window but found the rain had intensified, obstructing the glass with sliding torrents of water.

Whirling around, she demanded of Myrna, unable to hide her anger and resentment. "Then, I am a prisoner here?"

Myrna appeared genuinely shocked. "Prisoner? Nay, nay, everyone here has been eagerly awaiting you. His lordship has already sent word to Randolph of Varney to come north for the wedding, for it will be held barely a fortnight from today.

The entire castle has been preparing even before you were taken."

"I will marry no one."

"What?" Myrna became flustered, then disbelieving, finally utterly distraught in both word and manner. "But, Ainsley, you know you must! You've been betrothed to him since you were a child! We spoke of it often at the abbey, and you had no such . . ."

"I am already married to Rodric MacDonald." She came close to telling her about her baby but caught herself in time. She no longer trusted her old friend, for she was a Campbell. "I will not marry Randolph of Varney."

"Oh, Ainsley, what have they done to you? Why are you protecting the MacDonald cur after Hugh risked so many men to get you back? You belong here. You always will. You were forced to wed that awful man, were you not? You never would have done so without some sort of coercion."

Ainsley trod swiftly to the foot of the bed and drew Myrna down with her onto the brocaded bench. She took her face between her hands and attempted to make her understand. "Rodric is not awful. He is good and kind. He loves me, they all love me. Myrna, don't you see? Hugh Campbell has told us lies. Rodric and Ian told me the truth about my parents. I met my real father, Myrna . . ."

She fought to steady her voice as it cracked with a tumult of feelings . . . "Hugh hid me from him after my mother died. Ian and Meredith were married. Hugh stole my birthright. They don't fear me on Skye. They don't make me wear a cover over my eye or think me a demon. I love it there. I want to go back."

Her earnest pleas fell upon deaf ears as she discovered when Myrna spoke next. "Why, Ainsley, you surely cannot believe such blatant lies. How can you forget that Strathmorton has taken care of you since you were a wee bairn? Did he not send me there as your companion out of his deep responsibility for your welfare? And when I brought him word of your kidnapping, he was terrified for your safety. You must not let his enemies poison your mind against him! What gain would he have to engender such falsehoods concerning your parentage?"

"Because my marriage to Lord Randolph will safeguard his wealth and lands from English encroachment. He wishes to align me with English nobility because it will secure his own wealth, and because he hates any by the name of MacDonald."

"But of course he feels so. That is the way of the men and the world. As his ward, it is your duty to provide such alliances for your clan. You have always known such since you were a small child."

Myrna would never understand, Ainsley thought, spirits flagging as she realized her friend would never admit to Strathmorton's deceit. Sorrow overwhelmed her and she worded her next statement simply, as straightforward as possible, for in truth it was the only fact that mattered. "I am already wed to another. A man I love deeply, and will always love."

"A man who now rots in his grave, I will remind you, my Lady Ainsley."

Lord Hugh Campbell, Earl of Strathmorton, watched Meredith's girl jump up and turn to stare at him. Her lady-in-waiting, the young woman with freckled face and fiery hair who had apprised him of Ainsley's abduction, jumped up and dropped into a deep curtsy. The girl he had taken such pains to retrieve gave him naught but a silent, sullen glare.

For two decades, his stubborn pride had prohibited him from looking upon his only living kin, but now that he was finally face-to-face with his granddaughter, he examined her appearance hungrily, eagerly. A great, dreadful undulation passed up his spine then back down its length. God help them, but she looked so much like Meredith.

With vivid detail he remembered the moment he had sentenced the very child standing before him to death, the moment he had striven to forget but could never cleanse from his mind during endless long, guilt-stricken, sleepless nights, the last time he had seen his only daughter, Meredith. It came now as if yesterday. Meredith tossing feverishly, calling one name over and over. It was that name that made him do the unthinkable. She had not called for him, her father who had given her everything within his reach, but for Ian, her bloody MacDonald lover.

Stone-cold loathing swept his flesh even now, but he forced himself to recall his daughter before her bewitchment by his enemy, when she was young and lovely and thought her father the most wonderful man who trod Scottish soil. Hugh had doted on her, adored her, loved her to utter, all-encompassing distraction, but all that ended when he found out she was with child, the spawn of a foe. Even after so many years, the agony of her betrayal slammed hard upon his soul. He hardened his face, forcibly thrusting away silly sentimentality. He had no use for tender emotions. Not since Meredith had torn out his heart.

"I should welcome you home, granddaughter." Holding himself in strict control he bent forward in a slight bow from the waist. He tried to hide the ugly tide of resentment invading his bloodstream to run rampant through every part of him, but as he faced Ian's misbegotten bastard, he could only think of her extreme resemblance to Meredith, the fairness of her skin, the golden highlights shining from the honey-colored curls hanging down her back.

Ainsley met his stare, unafraid, unbending, out of eyes so strange in color yet hauntingly arresting, a gaze that had engendered the absurd fear of the witch of Kilchurn—a ridiculous legend, of course, but one that Hugh had encouraged to keep her safe and frightened behind the sturdy walls of the abbey until she was safely wed to the Englishman.

He felt like laughing now, but the sound would have come forth with bitterness, and complete and utter irony. For years he had followed every safeguard to keep her from betraying him as her

mother had, going so far as to lock her away. Yet
fate had seen the very same scene played out to
wound him again, as if a vengeful god still played
a wrathful jest. As he silently perused her, her
elegant chin rose a notch in the willful way of
Meredith at her most obstinate.

"Lord Ian is my true sire, and proud I am of
my father's bloodline, more so than of my mother's sad heritage."

No other utterance from her lips could have
engendered such cutting pain inside Hugh, nor
explode the rocket of black rage that accelerated
so violently to the surface. His chest heaved with
fury and his visible effort to contain it. Clamping
his jaw, he gnashed his teeth, grinding them together until his face hurt. His voice was so tight,
unnatural, that he hardly recognized it himself.
"You are a Campbell, and would be proudly such,
had the bastards of the Hebrides not filled you
with the lies that cause you to spout such
nonsense."

"You are the liar, Hugh of Strathmorton, and
no kin I claim to your line. You are the man who
sent my mother away to die alone and robbed Ian
all knowledge of his only child. You are the villain
who shut me inside a nunnery so that I would
never learn the truth of your perfidious deeds . . ."

"Enough!"

The one word wielded a harshness that instantly curbed his granddaughter's tongue, but
still she refused to lower her eyes shining with
open defiance. Her scathing condemnation
scalded him like hot broth thrown into his face.

For the space of several moments, he struggled to regain composure.

"You will return to reason once you stand at Lord Randolph's side as wife. Varney journeys from his London house even as we speak."

"I am legally wed to Rodric MacDonald, Lord of Arrandane."

"Legally? I think not. The marriage contract in my possession was made a decade ago and affixed with the royal seal." He frowned, tired of her tirade. "Little does it matter at any count, for the man you call husband lies dead and buried on the beachhead of Skye."

"He is not dead." Ainsley spoke in calm, succinct syllables, every word alive with steadfast conviction. "I will not wed another, never will I do such a thing. There is no way you can make me wed the Englishman."

Hugh could actually feel his own mouth twist with his inhuman attempt to control his anger. He could feel the blood rush up his neck and redden his face. Gasping, Myrna stepped away from him but Ainsley did not retreat. She held her stance, as her mother, too, had done when faced by his fury.

"Aye, granddaughter, you will do as I tell you, or suffer severe consequences. I warn you, my lady, they are dire ones, indeed."

"Nothing can be so loathesome as taking an Englishman before God when I am wed to a true Scot."

Hugh smiled at her extreme naivete. "You do not know me well, girl, or you would not profess such drivel. You will soon learn that I am not known for my patience, nor my mercy."

"Nor for your *honor*, my Lord Campbell," she tossed back, her expression molded with haughty disdain.

For a moment he stood unmoving, shocked by her insult, then his fists balled inward until his nails bit into his palms. She was a willful wench, but she would soon remember her place. She, as last remaining heir of generations of his bloodline, would marry the Englishman of Hugh's choice. He would see her do so before he drew in his last breath, by God as his witness, she would do as she was told.

"Guard!"

At his hoarse shout Myrna looked terrified, but Ainsley's stare was unwaveringly hostile. The soldiers he had posted to guard her door burst instantly into their presence.

"Seize the girl and follow me."

"Where are you taking me?" Ainsley said calmly as they rushed forth and caught her arms.

"You will soon know, my dear, and perhaps then you will be less contrary and wear more pleasant a visage in my presence."

"Rodric will kill you for this outrage" was her answer, head held high and regal.

Hugh's laugh was icy. "I fear naught from a sword wielded by the rotting arm of a corpse."

As the bearded Campbell soldiers dragged her up curving stone steps that led into the upper reaches of the castle, Ainsley made no effort to resist the brutal fingers clamped over her upper arms. Hugh led them at a swift march, and Myrna rushed behind them, clutching her shawl around her shoulders, wringing her hands and begging Ainsley to see reason.

Ainsley endeavored to hide the way Hugh Campbell's final words had devastated her hopes, but the words echoed around the corners of her mind like the clomping sounds of the soldiers' boots as they dragged her with them in a steady climb up a narrow stone staircase. She could not let herself believe Rodric was dead. He would come for her. She had but to summon her courage and hold out until he could rescue her.

Lifting her face, she tried to see the top of the circular steps. She was surprised they ascended in the old stone fortress, for she thought surely she would be imprisoned in some dank cell of the dungeon. She assumed the turret tower was one of the two forming the corner walls of the castle. She had looked over the abbey wall on many occasions and gazed at the old castle rising faraway in the misty loch. When her step faltered on the narrow treads, the kilted soldier gave her a sharp push that propelled her up the last few steps and out onto the very precipice of the castle.

It still drizzled, cold rain that drenched her gown within minutes as she was led across the narrow walkway. Behind her Myrna was still sobbing as if she already knew Ainsley's fate. Then Ainsley saw what awaited her. Her breath caught with horror. A metal box, perhaps five feet wide and six feet tall, was pushed out away from the wall, hanging on a metal pole suspended sixty feet above the waters of the loch with no shelter whatsoever from the inclement weather.

"Your new bedchamber, my lady," Hugh whispered close to her ear.

As one of the guards winched the cage back to where they stood and unlocked the chained door, Myrna thrust her woolen shawl into Ainsley's hands as she was shoved inside. Falling to her knees she held onto the sides as the tilting cage swung out again over the water.

She draped the long fringed shawl over her head, and Ainsley gripped her fingers tightly on the iron bars until the box righted from its swaying.

Her grandfather stood looking at her over the edge of the parapet. His call was half obliterated by the wind. "When you are ready to accept your responsibility, you may return to more luxurious accommodations. Let it be your own decision."

Ainsley watched him walk away. Myrna followed him, continually looking back at her friend with a sorrowful face. Ainsley's jaw hardened, then she squeezed her eyes shut. Rodric would come for her, she said firmly to herself, she knew he would come.

Chapter Twenty-one

❦

"I beg you, Ainsley, obey his lordship. I cannot bear to see you languish in this horrid cage."

" 'Tis Hugh who locks me here like an animal with only a bucket of brackish water and a chamber pot." Bitter, caustic anger fired flames inside Ainsley's breast. She gripped the bars and stared at Myrna, who stood on the parapet, protected from the cold drizzling rain by a tan tarpaulin the guards had stretched atop spears for their own comfort.

A shiver possessed her limbs, wracking feverishly through her body, and she knew she was very sick as her throat worked convulsively to force a swallow down that tight, parched passage. She wrapped herself tighter in the dry blanket Myrna had brought to her even as she knew that the length of wool would soon be as sodden as her dripping-wet skirt.

For nearly three days now she had suffered in the dreadful metal box beneath the lewd eyes and jeering taunts of the brutish guards. She had not been completely dry in all that time, for the weather was intermittently cloudy and cool. She longed for a sunny day that would dry out the dampness that was slowly, gradually penetrating to the very marrow of her bones.

Her palsied hands shook, from cold and fever, and her trembling was readily detectable as she placed her fingertips to her forehead and wearily massaged both temples. She had had very little to eat, had been desperate with hunger for the first day and night, but now with only a diet of bread and a few pieces of fruit to tease her appetite, her rumbling stomach was as numb and shriveled as wet leather broiled by the sun.

Her head pounded, a staccato drumbeat that caused the veins threading her temples to pulsate beneath her fingers, and she sought to pinch the bridge of her nose in the way Brother Alfonse had taught her, hoping that pressure would subdue the grinding ache. The remedy provided no relief, and though she suffered greatly, she rested her palm upon her abdomen and feared more the effect of the heartless abuse upon her unborn child. She could not let herself become so ill that she would miscarry her baby. And she was so weak already. Helpless, hopeless despair assailed her heavy heart, and she knew she would soon have to succumb to her grandfather's wishes.

"He seeks only to insure your happiness." Myrna was still trying, never giving up with her cajolery, but Ainsley welcomed her friend's visits, for she sneaked her the welcome dry blankets, usually with an apple or bunch of grapes secreted inside. Myrna continued with her pleas, tears welling up to glisten brightly in her eyes. "This union with Varney has been ordained since your birth; there is no good cause to continue to balk."

Ainsley drew in a long breath, a labored sigh that rattled the congestion plaguing her chest and brought on a sharp puncturing pain as if the point of a knife pricked her lungs. She forced herself to reply, if only to bolster her own dwindling resolve. "He took me from my rightful parents and subjected me to years of suffering persecution at the hands of nuns because my eyes were of two colors. The people of Skye bear me no ill but appreciate my efforts at the healing arts."

She pressed her lips tightly together as a rasping cough forced itself into her inflamed chest cavity, but she tried one more time to reach Myrna's good sense. "If Hugh bore such love of me, why am I here, chained inside this torturous device? Why did he not visit me at the abbey during all those lonely years? Instead of bringing me here to Strathmorton as his beloved granddaughter, which was my right, he sent you to watch over me in that loveless abbey."

Ainsley paused, hardly recognizing her own low, hoarse voice, but at Myrna's lack of response, she went on. "I will tell you the motive that held him. 'Twas because he feared his nefarious plots against my parents would be discovered and righteously avenged at the hands of Ian MacDonald." Surging emotion quit her voice, and her words came out as thick and stiff as aged oatmeal left at the hearth side. "Now you, too, after our years of friendship, do betray me by standing with one so cruel as to deny me the only happiness I have ever known."

Myrna's freckled face crumpled, hurt by Ainsley's contempt but unable to justify her disloyalty. She sank into the folds of her heavy-hooded cloak as if for protection against the harsh accusations, but Ainsley could not dredge up an ounce of pity. She shut her eyes against the softly uttered, self-vindicating speech that followed.

"My heart breaks that you think so poorly of me when I have always been your true and faithful friend. I wish only to encourage you to do your duty to Varney . . ."

"Whether I bear love for him, or nay? Whether I consider myself wed to Rodric MacDonald, my true love?" Swept with a fresh onslaught of indignation, Ainsley came close to admitting that she proudly carried Rodric's child, but she cut off her own revelation for fear she would be subjected to even harsher treatment at her grandfather's hands. Tears born of exhaustion, of illness and despair, threatened, overwhelmed her and began to roll down her cheeks. Too demoralized even to summon the energy to brush them away, she averted her face and fixed her overflowing eyes upon a point far across the misty reaches of the rain-blanketed loch. "Rodric is more a man, more a Highlander and man of honor than Hugh Campbell will ever be."

The censorious utterance brought a horrified gasp from Myrna. Her stammered warning came in lowered tones and with worried glances at the nearby guard post. "I beg you, Ainsley, hold your tongue, or he will leave you swinging over the water forever." Nervous now, Myrna pulled at her knuckles then wrapped her arms tightly around her shoulders. "The wedding on Skye is not legal. His lordship told me so himself. Your marriage contract to Varney was negotiated many years ago and sanctioned by the Church of England. I pray you be sensible, Ainsley, you are but a woman and cannot think to dictate matters such as this."

"I would rather die than take the Englishman into my bed." And that might be the ultimate result, an eventuality she would gladly accept if she was not with child.

"But, Ainsley, you are ill! I fear for you!"

Ainsley wished Myrna would go away. She dipped her hands into the rust-eroded bucket and smoothed palmfuls of cold water over her crimson-flushed cheeks. The fever seemed to smolder under her skin like glimmering embers beneath a half-burned log.

"If I succumb to such dire fate, 'twill be Strathmorton's doing alone. No one else's."

With those final words she twisted away and huddled miserably into the corner of the cage. Her back to Myrna, she closed her eyes and quickly fell into a fitful dose, barely aware when her friend left, sobbing softly into her open hands.

When next a low-timbered voice infiltrated the hazy edges of Ainsley's dream where she lay staked atop a bank of snow while soldiers warmed themselves by roaring campfire and partook of hearty beef stew, she ignored the intruding sounds until it became so harsh, so insistent that she had no choice but to acknowledge the source. She opened her eyes to a black, moonless night.

"Awaken, girl, do you hear? Strike the bars with your spear, man, and bring the girl around!"

As the cage shook slightly under ringing metal blows, Ainsley struggled to lift her head and stare groggily at her grandfather. He stood, bracing both palms atop the wall and leaning forward to peer intently at her. His deeply bronzed, well-furrowed face shone under the torchlight, his graying black goatee and mustache accentuating the angular lines of his craggy face.

Three torches, burning brightly with tar-soaked rags, flared past him and illuminated the half dozen bodyguards who always trailed in his wake. The flickering fires cast his looming shadow upon the stones behind him, jumping and darting in frightening, elongated shapes as if a giant gargoyle crouched behind him with malevolent intent. Groaning with pain, her body stiff from the cold, her mind cobwebbed with confusion, she pushed herself upright. On her hands and knees in the cramped cage she stared at him, thinking him a monster, completely repulsed by the degradations he subjected upon his own family, first his daughter and now her. How could he be so lacking in fatherly instinct? No human virtues found residence in his breast; no love of family, no compassion, no decency. He was the devil incarnate, just as both Ian and Rodric had described him to her, enamored of nothing other than political power and the wealth that it brought to the ruthless of heart.

"Leave me to the punishment you inflict with such pleasure. I am proudly a MacDonald, and I will be thus until I take my last breath."

Even in the red-orange glow of the windblown flames, she could see her grandfather's face contort, the mottled ire grimacing his features until he played the part of gargoyle in truth. With impassive disgust, she watched contained emotions ravage every inch of his face, turning him into a portrait of hostile, furious wrath. For a moment he struggled for his voice, then found it with words that made her blood tremble in its flow.

"Be forewarned, granddaughter, if you continue to flaunt your false marriage to the MacDonald as your reason for reneging on your marital duty, then I will order Rodric MacDonald's head carried before you upon a platter to prove the widowhood you deny so valiantly."

The threat was so measured, so intense, an acidic ache pierced her breastbone and struck her heart like the shaft of an arrow. Ainsley fought for breath. He was cruel enough to follow through on his pledge. She had no doubt that he would do so with enjoyment, but he would soon find Rodric MacDonald a most formidable foe, a warrior known far and wide for skill and bravery in battle. Praise Saint Columba that her husband had a fighting force to rally in defense of Hugh's claim upon her. She wove her fingers together and steadied her trembling by tucking them beneath

her chin. She began her silent litany again. Rodric
was alive. He would come for her.

"Get her out and be quick about it," her grandfather ordered angrily.

Shocked by the unexpected command for release, Ainsley clutched the side of the cage as she
was winched in with sharp, jerky tugs of rope that
sent her stomach into queasy turmoil. Her grandfather's eyes, black as twin obsidian stones, were
hooded and unabashedly hawk-like in his unblinking glower. There was no hint of feeling for her
in those small, awful orbs.

When the door was unlocked and forced wide,
she tried to stand but her legs were too wobbly to
hold her weight. Hugh flicked his hand, and one
of his bodyguards immediately supported her arm.
She could not walk with legs so long folded beneath her, but the soldiers had little mercy, half
dragging her between them as Hugh led the way
quickly down through the dark passages of
Strathmorton Castle, without a backward glance
to check her well-being.

In the interior courtyard two score armed soldiers stood readying themselves for a march. Amid
the sounds of creaking leather as men stepped
into stirrups and settled onto saddles, was the jin-
gling of metal bridles and harnesses and the ring
of hooves on stone as horses were backed up and
hitched to a small black traveling coach bearing
the Strathmorton coat of arms.

Escorted to the carriage and thrust inside with
little regard for her state of frailty, she was startled to find a black-garbed priest seated within.

On sight of her he immediately assisted her upon the seat beside him, grabbing up a soft blue blanket and draped it around her quaking shoulders. She recognized him at once as Father Fitzhugh, who had often performed services at the abbey. He had always been kind to her and a good friend to Brother Alfonse.

But the hasty flight through the castle had taken what strength she had left, and she could only stare mutely at him as he snatched up another quilt and tucked it warmly around her legs. She felt so ill now she had trouble with her concentration, but she fought fiercely to force her mind to function and realized that if Hugh meant to take her outside the fortress, an avenue of escape would be opened to her. She refocused her attention as the kindly clergyman began to speak. He, too, had dark eyes, but his were warm and filled with concern. The fact that he cared about her discomfort almost brought on a wellspring of tears, but what did he say? She must listen to him, though his words seemed to waver eerily through her mind.

"You must have courage, my child, for you have suffered much these last days, but 'twill soon be an end to your ordeal, God willing."

"Father Fitzhugh? Where are they taking me?" She peered into his kind face, very confused and disoriented.

"Out of Strathmorton. His lordship's spies have reported an assault force being landed at Taynuitt to lay siege upon Strathmorton. He fears being trapped here with you indefinitely if besieged by the MacDonald alliance."

"Rodric comes for me? He is not dead?" she whispered gruffly, emotions torn, so overcome was she by joy.

"Aye, my lady, he is alive and well enough to lead a formidable force to your rescue. That is why Hugh flees with you this night. We meet Randolph of Varney at Ayr, where we will see you wed and away to England before the first assault ramp approaches the walls of Strathmorton."

Too weakened in body and spirit to react with the outrage rolling inside her, she lay back her head and let herself weep with open despair, for with each passing mile she was taken farther out of the reach of her true husband.

The village of Ayr lay several days southeast of Strathmorton, on the west coast of Scotland facing the Firth of Clyde and the Isle of Arran beyond. Hugh led his force of forty soldiers and contingent of personal bodyguards through the town to the imposing facade of Loudoun Hall in the heart of Ayr.

As Father Fitzhugh assisted her from the coach, he explained that the house was one of many that Hugh held, inherited after the death of a distant Campbell kinsman, but Ainsley barely heard him, her fever intensifying as she was led to a second-floor bedchamber where she would be imprisoned until Varney arrived from the Borders.

For the next few days she stayed abed, resting and grateful for the remedy Hugh allowed the priest to fetch from the apothecary. She considered sneaking away but knew herself much too weak. Even more detrimental and frightening, since the jouncing coach ride from Strathmorton, she had begun to suffer periodic pains in her lower abdomen.

Then one afternoon, the serving girl who had been hired to attend her came with news that Lord Varney had arrived. The ceremony would be held that very afternoon at the nearby Auld Kirk. Trembling with the remnants of fever and a horrible sense of helplessness, she allowed the young servant to help her from her bed and into the plain white silk gown and matching scalloped-edged silk veil that Hugh Campbell had provided for the occasion.

Father Fitzhugh awaited her in the spacious front hallway, and she was glad to be able to lean wearily upon his arm. He rode with her in the heavily guarded carriage the short distance to the kirk. A great many kilted Campbell soldiers stood guard at the church, and she knew with sinking heart that she had no choice but to go through with Hugh's ungodly command.

Tottering slightly on her feet, she stared down into the dim reaches of the church. No one was in attendance except more armed members of the Campbell retinue. At one side stood a separate vanguard of scarlet-coated dragoons, small in number, whom she assumed had ridden escort with the Earl of Varney. Slowly filling with uncompromising dread, Ainsley hesitated at the portal, her chest heaving so violently that she feared she might faint.

"Have faith, my lady," whispered the kind-hearted priest. " 'Twill soon be over. And the Englishman seems a goodly sort."

At the far end of the church near the carved mahogany altar behind which tall white tapers flickered in their gracefully arched silver candelabras, she saw Randolph of Varney for the first time. He awaited her, half hidden in shadows. She could tell little about his person, other than he was tall and slim, dressed in the elaborate English style in slate gray surcoat with gold brocade waistcoat, a crisp, snowy white neck cloth folded at his throat.

Varney had turned now, apprised of her arrival and was peering intently at her, his face amiable enough in appearance with clean-shaven cheeks and neatly combed auburn hair that lay loose upon his shoulders. Her grandfather stood beside Varney with a black-robed Anglican priest who had arrived in the English retinue. The clergyman stood erect, an opened Bible cradled on his palms. No one else was present. No one to take her side or help her escape.

Ainsley looked again at the men waiting for her to make her way to the altar. Panic began to gain momentum inside her, like swiftly rising floodwaters. She could not repeat holy vows before God. She could not take Varney as husband without committing adultery. She could not do that. She could not!

Impatience carved a sterner expression upon

her grandfather's cold visage. His voice rang out in the quiet sanctuary, acutely annoyed in a way that was not concealed from those gathered around him.

"We await you, my lady."

A guard stepped closer, in warning, and Ainsley somehow moved her feet forward, eyes downcast, mind darting and searching for any avenue of escape. She stopped at Lord Varney's side.

"My Lady Ainsley," he murmured, bowing deeply and speaking to her in a deep, cultured English accent. "I have eagerly awaited this moment."

The Englishman took hold of her hand and pressed it firmly between his fingers. Every fiber in her body screamed to snatch her hand away and run, but before she could, Varney's other hand closed over hers, steady, firm, holding her steadfastly in place. The priest began to speak in a murmur, saying words she did not hear for the roar in her ears. Then it was over, the ceremony finished. God forgive her, what had she done?

In the aftermath as congratulations were being murmured, another different noise erupted outside the church, causing the priest to halt in his prayers of benediction. She did not recognize the sharp retorts as musket fire until the soldiers around her reacted, the sound of steel weapons shrieking free. Their nailed boots set forth a loud clatter as they headed for the doors, and Hugh of Strathmorton shouted a curse, foul and awful, his voice ugly with hatred as he ran for the rear of the church. Before he could gain the back pew, sword-bearing warriors burst through every portal, their bodies swathed in familiar bright red tartan, their war cries hoarse, gutteral, ringing to the rafters far above. Ainsley sobbed weakly, her knees sagging from beneath her when she saw Rodric at their head, sword upraised for fight, his beloved face dark and contorted with rage.

Chapter Twenty-two

𝒞

Rodric MacDonald's primary concern was to find Ainsley, safe and whole. His eyes cut frantically around the dusky interior of the sanctuary in search of his wife while his men surprised and disarmed the Campbell soldiers trapped inside the church. His biggest fear was that he had not made it in time, that she had already been whisked away to England where he would never be able to find her.

Or even worse, that she had succumbed to the illness her friend Myrna had described so chillingly when she had come to him near Taynuitt. The Campbell lass had wept hysterically when she poured out the story of Ainsley's ill treatment and Strathmorton's plan to wed Ainsley to Varney at Auld Kirk. Within hours Rodric was aboard ship sailing south to the seaport of Ayr with a landing force sizable enough to rescue her.

All his fears evaporated when he saw her at the altar. She was alive, thank merciful God. Almost at once his attention riveted on Hugh Campbell, who had stopped his advance ten yards down the aisle. He still held his sword in his hand. Rodric had no time to deal with him in the way he would like. Myrna had also informed him that a contingent of English dragoons from Fort William would arrive shortly at Strathmorton's request to escort Varney and his bride back to London.

Still Rodric hesitated, holding the basket hilt of his broadsword in a white-fingered grip. He fought his nearly overpowering desire to leap forward and plunge the razor-edged blade deep into the villain's breast. Around him his men waited as well, having already subdued Strathmorton's bodyguards and the handful of dragoons in Varney's retinue. They had forced them to their knees, the shouts and clomp of boots stilled, as all inside the church dissolved into an uneasy hue and the two leaders faced each other, weapons still in hand.

"The kirk is taken, your guards outside dead. I come for my wife, Strathmorton, with a force two hundred strong. Release her and live to draw your next breath."

Hugh's response was a short laugh, veritably dripping with contempt. "Take my sword, MacDonald scum, but you have come for her too late. She was wed to Lord Varney minutes ago as she was by proxy for nigh ten years past. You whored her by taking her to your bed."

The edges of Rodric's teeth came together so hard that his jaw jutted in an unnatural angle, but as he took a step toward the taunting man, Hugh, the coward he was, slung his sword upon the stone floor. It clattered loudly until it slid to a stop near Rodric's boots. Stooping, he snatched it up without pulling his eyes from the old man's face. Hugh smiled as he turned and stared at his granddaughter, who had wilted against the nearest pew. She gripped its wooden back, her face the pale and waxen hue of an ivory statue.

"Ainsley, come to me now!" Rodric ordered tersely, anxious to be away to the ship before the heavily armed dragoons from Fort William rode into Ayr. They had little time, and though Ainsley gave a muffled sound, she started toward him until the man beside her hooked her elbow and restrained her. He was tall, unarmed, and garbed richly in charcoal dark velvet with gold waistcoat. Randolph of Varney, Rodric realized with a stinging geyser of loathing.

"You cannot take her from me. She is my legal wife now under English statute."

Fighting for self-control, Rodric braced his feet, eyes as cold and hard as frozen silver coins. "Then, I will take pleasure in making her your legal widow under English statute."

Rodric's threat was uttered in so cold, unyielding a voice that Varney blanched underneath his swarthy coloring, his face whitening plainly for all to see. With only a moment's hesitation he released her arm, and Ainsley ran to Rodric. Inching fearfully around her glowering grandfather, she then rushed against Rodric's chest, burying her face against the thick brown leather of his metal-studded battle tunic. She clung to him, sobbing quietly, but his eyes remained on the bastards who had tricked and abused her. He hesitated there for one more instant, every fiber of his soul demanding that they pay with their lives.

All stood waiting as he fought to control the rage that had been simmering inside him for days while Ainsley suffered in their hands. If he killed them here, on holy ground, cold-bloodedly and in revenge, the dragoons would have reason to warrant his arrest, especially if he took the life of an English lord. Still he hungered for the pleasure of that sweet vengeance, but reason returned when Richard spoke lowly behind him.

"Time is short, cousin. The dragoons approach quickly."

"Take their weapons and bind them," he ordered abruptly, his left arm tightly around Ainsley's shoulder as he backed her away from her captors. He would wait to avenge his wife's honor in the clan war that their dastardly acts had started. Someday on the field of battle the bastard Strathmorton would meet his demise on the end of Rodric's own sword. "Then ride hard to the ship, for the dragoons cannot be far away, if Myrna spoke true."

As he backed out of the church, keeping Ainsley close, Hugh Campbell yelled, a shrieking curse, that echoed shrilly into the heights of the vaulted ceiling, damning his granddaughter to the depths of hell, the words ringing over and over again in the rafters high above. Ainsley's knees buckled beneath her, and Rodric swept her into his arms and carried her out of the church.

By the time they reached the longboat, which would take them to the ship anchored in a sheltered cove, Ainsley was so ill she succumbed to a fever-induced daze. Rodric held her himself as his men rowed hard for the craft, bathing her burning face with seawater, cursing Strathmorton over and over, regretting now that he did not kill him when he had the chance.

Once aboard he left Richard to attend the boarding of the men and hoisting of sail, and carried Ainsley down to the cabin he had prepared for her. She lay listlessly in his arms, limbs weak, flesh hot to the touch. He thought of her in the cage as Myrna had described, incarcerated like an animal and taunted by brutal guards. An English custom, he had heard, adopted by the swine Strathmorton.

Rage rose and he tried not to think about those things while he undressed her, murmuring soothing words as he carefully placed her arms in the full sleeves of the white nightgown. She began to shiver, though her flesh burned like fire, and he covered her with blankets. His eyes found the wedding gown he had just discarded upon the floor, and he jerked it up, wadded it to a ball, and threw it hard against the wall.

"Goddamn their souls," he ground out, low and hard and helpless, his jawbone grinding so hard together that a bolt of pain bladed into his temple. "Goddamn them to hell!"

His anguished cry penetrated Ainsley's torpor, and she sat up as if jerked by a chain. "No, no!" Her scream was short but frantic, her glazed eyes darting around in terror and confusion, and Rodric died a little inside as he quickly enfolded her into his arms.

"Shhh, my love, you're safe now. I'm right here with you. No one is going to hurt you anymore."

Ainsley sobbed one time against his shoulder, and he stroked her hair and murmured soothing reassurances that did not prevent her shivering. She would be all right, he told himself firmly, gently lowering her back to the pillow. She clutched at him, and he wrapped his fingers around her hand tightly.

"It's all right now. Don't be afraid."

"Rodric, Rodric?" She strained upward, eyes trying to see him. "Don't leave me, don't leave me . . ."

Wincing, blaming himself for all she had suffered, he placed one knee on the floor and gently swabbed a wet cloth against her hot forehead. "Lie still, Ainsley. I'm not going to leave you." She relaxed a bit, and he went on in a low, soothing whisper. "We're at sea now, love. We'll soon have you back on Skye where you belong. You must rest now. You're very sick."

Ainsley seemed to hear him, for she quieted while he bathed her face and arms, attempting unsuccessfully to cool her heated body, but her mind eventually succumbed to the fever once more. She tossed and turned and cried his name, and he set his jaw and vowed vengeance with a viciousness he had never had before.

Outside the closed door of his bedchamber at Arrandane, Rodric paced in an endless march up and down the corridor. Breanne stood against the wall, wringing her hands with worry while Ian sat with haggard face upon a bench beside the door. He had returned with her three days before. She had become more ill while upon the ship and had steadily grown worse instead of better since their arrival on Skye.

So stricken by regret and worry that he could barely draw lucid thoughts, he let his worse fears surface and was instantly consumed with dread. She had begun to bleed in the last few hours, her abdomen cramping with pains that made her cry out with agony.

Oh, merciful God, what if she lost their baby? God help him if she died, for he knew not what he would do without her. The shock of losing her completely immobilized his muscles, sent his face pallid and beaded with cold sweat upon his brow and cheeks. Convulsively he forced a swallow down through a throat swollen from emotion, his guts wrenched with a kind of fear he had never faced before. Steely fingers squeezed tightly around his heart until he feared the beat would still and leave him to face his own death.

As Ian shifted miserably in his chair, the extreme irony of the situation burrowed unwanted into his mind. Ainsley, the Lady of Legend on Skye, who had helped so many others with her potions and the touch of her fingers, could not help herself in this moment of despair.

When the doorknob rattled, both Breanne and Ian jumped to their feet, but Rodric turned slowly, paralyzed with unbridled dread as he faced Ellie. The gentle old woman wiped away a tear rolling down her cheek. Wordlessly she shook her head.

"I am so sorry to tell you, my lord, but your lady has lost the bairn." Breanne sobbed aloud, but Rodric barely heard her as the old nurse continued in a terrible voice. "I did all I could to save the wee thing, but my lady's fever was too high and she too weak to fight the sickness."

Rodric could do nothing but stare at her, could say nothing, could not move. He felt a hand on his shoulder and knew somehow it was Ian, but he had only one thought, one concern as the muscles in his jaw seemed to work of their own accord, twitching in spasmodic jerks as he tried to come to terms with his loss. His voice was unnatural, hoarse, a sound he did not recognize.

"What about my wife?"

"Her fever has broken at last, which bodes well, but she is very weak. We must all pray that she finds the strength to survive."

Rodric had to know. "Does she know about the babe?"

Ellie nodded sadly. "The poor child knows, my lord; she made me tell her."

Rodric nodded stiffly, pausing to glance at Ian before he inhaled a deep, fortifying breath. He entered the sickroom, then quietly closed the door behind him. He stood just inside, staring across the room at Ainsley. She lay on her side on the bed, facing away from him, curled in a fetal position. He winced at the vulnerability of her pose and cursed himself for not protecting her. If he had been at her side, she never would have been taken from Skye in the first place, never would have suffered the degrading abuse, never would have miscarried their child. Somewhere deep inside his soul he wept about that, for what he had not done to protect her.

Soundlessly he crossed the room and stopped beside the canopied bed, where they had laughed together on their wedding night, where he had kissed her for the first time and held her after she had slept, where for the first time he realized the marriage would be more than an alliance, a bond of love that could be cherished above all else. Her gold-streaked hair lay loosened now, as it had then, curled in riotous honeyed glory over the feather pillow, her lashes long, the color of burnished gold, covering the beloved eyes that had caused her such grievous treatment throughout her life.

Suddenly he had to hold her in his arms, had to have her close against him where he could hear her heartbeat, feel her breath against his cheek. He sat down on the edge of the mattress, then stretched out behind her, cupping his knees close behind her slim thighs, drawing her back against his chest with one arm. He found her hand, where it lay limp against the sheet, palm open, and he curled her fingers up beneath his own longer ones. She awoke with a moan and murmured his name.

"Aye, my sweet, 'tis me. I want to hold you while you sleep."

She struggled to roll over to face him, and he helped her. When they lay face-to-face, he smiled tenderly and brushed a strand of hair from her face. He could still see the low-grade fever burning brightly inside her eyes. Bluish crescents of fatigue formed shadows beneath her eyes, and he brought up both palms and pressed them gently along the fragile cheeks. Her skin felt hot and dry but so very soft.

"How do you feel, my love?"

Ainsley stared at him without speaking, and he caressed his thumb over her soft lower lip. Again the extent of his love sent a thrill through him, expanding beneath his breastbone until his chest was full of it. His breath caught tight, and he could not speak.

"We never even got to see him." Tears welled up in her eyes, filling them with liquid until they overran her lashes and fell down over her cheeks.

Rodric nearly choked on his own rising grief. His breath caught so tightly that he could not speak. When he did, his words sounded bent and broken with regret.

"Try not to think about that now." He ground his teeth, swallowed, forced down his feelings. "You've got to save your strength and get better."

The tip of her tongue emerged to moisten her parched lips. "I feel empty."

Rodric shut his own eyes and pulled her head against his shoulder, unable to watch the tears rolling down her face. He clutched a handful of her silky hair and fought the sobs threatening the back of his throat. His lips compressed, tightening his jaw, as a lump the size of an orange rose to block the base of his throat.

"We'll have another baby someday," he got out somehow, but he knew such words could not comfort her anymore than they did him. They had lost their firstborn, the child conceived as they discovered their own love for each other.

He combed his fingers through her hair with long strokes the way she liked. "Just get well, Ainsley, my love. I need you to get well."

After a time, she quieted and finally slept peacefully inside his embrace, but he did not close his eyes for hours. He stared out the windows overlooking the sea until the first faint rays of light filtered through the panes of glass and painted the ceiling with the soft pinkish-yellow hues of earliest dawn.

Chapter Twenty-three

Within the great hall of Arrandane, beneath the towering stained-glass windows, Ainsley stood looking out over choppy waves sailing landward from the open sea under a dome of skittering, black-humped storm clouds. Nearly six weeks had passed since Ainsley had been brought home to Skye, and still she was caught in a dreadful, immobilizing web of melancholy.

Outside, where twilight fell like a slowly lowered theater curtain, gray fog obstructed the jutting mountains and plunged the inside courtyard into black relief. On the steep slopes rising in her view, the darting flames of hundreds of campfires stretched in a glittering trail from the walls of the keep to the ancient Norse ruins, where Rodric had followed her on their wedding day.

Company after company of clansmen—MacLeod, MacKinnon, MacNeil, Fraser, MacCodrum—had gone on the march, converging at Arrandane for the assault of Hugh Campbell's force. From the foothills to the sandy beaches of

Maycairn, as far as the eye could see, soldiers had struck their tents of tanned leather in readiness for battle. Despite her lingering fears, it was truly a glorious sight indeed to find such a diverse collection of clans with pennons of every different hue, gathered as one, prepared to fight to the death. *Because of her.* A fluttering spiral of guilt delved deep into her stomach, and she quickly crossed her hands at her waist and thought of the innocent child who had not been given the chance to live.

Catching her lower lip between her teeth, she blinked back an onslaught of hot tears and tried to remember all of Rodric's soothing reassurances. She was trying desperately to come to terms with the loss of her baby, but deep inside her heart she mourned daily with such aching, cutting agony that the grief never seemed to leave her. Nor would it, she feared.

Oftentimes she was left to sit alone, or work alongside Ellie and Breanne in her garden of medicinal plantings, while in the courtyard Rodric pressed into motion his great attack on the mainland. There, among the shady, fragrant plants and climbing vines, with a piece of oleander or mandrake forgotten in her hand, she would sit on her heels and sadly conjecture what the tiny baby would have looked like. Would he have been a boy, dark and handsome with eyes of pure gray? Grown into a tall, strong son, would he have stood alongside his father and grandfather as the chieftains of MacDonald?

There were times when she wondered if Rodric,

too, suffered the anguish that she did, but knew inside her heart that he must, though he tried valiantly to hide it. Beneath the sweet, caring words and under the tender smiles, there was something in his eyes that had not been there before she had been taken from Skye, a dark shadow of pain, and even worse, a pinpoint of fire that brightened his eyes with hunger for revenge. She exhaled deep and long, and concentrated her will upon pushing the sorrowful thoughts out of her mind.

At the long mahogany table inlaid with onyx squares sat the war council. Chieftains every one, they were men of authority and regal bearing, proudly wearing their tartan plaids, their wool bonnets adorned with eagle feathers denoting their rank. Weapons sheathed, faces somber, they heard in concerned silence the latest tale of Campbell atrocities from a MacGregor courier. Still fighting exhaustion and the shallow spear wound in his thigh, he had recently arrived from the wartorn peninsula of Argyll, where Hugh Campbell had wreaked havoc ever since Rodric had humiliated him in the Auld Kirk at Ayr.

His face rigid with furious disgust, Rodric shot to his feet, startling everyone when he brought a doubled fist down so hard upon the table that the sound reverberated into the depths of the long room for several seconds afterward. "They're damnable devils, every bloody one of them! How could they do such a thing? Massacre women and murder innocent children who have done nothing against them!"

Her father rose as well, his voice, usually calm and steady, was embroidered with tight strands of constrained anger. "They left no one alive in the village of Taynuitt? Not even bairns of the cradle?"

"Sire, 'twas a complete and blood-crazed massacre ordered by Strathmorton himself in retaliation for their help in the docking of MacDonald ships." The soldier's voice choked as he continued the telling of the loathsome deeds of which he had borne witness. "One poor lass was big with child. I saw such butchery with mine own eyes."

Every muscle in Ainsley's body contracted with acute horror. Her shoulders tensed and slumped forward with the terrible visual image imposed inside her brain, and she squeezed her eyes tightly together, as she put her fist against her mouth to fight the nausea rising in her belly. Another wee babe robbed of life. *Because of her.*

"The corpses were hacked brutally and left for carrion where they lay," the MacGregor went on until Ainsley wanted to cover her ears with her palms to block out the terrible words. "Every croft between Strathmorton and where we took to sea was torched, the fields burned, the livestock rounded up and stolen. The Frasers were hit worst with most of their winter crops destroyed."

"Have those homeless brought here and to Dunvegan for wintering until we can stop Hugh's rampage." A short pause ensued in Rodric's remarks as Ainsley suddenly turned around. Their eyes met, and she knew he questioned whether she could hear more. Though he wished her close by so that he could know of her safety, he carefully tiptoed around her raggedly fragile emotions, in his vigilant endeavor to protect her shattered psyche.

"And the terrors do not stop there, my lords," the young courier cried, coming to his feet in spite of his recently injured thigh. "Hugh Campbell is readying his army to sail upon the Hebrides. 'Tis said King William himself is mightily angered by the affront of the Highlanders against Varney as English lord and noble, and will join Strathmorton's fight against us with warships of the Royal Navy."

"If that rumor be true, then let the English curs come. Our alliance makes us strong enough now to face them in numbers, and Strathmorton has gone too long without recourse for his treachery against his fellow Scots."

Ainsley could listen no longer. Overwhelmed by weeks of restrained grief and loss, compounded fiercely by the guilt of knowing she was the cause for the ravages of the brutal war, for every man, woman, and child killed or murdered in the growing strife, she fled the hall and words of war, taking the staircase with all the haste she could muster, not lessening her step until she reached the sanctuary of her bedchamber. She threw herself facedown upon the soft feather mattress, and though tears welled and burned like trapped acid behind her closed eyelids, none fell as night drifted in a dark shroud against the windowpanes.

When Rodric came to her a short time later, she still lay with her face upon the pillow in total darkness, comforted by the inky blackness. She neither moved nor spoke as she heard him light a wick and dim light flared at the bedside table behind her back. Soft sounds followed, of leather sliding on metal as he unbuckled and removed his belt, of fluttering flannel as he unwrapped the plaid, then lastly the thud of heavy boots hitting the floor. His side of the bed dipped, then she closed her eyes at the feel of his hands on her shoulders as he drew her back close against his long length of his body.

"I look forward to this moment throughout the entire day," he whispered softly as he buried his face in the side of her neck.

"Yet you will abandon me here to fight my grandfather."

His sigh was audible, a deep breath that fanned into her hair. When he shifted to his back, he kept his arm tightly around her, bringing her to lie close against him. She positioned her cheek and palm against the warm bare skin of his chest, and he stroked her hair back in silence for several moments before he said very softly, "I must fight for what is right, as must any honorable man. You must know that to be true, my love."

" 'Tis because of me that so many Highlanders have suffered and died." Her mind evoked a picture of their own dead child, but she could not bring herself to mention that, both for Rodric as well as herself.

"Nay, not because of you. Because of Hugh Campbell and his greed for power. This time he will not take what belongs to others without paying a price for his perfidy. He must be stopped."

"But what if you are killed? What will I do?" she asked him with low, breathless dread, while inside she screamed at him: Don't you understand? I cannot bear to lose anyone else I love! Please don't put yourself in danger!

Sensing her inner despair, his arm tightened around her. "I will come back, and you will be here safely awaiting me."

When she did not answer, he tipped her chin up so that he could kiss her lips. He pressed his mouth to hers very softly, almost tentatively at first, tasted the tears now seeping from her closed eyes, then wiped them away with a gentle forefinger. Ainsley clung to him, and looped both her arms around his neck, wishing she could hold him there against her forever. "I am afraid for you," she managed somehow, her words thick, hoarsened by what could happen to him. "Hugh is a powerful man and ally to the English monarchs. If he brings the dragoons against us as the MacGregor said, we cannot win the fight. They are too mighty even against our united clans."

Rodric made a weary sound, one that tugged at her heart, but he rubbed his hand up and down her spine, absently toying with a silky strand of her hair. "War has been declared. Hugh has stormed a swath of blood and gore through our fellow clans. We cannot ignore his crimes any longer. 'Tis not just Ian and I whom he has wronged in his treatment of you and your mother, but all the Highlanders who have fallen before pennons bearing the Campbell boar. He is like a festered wound in our midst that will slowly rot all of Scotland if left to do his crimes."

Ainsley thought for a moment of all the blood he had spilled, all the people he had hurt or destroyed. "He is a terrible, evil man. I am ashamed that his blood flows through my veins."

"You are of MacDonald blood now, my love. You are my wife, my heart, everything I have ever wanted, ever needed, or dreamed of in my life . . ." His words stopped only when his mouth took hers, stealing her breath as she lay still and receptive to his caressing palm and seeking fingers, sliding over her bare flesh, turning her skin hot and trembling and full of need. She wrapped her fingers in his hair as his head moved across the silky skin of her breasts, tasting, closing over the hardness of her nipple.

She loved him, loved him so deeply that he seemed a part of her being, their hearts fused into one beat. She brought his face back to hers, kissing him eagerly as he braced atop her on his elbows, wrapping her legs around his waist and drawing him deep inside her body as he was already inside her soul. Her pulse pounded as he moved into the dance of love, and she ran her palms over his hard flesh, their lips searching bare skin, exploring hollows and curves, trembling with the love gripping them, eager, hungry, overwhelming, until the tempest broke between them, inside them, like a fast, swirling maelstrom that drew them up and over the edge into the sparkling sunburst of mutual ecstasy.

*   *   *

When Rodric opened his eyes, Ainsley was snuggled in a safe, silken-limbed embrace close against his side. So content was he that several seconds flitted past before the tolling of the alarm bell filtered into his consciousness, loud, insistent, the warning of enemy attack. Shocked instantly into wakefulness, he leapt from the bed and strode naked across the room. He flung open the windows upon the early dawn light and stood stock-still, stunned by what lay before his eyes.

"God have mercy on us," he muttered under his breath, but his voice held such appalled disbelief that Ainsley came running to the window, wrapping her robe around her as she stopped beside him. Her face bleached as white as chalk when her eyes found the four English warships anchored in the waters offshore, cannon canted to target on the keep of Arrandane.

Leaving Ainsley to don her clothes with fumbling fingers, he threw on his shirt, belted his plaid, and pulled on his boots, then made his way rapidly down into the courtyard where he found the entire population of the castle in complete uproar. Women ran after children, donkeys brayed in alarm while chickens scattered and squawked as he strode purposely through them. He climbed straight to the battlement wall, where a handful of chieftains already had gathered to ready their men in the defense of the castle.

Joining them, his face soon shared their expressions of heavy strain because he knew as well as they that even their congregated force was no match for the armed frigates with their long rows of cannon aimed upon their ranks. Such powerful guns could blow a hole in the fortress with one barrage, and once the walls of Arrandane lay in ruins little could be done to stop the onslaught of English soldiers. He had never expected such a swift response from King William, nor such a concerted show of arms against one side. The Crown had answered Hugh Campbell's cry for help with force enough to stamp out the MacDonald forces in one fell swoop.

"We are lost." Ian's voice murmured from just behind him.

Rodric refrained from answering, his eyes locked upon the trio of longboats sliding to berth on the strand far below. He took the long brass eyeglass Ian handed to him and peered through it at the score or more red-uniformed dragoons that scrambled into the shallows and dragged the boats upon the beach. An English officer with gold epaulets festooning his scarlet jacket held up the banner that designated him as emissary from the Royal Court of King William and Queen Mary.

"Hold up, Ian, perhaps we are overanxious in our fear of attack. 'Tis a messenger who comes as leader. Perhaps they intend no attack upon our forces but a chance to act as intermediary."

"Are you daft, man? A mere messenger needs no escort of four fully armed warships? They mean us harm, there is no other message could be."

"Well, we will find out if you are right soon

enough. Dispatch a contingent with mounts to escort the emissary and his guards into the castle."

Within the hour the royal ambassador stood at the forefront of the great hall where the Highlanders sat around the table in full battle regalia. Ainsley stood with Breanne and the other ladies near the windows, her hands clasped tightly together as the small, precise Englishman strutted forward in his gigantic white-powdered curled wig and unrolled the parchment stamped with the royal seal.

"Hear ye all and give credence to this command from Queen Mary, wife of King William, exalted ruler of England and Wales, and crowned monarch of Scotland. It is with extreme dismay that Her Royal Majesty looks upon the internal fighting of the Highland clans one against the other. In order to seek a peaceful resolution to the strife between the clans of Skye, their allies and kin against the esteemed Earl of Strathmorton, Hugh Campbell, his allies kin, and supporters . . ."

When the man paused to gulp air, Ainsley waited with held breath and tightly clenched fingers for fear that he would finish with writs of execution for her father and her husband. Astonished, she gaped openly when she heard her own name ring out in imperial tones to shatter the tense hush of the assemblage.

"In accordance with the wishes of the Queen, Lady Ainsley Campbell will be brought to London under escort of the Royal Dragoons and upon Her Majesty's Ship *GOLDEN LION* to Windsor Castle

in Londontown, her fate and state of wedlock to
be decreed there by royal order."

Rodric shot to his feet, causing the cocky emissary to stutter in startled dismay as he continued.
"Secondly the following Scotsmen will accompany
her, under guard and unarmed, those to include
Lord Rodric MacDonald and Lord Ian MacDonald of Skye. Lady Breanne, sister of said Rodric
MacDonald, and Lord Richard MacLeod of Dunvegan, and as many clansmen as deemed necessary by such chieftains to sustain the security of
their person and retinue. Let it be known that
these are the commandments of the queen on this
year of our Lord, sixteen hundred and ninety
one."

No sound could be heard as the stuffy little
magistrate rerolled the scroll and bowed to the
assembled leaders. It was Rodric who slowly rose
to speak in their behalf.

"And if we refuse to abide by this decree?"

"Then we are ordered to fire our cannon at the
walls of Arrandane until not a single stone re-
mains standing. The same order is given to the
Clan MacLeod in regard to Dunvegan Castle."

"Then, we have little choice but to obey our
queen," Rodric replied with a short answering
bow, and not a little sarcasm.

"Thank you, my Lord MacDonald. Berths have
been readied on Her Majesty's flagship for all of
you. We will await you shipboard, for we intend
to set sail upon the outgoing tide."

Ainsley sat quietly, relieved that no death warrant was issued, but Breanne turned to her, brown eyes huge with fright.

"Oh, sweet Mary, we are to be taken to England. What will happen to Scots such as us in that wicked place?"

Chapter Twenty-four

Aloft, far above where Ainsley stood with Rodric at the forecastle rail, two and three billowing banks of square sails were full-blown on the foremast and mainmast as the *Golden Lion* plowed southward toward the port of London. The 660-ton frigate was commissioned by Queen Mary herself, armed and swift, and when Ainsley gazed aft, she could see the four-pound guns—fourteen strong, seven port, seven starboard—that guarded the flagship from attack by Spanish galleon and French sloop alike.

Moments ago Rodric had pointed out the heavier artillery, cannon on the gun deck below, their barrels pointed out over miles of rolling, white-capped, green-gray waves. Three smaller vessels, though similarly armed as warships, cleaved the waves on either side of the frigate's churning wake. Ainsley hugged her shoulders, shivering as she realized with growing trepidation that the mighty ships, though impressive, were only a small part of the Royal Navy. How little defense the Highlanders, and in truth, all of Scotland, had before their wrath!

"Are you chilled?" Rodric asked, his voice concerned as he slid an arm around her shoulders and brought her in close against his side. He had been ever vigilant about her health since the miscarriage, and she knew he worried that she would have a relapse of fever.

Ainsley smiled up at him and tugged the soft black velvet folds of her cloak tightly around her. She pressed up closer, wanting the comfort of touching him and drawing from his strength. She felt afraid, wary of the strange summons that was bringing her into English waters. " 'Tis the fear of what awaits us in London that makes me apprehensive."

"The queen's interest is benign, or she would have had you arrested and brought before her in chains. Perhaps Her Majesty intends to help you in your fight with Strathmorton. 'Tis said she sometimes takes the side against those whom her husband supports, if she feels their plight a just one. If she does take your part, 'twill make our plea fall easier upon the ears of the king. The English royal line flows through Mary's veins, and 'tis said he listens to her when she feels strongly about a petition."

"But why ever would she be interested in me? I have never met her or even a member of her court. How could she know that I exist?"

"In Hugh's petition to William, he would expound on your descent from the thanes of Strath. Perhaps Mary feels a distant kinship as a woman of royal descent, and feels your wishes deserve hearing as well as Strathmorton's, or it could be that she is touched somehow by your suffering and wishes to help you."

Ainsley supposed any of those explanations could be true, but she found them more than unlikely. The terror that haunted her nightmares was that the English monarchs would turn her over to Hugh and force her to honor her coerced vows to Varney. The idea struck her numb with horror, but William and Mary had the power to do so. She couldn't do that, couldn't let them make such a decision. She would throw herself on the mercy of the queen; she would beg upon her knees if she had to.

Determined to shake thoughts of that abhorrent fate out of her mind, she turned her head and regarded the captain of the *Golden Lion*. The moment they had climbed aboard, he had been at their service, introducing himself as Sir Christopher Briggs, loyal servant of the king and courier of the queen. He had been courteous and respectful, as if he did consider them the queen's own guests.

In truth, he impressed upon them that he had been given no explanation as to why Ainsley was required in England. However, Ian felt certain Sir Christopher knew more than he intimated, and now stood with the captain on the poop deck deep in conversation, no doubt striving to extract the true reason for the queen's command. Again Ainsley forced herself to share Rodric's optimism about the situation.

A few yards away, near the main hatch, she saw Breanne and Richard moving along the railing together, smiling and strolling as if they enjoyed a leisurely walk afield upon a balmy summer eve. They, too, seemed to think if the English meant ill toward them, the ship would have fired upon Arrandane, but she had heard too many frightening stories of the wicked English and the awful things done by them. Thus far, however, Sir Christopher and the members of his crew did not appear to be the ogres the abbess had described them to be.

On the two-day voyage, they had dined with the captain in his quarters, had been given extravagantly luxurious cabins themselves, though she had been forced to share a cabin with Breanne instead of Rodric. She missed him in bed at night when she lay lonely and worried, but he was with her the rest of the time. That, too, boded well about the queen's intentions. Their every wish had been provided, but why? The questions continued to run like a chanted mantra through her head.

"Don't brood so, Ainsley. Have faith. We have the truth behind our feud with Strathmorton. Hugh's story is riddled with evil deeds and falsehoods. The truth will prevail. The queen is said to be fair. We will tell her our side and ask her to intercede in our behalf."

Rodric smiled as he pulled her in front of him, settling his palms lightly upon her shoulders. She leaned back against him, taking succor in the solidity of his chest, then entwined her fingers with his long ones. "I am so afraid I will lose you."

"Never will that happen, my love, not while I can lift a sword against any man who tries to take you away from me. The queen means us well. I can feel it instinctively. There is something in our case that intrigues her, though we know it not yet, we will upon the morrow."

Ainsley tipped her chin upward so she could look into his eyes. " 'Twill be Hugh's word against us, with Varney to verify his every accusation. He has been a staunch ally of the English since before I was born."

"The queen will be pleased that I showed mercy to Strathmortin and Varney when they meant to force you into an adulterous marriage. That, too, will work in our favor. If I had slain them, she would have no choice but to condemn me."

"What if I am given to Varney?" Her words were low, barely audible.

Rodric would not meet her eyes. He stared out to sea. His voice was quiet but with a iron quality that gave her comfort. "I will never let anyone take you from me. Never."

The utterance was calm and controlled, but she knew that whatever awaited them at Windsor would determine the course of their lives. Rodric would be imprisoned or worse, executed, if he defied the Crown. Shaking with horror at the thought, she turned his arms and wrapped her arms around his waist. Ainsley would beg to return to Skye with her husband. Mary was said to be happy in wedlock with the king. Perhaps she could understand Ainsley's love for Rodric. She shut her eyes. Mary had to help them. She had to.

*   *   *

It was mid morning the day they arrived in the great hole of the Thames River where a forest of masts lay anchored in the deep gray water. An ornate black carriage awaited them, emblazoned with the royal crest and surrounded by an armed escort of English soldiers. The city was overhung with a great fog of black coal smoke, teeming with people and all sorts of coaches and drays, and they all could not help but exclaim over the immense size of the capital as they were driven through its narrow, twisting thoroughfares.

Little was said, however, as they rode through the enormous gates of the palace, but Rodric took her hand as the well-sprung conveyance took them up the cobblestoned driveway to a covered portico that led into a domed receiving chamber with great arched windows.

A magnificently bewigged royal official, garbed all in scarlet and gold braid, met them and led them through long marble corridors adorned with life-size paintings of splendidly appointed English royalty. White and gold damask divans and chairs set in profusion along the way, and Breanne looked at every antique piece of furniture, every Chinese vase and gilded lion in awestruck delight. Ainsley, however, barely noticed anything as Rodric kept a firm grip on her elbow. Inside an enormous antechamber with dark blue and silver wallcovering and dozens of silver candelabras, they were ordered to wait.

Nearly an hour passed while they wondered what would happen next until the official with the huge curly white wig returned. He walked straight to where Ainsley sat beside Rodric and bent in a low, courteous bow.

"Her Majesty wishes to see the Lady Ainsley Campbell."

Rodric stood as if to accompany her, but the courtier politely held up his palm in a gesture of restraint. "Alone. I can assure you, my lord, that Lady Ainsley will be quite safe while under the auspices of the queen."

Rodric frowned and gave her fingers a comforting squeeze, but Ainsley's knees were so wobbly they nearly gave way when she followed the man, very aware of the trio of palace guards marching behind them in a fierce clomp of polished boots. They finally entered a double white door, and the man stopped just inside the portal.

"Lady Ainsley Campbell, recently arrived from Arrandane of Skye, Your Majesty."

"Please bring the child forward" came a soft voice, but one that held an inexorable thread of authority. Ainsley moved deeper into the room, her trepidation growing with each halting step forward.

The chamber was lavish beyond all description, ivory and gold and crimson, rich woods, magnificent tapestries and paintings by the masters. Mary, the Queen of England, sat on an ornate velvet chair near a roaring fireplace. Her feet were propped upon a low hassock edged with long golden satin fringe, her lap covered with a paisley silk throw. She gestured with one ringed finger for Ainsley to come closer.

Ainsley obeyed, realizing that at least eight other women stood near the queen—her maids of honor?—one of them even was seated in a smaller velvet chair to her right. She paid little heed to the ladies-in-waiting, however, her full attention riveted upon the most powerful woman in all of England and Scotland. Mary was a large woman, perhaps five foot eleven or more, not heavy but big of bone, and dressed all in dark purple with a beautiful gold lace flounced shift that showed through an opening down the front and peeked from the flowing elbow-length sleeves.

A turban of gold satin could not hide an abundance of dark hair. She looked to be around her thirtieth year or perhaps less, a handsome woman with fine brown eyes that seemed a bit red, as if she suffered eyestrain. Ainsley was pleased that Her Majesty was smiling broadly, seemingly quite happy to see her.

"Come closer, Lady Ainsley, let us look at you."

Ainsley obeyed, nervously twisting her fingers together, uncomfortable as the queen looked her over. Suddenly Mary waved all the women away with a flick of her left hand. Only the one sitting silently beside her was allowed to remain. Ainsley darted a brief glance at the other woman, but instantly returned her attention to the queen when Her Majesty spoke once more.

"I suppose you are quite beside yourself as to why I would command you to come in audience before me?" the queen inquired, quite low.

"Aye, Your Majesty." Ainsley took a deep breath and forged on, having rehearsed her plea a thousand times on the voyage south. "But I am so very pleased that you did so that I might beseech you to return me to my true husband. I am terrified that you will listen to Hugh Campbell's lies and force me to leave Rodric and cleave into Varney, a man I neither love nor wish to wed."

A short silence ensued after her breathless entreaty. "Then you do my judgment ill, my dear, but there will be time to consider those heartfelt woes at a later hour. At this moment we have more pleasant business to attend."

Ainsley's facial muscles fell into complete astonishment, and she stared nonplussed at the queen, who was now smiling as she fussily re arranged her frilled satin underskirt with bejew eled hands. She stole a sidelong glance at her heretofore silent companion. "I have brought you here, my dear Ainsley, to meet someone very special to you. She was waiting many years for this moment, so I will not make her suffering last one moment longer. This kind lady at my side is my faithful companion." A short pause ensued while her attendant rose. "Prepare yourself to be shocked, my dear Ainsley, for this lady is your mother."

Ainsley was so stunned in that first moment that the floor seemed to tilt beneath her feet and slide her backward across the glossy marble floor tiles. She could not move, could not speak, as slowly she turned her head and stared with intrepidation into the other woman's face. She could not look away in that moment, even as tears rose in the other's eyes, for it was as if she looked impossibly upon her future self.

The woman portrayed in Ian's locket did stand in the flesh before her, the same if not for a few streaks of gray in her dark blond tresses, a web of fine lines drawn at the corners of her eyes. It was Meredith. It was her mother, she would recognize her anywhere. Oh, God help them all, it truly was her mother.

"Your name is Ainsley?" So soft were the words that Ainsley could barely hear the query, but the voice was warm, trembling vibrantly with emotion. " 'Twas the name I chose, but I feared my father would not pay heed to my wishes."

A terrible ache started up deep inside Ainsley's breast, filling her both with joy and sorrow, and she stumbled the few steps to her mother and dropped to her knees at her feet. She sobbed as she clutched the folds of her black silk skirt. Her mother sank back into her chair and cried herself as she stroked Ainsley's fair hair. Both women wept unabashedly for the first few moments, then Meredith cupped Ainsley's chin and gently wiped away the tears rolling unchecked down her daughter's cheeks.

"Please, darling, do not cry. 'Tis a happy moment, this reconciliation; one I never expected to enjoy. I knew not that you existed until nigh a few weeks ago."

"They told me you were dead, too," Ainsley sobbed out, unable to stop crying. Her emotions were torn apart, as shredded and raw as if ripped open by a pistol ball. "Everyone thought you were dead, my grandfather, Ellie, Rodric, all of them . . ." Ian's name faltered at the edge of her tongue, and she wondered if her mother knew about him, that he was here, just a short walk away. Her tears stopped, but her mother was smiling now.

As Meredith spoke, Ainsley examined every inch of her face, astonished all over again that she was alive, sitting there before her, touching her with a mother's gentle compassion. Her heart twisted again, renewing a deluge of glistening teardrops.

"Father told me you were dead, and poor dear Ian as well," Meredith was whispering in a hoarse, stricken voice. "He was so ashamed of my elopement with Ian that he shipped me away to a nunnery immediately after you were born. I was so ill I almost died on my way to the Spanish Netherlands, but it was there I stayed until long after Her Majesty married the Prince of Orange and heard of my plight." She smiled aside at the somber queen. "She took pity on an Englishwoman condemned for life inside a foreign nunnery and sent for me. I've been with her ever since, out of the goodness and mercy of her heart."

"He sent me away, too, to the abbey of Kilchurn, but he told me you were dead. That both you and my father were murdered in a MacDonald massacre. I never knew differently until Rodric came for me and took me to Skye."

"My poor baby. How I grieved for you all those years ago. Mary sustained me with her kindness and sympathy, and when she became queen, she brought me home with her. But I told no one of my past. I knew not that you were alive and grown into a young woman, not until Father petitioned William to condemn Rodric MacDonald to death for kidnapping you from the abbey. He also wished Ian sanctioned and imprisoned . . . that's when I knew Ian survived . . . I could not believe it, I could not imagine him finding you after all this time . . ."

Ainsley heard the way her voice quavered as the words dwindled away, and the way she bit her lip, overcome by emotion. She smiled through her tears. "Mother, mother, Ian's here with me! He's outside waiting! You can see him again now—this very moment!"

Ainsley's mother's face did not reflect her daughter's excitement. She turned quite white and stared wide-eyed at her daughter as she slowly brought both hands up to cover her mouth. "Nay, I could never see him . . . not after so long. It's been too long, too much time has passed."

"But he still cares for you. He has always loved you. He gave me this the day we met. It was the first time he took it off since they told him you died." She quickly gathered the locket out of her neckline and slipped the gold chain over her head.

Meredith took it, cradled it reverently inside her hand, and sprung the clasp. Then a sob escaped her as she bent over, rocking as she held the ornament against her forehead. Ainsley touched her shoulder comfortingly, but all the while she kept thinking, it couldn't be true, it couldn't be her mother sitting before her, but it was! She was here, flesh and blood and tears!

"Is he well? Did he remarry?"

"He is well but for a lingering sword wound in his thigh, but he never stopped mourning you. That's how I found out the truth of my parentage, when he sent Rodric to bring me home to him. He still grieves for you, everyday, but he'll be so happy to know you're alive! We must go out and tell him how wonderful . . ."

But Meredith burst into tears, hard, wracking sobs into her hands, until Ainsley wept, too, and held her mother tightly to her breast. Neither of them knew when the queen slipped away into the adjoining chamber, dabbing at her own tears as they consoled each other.

Rodric paced from door to windows, then back again, over and over. Ainsley had not come back yet, and it had been over three hours. No word had been sent revealing her whereabouts, but the rest of their party had been escorted into a great receiving hall where the king and queen held audience.

Fearful that she might have already been spirited away and given over to Varney, he continued to prowl, his jaw locked with anxiety as Ian, Breanne, and Richard sat together on three of the hundreds of plush gold and white armchairs lining the walls. All around him milled other petitioners, too many for him to count, and though he had searched their faces, he had not seen Ainsley anywhere among them.

Most of the people around them stared curiously at his red-belted plaid and knee-high boots, but he wore them proudly, inwardly contemptu-

ous of the London lords and ladies in their out-
landish costumes of jewel-colored silks and collars
of lace, and hideous white-powdered wigs that hid
their true hair. The women were as gaudy as pea-
cocks with giant coiffures and all manner of feathers and jewels and even bizarre decorations such
as bird's nests and miniature ships affixed to beau-
tify their elaborate periwigs. He paid them little
heed, however, as he wandered among them
searching desperately for a glimpse of his wife.

Trumpets blared, stopping the loud buzz of conversation throughout the hall, then rang in royal
fanfare as King William and Queen Mary of England entered with regal pomp and circumstance,
followed by all manner of lords and ladies selected
as their favored retinue. Rodric turned and eyed
the lavishly adorned royal company with cynical
disdain, until he saw Ainsley. He gaped at her
in shock as she swept into place as one of the
honored few.

Thank the saints, at least she was still in the
castle and safe, and not miles away in Varney's
clutches. She stood alongside another woman
dressed all in black, which made her stand out
from the other vibrantly adorned ladies, and he
saw at once that she searched the assemblage for
his face. Smiling, he wended his way through the
crowd and closer to the front where she could see
him. When their eyes met, she presented him
with a brilliant smile, which reassured him immediately, then turned her head as if looking for Ian
and the others.

Reassured that things had gone well in her audience with the queen, he breathed a bit easier and motioned for Ian, Breanne, and Richard to come forward and stand with him. They formed a tight knot close to the front, watching as the king rose and stepped upon a raised dais draped with purple velvet and gold fringe. He was slight, stooped in the shoulders, and to Rodric's surprise wore no periwig but stood before them with his own dark hair as if he cared not for the affectations of the court.

William wore his royalty as regally as he did his purple robes, along with his wife, the queen, who sat in a matching throne at his side, a tall and elegant woman who surveyed the crowd of petitioners with cool detachment. Her ladies-in-waiting surrounded her like butterflies around a bush of blooming roses. He prayed that Ainsley's ease meant Her Majesty intended to help them in their plight.

"Upon the matter of the warring Scots," the king said at length in a strong Dutch accent that hushed the gathered petitioners to dead silence. "I would have the involved parties brought forward, where I can take proper notice of their pleas."

Rodric kept his eyes on Ainsley as he moved with Ian to the forefront of the crowd. Richard stayed in the background supporting Breanne's arm, but Ainsley still smiled as if she had not a care in the world. His own features went hard and his jaw clenched tightly when Hugh Campbell stopped within yards of him, directly in front of the king, Randolph of Varney standing erect and haughty beside him.

"In private chambers I have listened at length to Lord Campbell of Strathmorton's complaints against the chiefs of Clan MacDonald and their allies of war, and I must say that his accusations are dire ones indeed. Is the lady responsible for this bloody feud here as I commanded?"

"I am she, Your Majesty." Ainsley stepped forward and curtsied gracefully. To Rodric's shock she still wore a confident smile. What in God's name had come over her? She had been a bundle of nerves, nearly paralyzed by her fear, only hours ago. Surely the queen had promised to help her. What else could have calmed her thus?

"Is it true what has been reiterated to me? That you are married twice, first to the Highlander Rodric MacDonald and then to an Englishman, Lord Randolph of Varney?"

The buzz of shocked exclamations erupted then lowered to the hiss of scandalized whispers among the onlookers. "Nay, sire, I am wed only to Lord Rodric MacDonald. 'Twas a marriage arranged by my true father, Lord Ian MacDonald of Arrandane."

"Lies! She is my granddaughter, and the true tale is as I have told Your Majesty. It was by the hands of MacDonald savages that my daughter and her husband were cut down by sword in a cowardly raid upon my lands. I have kept the child safe inside a nunnery for fear of their retribution until she could be wed to young Varney as I contracted with his father years ago!" Hugh Campbell strode forward as his furious denials echoed from one end of the chamber to the other.

The king's voice, curt, sharp in tone, brought him to an instantaneous standstill as several of the royal guard drew swords and held them poised in Hugh's direction.

"Enough, Strathmorton," William continued in a softer voice, "I will hear both sides of this festering altercation. What have you to say to these accusations, Lord Ian of Arrandane? Is this woman your child as she purports to be?"

Ian stepped forward, and when Rodric glanced back at Ainsley, she was not even watching her father at such a momentous occasion but was smiling at the woman beside her, the one in black. He frowned when the two women entwined their hands.

"I was wed to Lady Meredith Campbell, proudly wed, though in secret because the age-old animosity between our clans made it impossible to reveal our love, for fear of retribution by our families. Despite the fact that she was wife to me, she was taken by her father, Hugh of Strathmorton, and hidden from me."

His voice seemed to falter from emotion, but he quickly got hold of himself and pressed on. "Only this past year did I learn that she bore a child to me before she succumbed to a death from childbed fever—a daughter, Lady Ainsley of Arrandane, whom Hugh Campbell locked away from her rightful family, as he just now openly admitted before his God and king alike. He is the perpetrator of great wrongs against mankind and his own countrymen, both to me and my only child, and most of all to his own poor daughter, whom he murdered as surely as if he had driven a knife into her heart."

For the first time Queen Mary joined the discussion. After the deep and angry tones of the gentlemen, her voice seemed very low and softly melodic. Nevertheless there ran a thread of unflagging steel in her voice. Rodric heard it well and named it as anger. "And how did you come by the knowledge that you had this long-lost daughter, Lord Ian?"

" 'Twas on the oath of a servant, Ellie MacLeod, who witnessed the child's birth herself . . ."

"He takes falsehoods from the mouth of an ignorant nursemaid. My daughter Meredith was killed by the MacDonalds, and I challenge anyone to prove otherwise."

"I can prove otherwise."

To everyone's shock, the challenge had come from the black-clad woman at Ainsley's side, and when she took a step toward Hugh, her voice rang loud and clear without fear. The woman was slight, not even as tall as Ainsley, but Ainsley stood as an obvious ally, now supporting her elbow. Rodric could not see her well, but she was older, with blond hair parted in the middle and forming wings that disappeared into a black-veiled hat. Beside him, Rodric heard a strangled sound and turned swiftly to find Ian quite distraught.

"My God, no, it cannot be, it cannot," he was muttering through lips that barely moved. "Meredith? Oh, God, is it you?"

Stupefied, Rodric swung back around, his stunned attention riveted on the woman at Ainsley's side. His wife nodded, her face wreathed with joy.

Tears rolled down Meredith's face, but her sorrow was silent and incongruously veiled by a smile. She moved off the dais and slowly walked toward Ian, the shocked audience parting in wonder until she stood before the husband she had not seen in two decades. Wordlessly he opened his arms and enfolded her against him, where she buried her face in his neck as he held her close. They rocked back and forth where they stood, wordless in their wonder, mute in their joy.

"You do not recognize your own dead child, Lord Campbell?" the queen intoned with audibly rising anger in her query. "Nor do you, I suppose, recall that you sent her away those many years ago to a nunnery in the Spanish Netherlands to live out her life in shame and loneliness? I found her there not long ago and heard her sad story of her own father's betrayal. You told her that her infant daughter died at birth, did you not, my lord? That you had had Ian MacDonald assassinated for the sin of their elopement? Are you ready to be held accountable for your own crimes, my lord? God will be your judge for all eternity, but no longer will I allow you to destroy the lives of the members of your family."

Hugh staggered backward a step, his face whitening to bloodless hue under the weight of the queen's merciless indictment, then he turned and thrust his way forcefully through the crowd of his whispering peers.

Rodric was free to go to Ainsley then, and he

supported her as she watched her mother and father remain locked in their disbelieving embrace.

"It's true, Rodric," she whispered softly, her eyes shining. "It's my mother, my own mother."

Rodric smiled at her as the happy couple drew back a space and stared speechlessly at each other.

"I have thought about you every day since you were taken from me," Ian said low, hoarse, thick. "Come, let me take you home to Arrandane, where you belong. You and our daughter."

When Ian and Meredith turned and opened their arms, Ainsley ran into their embrace, and Rodric fought the burn behind his own eyes as he watched a family reconciled, after endless years of lies and deceit, after countless wrongs and intrigues against them. Finally, at long last, everything was as it should be. Thanks be to God for such a wondrous answer to all their prayers.

Epilogue

The day on which Ainsley's parents reconfirmed their marriage vows dawned bright and beautiful. They had returned to Skye not long after their reunitement in London, and Ainsley now stood in the chapel of Arrandane, blinking back happy tears as she watched her mother, who was adorned in the same dress of ivory satin that Ainsley had worn when wed to Rodric, her coiled hair covered by the beautiful veil of lilacs on lace handworked by Rodric MacDonald's great-grandmother.

Ainsley's father stood proudly at Meredith's side—in truth, he had hardly left her presence since that fateful moment at Windsor, as if fearing she would somehow disappear once again. As the vows were repeated, a gold band was given with gladness and was taken with joy. Through a sheen of teardrops, Ainsley smiled up at Rodric. He lifted her hand and kissed her fingers.

"Few can say they stood attendant to their parents' wedding," she whispered in a hushed tone.

"Nor can they say the chapel was like an armed camp." He placed his hand on the hilt of his sword as he spoke, his gaze moving suspiciously past her to the other side of the church.

Ainsley followed his regard but suffered no fear of what she saw. During the week that followed their audience with the English monarchs, before they had been allowed to weigh anchor for Scotland, King William, at his queen's behest, had made a decree that startled both MacDonalds and Campbells. With final royal command he had deemed Hugh Campbell and his retinue to stand as witness upon the recommitment in marriage of his daughter to her true husband.

Now, gathered upon the pews on the right-hand side of the church aisle, where she sat hand in hand with Rodric, the red with green, navy blue, and white-striped MacDonald tartan was sported, in yet unheard of proportion, in the form of shawls, dresses, belted plaids, and even the feathered bonnets of the men. Intermixed were patches of the yellow MacLeod weave as well as others from the united clans of Skye.

But on the distant side, where sat her grandfather and his Campbell clansmen under force of royal command, navy blue with stripes of green, white, and yellow swathed the sullen onlookers. They wore no weapon, also by decree, while every MacDonald in evidence was armed to the hilt, often fingering their broadsword and dirk as if itching for a rallying battle cry. Both sides eyed the rival clansmen with fierce distrust, but so far none dared to cause an outcry, no doubt because of the contingent of royal guard who rode escort to Strathmorton's visiting party.

No bloodshed would occur on this happiest of days, and hopefully not for many more to come, for the English Crown had forced this alliance of their clans and the peace would hold for a time at least, now that much of Hugh's power had been stripped from him. The other Campbell clans, of Argyll and Glenorchy, had inherited some of his confiscated lands and properties, and considered it their fortune good that someone else had dealt with the most troublesome of their kinsmen.

"I think we should sneak away to the lodge and renew our own wedding vows," Rodric said, his lips touching her temple as the priest ended the ceremony. Ainsley nodded with not a little eagerness and allowed him to lead her down the side aisle with willing abandon, stopping briefly to watch her mother and father share the most tender of kisses. She had a family now, one she had always longed to have, parents who lived and breathed and loved her as their only child. She had an adoring husband at her side, and someday soon she would conceive again, a baby of her own to raise on this beautiful isle.

She smiled when Rodric stopped in the corridor outside as the chapel bell rang out over the castle towers and drew her behind a tapestry to steal a kiss. The mingling of their lips was long and leisurely, and the most beautiful kind of joy warmed her inside when she thought of the wonderful life they would share together here at Arrandane.

"I can think of nothing but you," Rodric was

murmuring. " 'Tis those bewitching eyes of yours, I think, that entrap me."

"Then, I shall never cover them again, for I wish to have you under my spell," she replied throatily before his mouth closed over hers and she forgot everything but how much she loved him.